The Shadowed Eye

Also by Matt Beighton

Poetry
Tig You're It: And other poems from the playground

The Shadowland Chronicles
The Spyglass and the Cherry Tree

Monstacademy Series
(Ages 6+)
The Halloween Parade
The Egyptian Treasure
The Grand High Monster
The Machu Picchu Mystery
The Magic Knight

For Younger Readers
Spot The Dot

Matt Beighton

The Shadowed Eye

THE SHADOWED EYE

Printed in the United Kingdom
First printed 2019

A CIP catalogue record for this book is available from
the British Library.

ISBN: 978-1-9161360-0-7

www.mattbeighton.co.uk
www.greenmonkeypress.co.uk

For Phoebe and Willow

The North Wood
North Bay
Balzor's Straight
Kobold
The Hidden Wall
Glen of Tears
Port Escrildor
Theandro
Landragog
Tor
Druidmotte
Dune
Wizened Peaks
The Wandering Place
Alastor
Golmankin Range
The Silver River
Fenkur
Lörieas
The Gloom
The Shadowlands
(where the spirits roam)
Hillmoss
Rivergold
Salabah
Liorath's Peak
Tunlef
Scirion Mountains
Carak Tak
Malagao's Folly
Beilmor
Orcwood
Keredor's Pass
Crazak D'Ur
Orctooth Range
Phoenix Falls
Bay of Sorrow
Westport
Kanthor
(The lost realm of the Elves)
Huruzan
(The realm of men)
The Longman Trail
The Kraken Dance
The Solar
Eragor
(Walled city)
Horongor
(The Burnt Fort)
Milsandor
(The Royal City)
Realm of Milsandith

It Begins

A small shadow crept through the dense forest, careful not to make a sound. Overhead, a moonless night shrouded everything in the darkest of blacks. The goblin was just one more shadow amongst many.

Nervously, he reached up to his brow and wiped away the sweat. On his wrist, a tattoo of the dark outline of an eye seemed to glow. He had to keep reminding himself that this is what he had been training for. He had joined the rebellion for nights like this. He was about to make a real difference. This was no place for nerves.

Up ahead, the guard had paused in his long walk around the towering wooden wall that added the depth of the shadows. The shadow shielded his eyes as the guard struck a match and lit a pipe. He didn't want to lose his night vision. He knew he'd need all his wits about him tonight. Animal noises in the distance seemed as though they were on the other side of an ocean. The goblin felt his tongue stick to the roof of his dry mouth. His stomach knotted itself together, and his hastily eaten supper threatened to make another appearance.

Panicking once again, the shadow reached into the cloth bag that hung at his waist. He felt the reassuring weight of the knife against his hand. He drew it from the bag and gripped it firmly in his palm.

Like a snake in the grass, the shadow moved across the muddy track making its way slowly, inch by slow inch, towards the guard. Before the guard had time to realise what was happening, the shadow rose from the floor and plunged the knife into the back of his neck.

The goblin twisted the knife and felt the guard shudder and relax in his grasp. He dragged him into the trees and covered his body quickly with a pile of leaves. With shaking hands, the assassin pulled a small paper tube from his bag and ignited the short fuse with the guard's smouldering pipe ashes. It sparked into life and he held it high above his head and closed his eyes as the green firework rocketed into the sky and exploded. In the distance, further explosions signalled that the goblin's allies had also succeeded.

There was no need for secrecy, and the goblin raced with all the speed he could manage towards the source of the other explosions. As he approached, he saw his allies in a battle with the guards on the main gate into the wooden fortress.

The goblin grabbed his knife and set about the guards from behind, though, in truth, his allies had already killed most of those who had chosen not to flee. Within the walls, sirens started to scream their warning; somebody had made it as far as the inner guard towers to raise the alarms.

"The guards are dead! Through the gateway!" screamed one of the goblins in the darkness. "You know what to do. We are here for one thing and one thing only. We don't leave without Akeldama!"

The other goblins responded with a loud war cry and made their way towards the unguarded gate.

"We did it, my friends," the leader shouted as he shepherded them through to the other side of the wall. "The Holden Wall is fallen!"

Far below, in the middle of the goblin village,

his brothers were already piling the broken timber snatched from pillaged houses into a large fire. From here, it looked exactly like an eye, watching to see what would happen next.

The branch underfoot creaked as Salismir Unt eased his legs into a more comfortable position. The hobgoblin had been hiding at the top of his tree for most of the night. As the sun threatened to make an appearance over the horizon, he was more than ready for his replacement to take over.

He knew it would be worth the wait. Hidden away in the trees around him were a dozen of his most trusted brethren. Their band of hobgoblins had been scouring the forests north of Athancor for generations living mainly on the animals and trees.

Every now and again, a rich merchant would leave Athancor and make their way to the bustling trade town of Hurathi, nestled in the curves of the aptly named Long River. Salismir and his brothers had long considered these merchants fair prey, and many a rich courtesan had died with the brigands' voices echoing in his ears as his woefully unprotected carriage came under their attack.

Salismir had been taken in by the Brotherhood

of Grield as a child after he had been cast aside from his own village for practising witchcraft. Ever since he could remember, the hobgoblin had been able to produce a powerful aura whenever he concentrated.

Unfortunately, he had never been able to control it. It had been a warm day, unusually so for autumn, and the grain had been ever so dry. It hadn't mattered. The harvest had been put aside to see them through the winter and he'd set fire to it all.

"Burnt until dead!" the village councilman had cried as he stood tall over Salismir, the tiny hobgoblin pinned mercilessly to the wooden post. Salismir could still hear his voice echoing around the crowd as they brayed like donkeys for his death. He could still feel the tears running cold against his cheeks as he fought down the rising bile in his stomach. He mustn't show fear. He mustn't bring further shame to his already wounded family who he could see looking over the horrible scene unfolding in front of them.

Panicked in case he decided to cast a spell upon them all, they'd dragged him away to the burning post that very afternoon and doused the mound of wood in tar and oil. Normally in the village, a criminal would be given a chance to utter any final words, to repent for what they had done or to offer themselves to their gods. Salismir had been bound about the mouth with rope. Anything he had to say would endanger the village, he'd been told. He had nothing to say that they wished to hear.

The heat of the burning wood had been intense as soon as the flaming torch had been thrown onto the pile. He'd felt the flames lick against his clothes and his skin blister at its touch. Whenever he closed his eyes at night, he saw the red wall in front of his eyes and the ripples of the air as the heat rose and surrounded him.

He was still unsure of what had happened next. All he could remember was hearing a loud scream from the woodland behind the crowd followed by the panic of people scattering. As he'd passed out from the pain, he'd felt the bonds around his wrists give way and the feeling of falling forwards into the darkness.

When he'd awoke, he'd been lying in a soft bed being tended to by a hobgoblin he soon came to know as Jorn the Bandit. He was the unelected leader of the Brotherhood of Grield and made sure that Salismir made a full recovery. He'd taught the young hobgoblin how to use a throwing spear and how to hide in the woods like a shadow. Eventually, Jorn had allowed him along on their skirmishes to the woodland edge to attack and pillage the passing traffic.

That had been a long time ago. Salismir owed Jorn

and the Brotherhood everything. If sitting painfully in a tree was part of paying that back, then he considered himself happy to do it.

Just as he was thinking about changing his position once again and maybe moving to a lower part of the canopy out of the biting wind, the sound of horses approaching at speed caught his attention. He whistled softly under his breath and signalled to the watchers lower in the trees that something was approaching. According to Jorn, a new army had started to form further east of Athancor in Soulaman, and he was expecting a lot of gold to be travelling back and forth along the main route to Hurathi. This could very well be one of their money trains. They'd certainly be traveling at speed, not wanting to delay with such precious cargo.

As the horses rounded the bend and came fully into view, the fighters at the foot of the trees were primed and ready with their long throwing spears ready to skewer the horses as they passed.

The attack on the carriage was swift and deadly. It was well-rehearsed, and soon it lay empty. This one had been well armed with a dozen strong men riding pillion, clinging to the canvas sides, along with the heavily armoured driver. Once the horses were lying dead on the ground, the men never stood a chance.

The hobgoblins had been merciless in their work.

Salismir hopped down from the tree and followed the other brothers to the rear of the cart where Jorn was hammering open the chest that formed the sole item of cargo. When the old steel finally gave way and the wooden lid was thrown back, there was no pile of gold to be found.

In fact, the chest was almost empty.

All that rested inside the wooden case was a dark, cloudy black sphere of semi-transparent glass with a noticeable chip on the surface.

A thunderstorm raged across the grey sky pelting the land with hailstones. An enormous stone tower rose from a sea-swept clifftop and speared the leaden clouds. Rain and hail lashed against blue-green metal walls that were pitted with barred windows that did nothing to protect the inmates from the swirling tempest outside. Feared by all but the most insane, the prison was nicknamed the Solar. Legend said that the walls rose so high that those in the topmost cells could kiss the sun.

Inside the prison, a riot had been raging for the better part of the evening. The Solar was used as a final destination for the worst criminals of all races, many of them with magical powers that rivalled those of the greatest druids. Inside the Solar, however, those powers were rendered impotent by the layers of copper that lined the outer walls. The once polished metal had tarnished over the centuries to a mottled turquoise, but it still served its purpose of earthing all magical power in the vicinity. Outside, it merely served to ground the lightning that continuously struck the tower.

The most powerful of all the inmates wanted nothing to do with the riot. Damphir was a powerful sorcerer. He was also hundreds of years old and very patient. He was too close to ruin it now. He sat quietly in his cell meditating whilst around him the wardens took out their anger on those inmates too slow or confused to make good on their escape plans. They wouldn't make it to the front gate anyway. They never did. Besides, he had plans of his own.

It took a while, but soon he could hear the sound that he had been listening out for. The slow, rhythmic crack of leather straining against the howling wind carried over all of the other noises that surrounded him; above the din of the riot taking place outside his cell, above the bellowing thunder echoing across the plains outside the open window and above the roaring of the waves throwing themselves at the mercy of the sharp rocks far below. Damphir smiled to himself and stood quietly from his bed. He reached under his flattened pillow and pulled out a heavy, leather-clad book onto which was branded the title: *Eternis Mortus*. He thrust it into the folds of his robes and pressed himself against the bars of his cell. He closed his eyes.

As he focused, he reflected on the limits of the prison that held him. They might be able to stop his magic, but they had forgotten that Damphir was also a powerful seer. He could use his mind to control those under his influence. Their defences were powerless against his mind and so he'd forged his plan. When he'd been captured all those years before, he'd left behind a servant, a weapon. At the time, it had been no more than an egg, but a lot of time had passed since. Now he could leave this wretched place.

Damphir covered his face as the outer wall of his cell exploded and the large stones collapsed and fell the hundreds of feet to the ground below. He made his way to the gaping hole and stood on the precipice and stared into the night sky. In the distance, a shadow moved in front of the clouds and circled away behind the tower. The seer crouched down and waited, his eyes closed, watching the future unfold before him.

When the time was right, he leapt out into the void, his dark cloak billowed behind him and whipped in the wind. Time slowed, and he seemed to hover in mid-air. Just in time, the large shadow rounded the corner of the tower with a roaring scream. Damphir reached out quickly and grabbed hold of the thick green skin that rippled under his body. With a loud clap, the dragon flapped its wings, and Damphir escaped into the darkness.

A Burning Eye

The council of goblins sat quietly around the large wooden table at the centre of the room. Snudge, the leader of the G'Oräk, and therefore the leader of all those present, took to his feet and made his way over to the window that overlooked the woodland beyond his home.

"When the Dark Queen was destroyed, the power that formed her soul wasn't. It left her body and fled as far as it could, but it *will* rise again. We have known this for a while. Even without Akeldama, it will find a way to draw evil to its banner.

"The dark powers are like a magnet. It has been over a year since she was defeated and into the vacuum have poured a thousand kings, overlords, warlords and general opportunists who have sought to rise to the top in her absence.

"At the moment, nobody has found that wretched stone, and so the power is shared relatively equally between all of the clans. Nobody dares to fight the others, at least not in a full-scale war. Not yet anyway. There have been small skirmishes here and there, and some groups have been wiped out altogether."

"How do you know all this?" asked one of the goblins seated around the large table.

"Since we lost Akeldama at the base of Liorath's Peak, I have had scouts out beyond the Wandering Place. Some of them have roamed very far south indeed. Not too long ago, we only needed to know what was happening as far as the edge of the North Wood, then, with the rise of the Dark Queen, we knew a little bit more, just beyond the range of Liorath's Peak.

"Recently, there has been an uneasy peace, and, perhaps as my own failure, we have grown complacent. Now, I need to know how the entire world is turning; who is fighting whom, who is in league with which band of orc and who, most importantly, is searching for the stones of power."

"Do you think it will come to war? After all we did before to prevent it?" continued the first goblin.

"Snowbroth, you have been walking this world for many more years than I, and you know how these things go. For now, I hope that war can be avoided—"

Snudge's speech was interrupted as siren sound filled the house around them and echoed through the woods beyond. A soldier goblin, stationed as a guard on the front door, burst into the meeting room dragging a bedraggled and wounded guard behind him.

"Sirs," the injured goblin started, "they are here. They have taken the Holden Wall! I'm so sorry, sirs. They've killed everyone. Goblins, sir, goblins are attacking us. They're inside the wall. We're at war!"

The goblins around the table erupted in panic, many drawing their weapons where they stood.

"Enough!" screamed Snudge over the growing noise. "Enough! Everyone, take to your homes and alert your families. Make sure that they are safe and hidden. We do not know who or what is behind this breach. Until we do, we must defend what we can."

The assembled goblins scrambled for the door as quickly as they could, pushing and shoving each other in a bid to escape first. As the crowd streamed past Snudge, he grabbed one of the few who had remained seated.

"Weard, you know what this means?" Snudge addressed the G'Oräk healer, one of his most trusted advisors.

"Indeed, sir, but you know we promised—"
"We promised only until there was no other choice.

We need her, Weard. We need her to finish what she started."

"Of course," the healer answered. "Consider it done." A few seconds later, the healer was gone.

Snudge walked over to the window and looked out onto the town of Holden beyond the trees. In the middle of the town square, a fire had been started. It burned in the shape of an eye.

"This test is an hour and a half long, and there will be no toilet breaks, no leaving early and no talking. Is that understood?"

Skye Thistle joined in the rest of her class parroting back their understanding and in writing her name and school details onto the front of her last exam paper. By now, they all knew what to do, and Skye felt that the teachers were as bored as she was by the whole thing.

This was it, though. Her last ever test at this god-forsaken school. After the summer, she would be nearly sixteen and going on to college. Skye couldn't wait. Her nemesis Keith Boggart and his cronies had no desire to stay in school any longer than needed, and so she'd be free of their bullying forever. It sounded amazing. Arthur was equally excited because their new school had lots of different sports teams, and he was convinced that he would walk on to all of them.

"Children," the maths teacher continued, "it is now ten a.m. You will have until eleven thirty to finish the test. I do ask, if you think that you have finished early, please check your answers."

Skye laughed at this. She had managed to sneak a look over her table to check on Alicia Reece's paper during the last maths test. She had put some ridiculous answers which Skye was glad about. Alicia fancied Keith Boggart. In Skye's eyes, that meant that she deserved any other foolish decisions that she made.

The teacher indicated that they could start their test, and Skye dropped her head to read question one.

There was nothing on the test that Skye didn't know, and she had finished, checked and double-checked her paper before they were even halfway through their allotted time.

"If only the English and history tests had been this easy," she grumbled to herself which earned her a sharp shush from the teacher. With nothing else to do, Skye took to staring out of the window onto the school field and letting her mind wander back to Ithilmir. She wondered how her friends were doing. It had been just over a year since she'd first looked through the spyglass and found herself whisked away to another world, and she'd been back maybe a dozen times since then. *How long has it been since my last visit?* Three months? Four? Probably even more, if she was honest. School had taken up a lot of her time lately. Had Snudge managed to find Akeldama since she last visited? She knew that he was sending out regular search parties, but he was becoming less hopeful each time.

"So long as nobody working in alliance with the Dark Queen finds it," he had told her once, "then we have nothing to fear."

Skye hoped that Snudge was right. She hated to think of any harm coming to her friends whilst she was away. In many ways, it was harder being on Earth than it was to be on Ithilmir. She knew that whilst she was away, time stood still on Earth, so nothing bad could happen to her family and friends. However, she knew that this wasn't the case the other way round and that with every moment that she was away from Ithilmir war could be breaking out.

It was whilst she was in the middle of this particular daydream that something moved in the trees at the bottom of the school field and caught her eye. She told herself not to be silly and that it was just because she was thinking about Ithilmir. Nevertheless, she couldn't take her eyes away from that particular tree. She was sure that she could see, about halfway into the canopy, a small, wiry creature that looked remarkably like her good friend, the goblin Weard. Skye knew better, though. The goblins had promised never to return to Earth as they didn't want to draw the queen's attention to the link between the worlds, and they wanted to allow Skye to lead as normal a life as possible.

Skye shook her head and returned to checking her answers once again to pass the time.

When the exam was over, Skye and her class piled out into the playground. Arthur came running over to her to moan about how hard it had been and how he had definitely failed this one. Skye sighed with resignation and tried to keep one eye on the trees whilst Arthur went through the test question by question.

"Skye, are you okay?" Arthur asked after talking at her for nearly a whole minute with no reply.

"Huh? Oh yes," she muttered. "Excuse me a minute, will you?"

Without waiting for an answer, Skye walked over to the tree where she was convinced that something had been lurking and started to throw sticks up into the branches. When this failed to reveal anything more than a startled squirrel, she started to look for a way to climb the tree herself.

"The reason I ask," Arthur started when he finally caught up with Skye, who was stuck a few feet above the ground, "is that this," he indicated Skye's general behaviour with his hand, "is not normal behaviour."

Skye sighed and slumped back down on to the grass at the foot of the tree.

"It's nothing," she said. "Honestly. How did you find the test today?"

"I already said it was impossible. Nobody could answer those questions and…" Arthur trailed off again as Skye was staring past his shoulder and into the hedges behind the tree. Without taking her eyes away, she crept slowly towards the bushes and thrust her hand into the branches. Pulling it back out with all of the flourishes of an accomplished magicians assistant, Skye held a small piece of torn cloth in front of her.

"What on Earth is that, Skye? You are being really weird, even by your standards. And why are you smiling so much? You look odd!"

"I'm not smiling," Skye said whilst smiling from ear to ear. "It's just nice to know I'm not going mad."

"Not going mad?" Arthur mocked, "*Not* going mad? Oh, well, at least you're *not* going mad at the minute. I'd hate to think you *were* going mad."

"Arthur, what are you on about?" Skye asked, snapping out of her daydream. "Let's go and get some lunch. I'm starving." She headed off towards the canteen, allowing Arthur to fall in beside her.

In her pocket, a silver handprint glowed faintly on the scrap of dark fabric.

Disbelief

Skye barely had time to shower after returning home from school later that night, before she was bundled into the car and dragged out to dinner at the Swan and Turnip, a local restaurant that thought simply naming the meals in French would improve the quality. At least Arthur and his parents were being dragged along as well.

Once they'd all been seated and their food had arrived, the parents indulged themselves in small talk about the recent exams and the disaster that the new government was already making of the country.

Skye sat back and tried to piece together the events of the day. She was surer than ever that it was Weard who had come to see her, but she couldn't understand why she hadn't made more effort to find her. Skye knew that she couldn't wait forever. She promised herself that she'd travel to Ithilmir as soon as she got home whether Weard had contacted her or not. She couldn't go on not knowing.

Whilst all of this was going through her mind, she realised that she had been focussing on a point towards the bottom of the bush just outside the large picture window next to their table. Skye couldn't be sure, but she thought that she could just make out a couple of bright green points of light just beyond the branches and leaves, as of a pair of green eyes staring straight at her.

"Erm, excuse me a minute," she apologised to the table. "I just need a bit of air. I'll be back in a minute."

Without waiting for a response, Skye got up from the table and slipped out into the garden. Not wanting to seem too crazy, she took a more roundabout route to the bush in question. When she reached it, she sat down on the grass and faced it. She didn't need her parents seeing her talk to a tree after all.

"I know you're here, Weard. You may as well show yourself," she said.

For a while, nothing happened. So Skye sat and waited.

"I know you are here, Weard. I found a piece of your cloak in the bush at my school."

Skye heard a sigh from the bush as the goblin

finally broke her silence.

"Hello, Skye," whispered Weard. "I am sorry that I am here. It is with a heavy heart."

"What is wrong?" asked Skye, eager for any news.

"There is trouble on Ithilmir. You are needed. Snudge has asked me to fetch you, as soon as you can."

"Is it the Dark Queen again? Has she come back?" Skye asked nervously, not daring to look back at her mother as she spoke of her shadow image back on Ithilmir.

Weard stepped from the shadows of the tree and gave Skye a hug.

"I know that you are worried about the link, Skye. I understand. I cannot say too much, but I believe that the darkness is once again rising. Whether it is the queen who is leading it, I cannot say for sure."

"I can't come until I get home. My only portal is there. I'll have to find a way to get home more quickly," Skye finished, thinking hard.

"No, enjoy your evening, Skye. It may be a while before you see your family again. You have a little time at least, I hope. Besides," the goblin pointed behind Skye, "I think you'll have some explaining to do first."

As she finished, Weard disappeared back into the trees. Skye spun round to see where the goblin had been pointing. Her stomach sank as she found herself looking straight into Arthur's face, his mouth hanging open with surprise. Skye was stuck for words, so she decided to wait until Arthur recovered himself before attempting to explain everything.

"Skye," he began before falling silent again.

Arthur got no further as their parents called them back into the building to inform them that they were going home. To Skye's dismay, her parents invited Arthur and his parents back to their house for drinks. How could she possibly sneak away to Ithilmir with them in the house? She knew that she would have to think on her feet to solve this one and tried desperately to think of something on the short car journey home.

Skye and Arthur were barely through the front door when Arthur dragged Skye away from her parents and up to her bedroom.

"Right, Skye," he started as soon as they were alone, "what on Earth was that thing?"

"That thing," Skye answered sharply, suddenly annoyed, "was a close friend of mine. She's a goblin – a G'Oräk in fact – called Weard, and she has saved my life more times than I'd care to count."

"Saved your life? When have you needed your life-saving?"

"Just forget it. You wouldn't understand. You wouldn't even believe me. Nobody would."

"Try me," Arthur said, "After what I've just seen, I'll probably believe anything."

Grumpy at his presumption, Skye once again told Arthur the story of her first adventure in Ithilmir. She was desperate for him to leave and to head straight back to her friends to help them, so it wasn't a long tale.

"So, you killed things?" he said, still sounding suspicious. "With a sword?"

Skye didn't bother to answer him. Instead, she reached her hand underneath her mattress and pulled Burrower out from its hiding place. Skye had been very careful when choosing where to hide her trusty sword. Of all the things that she had brought back with her, a sharp weapon was the one most likely to upset her mother.

Arthur stood speechless in front of Skye, his eyes fixed on the blade in front of him. Skye held the blade and offered Arthur the handle. He took it and swung it in front of him a couple of times, knocking over a lamp in the process. Arthur ran his fingertip along the blade and sucked it quickly as it started to bleed.

"What is that doing?" he said, breaking the silence by pointing at the ring on Skye's finger. It was glowing.

"I've no idea," she offered. "It does it from time to time. It is a sliver of stone broken from the evil glass orb. I don't know what it does."

"Isn't it dangerous then? To wear it?" Arthur asked.

"Don't talk to me about dangerous, Arthur. You have no idea."

"Show me then," he said with a bluntness that shocked Skye.

"What? How?"

"Take me with you. I heard you telling the goblin that you would go back as soon as you got home. Let me come with you."

"I don't know," Skye said, uneasily. "I don't know if we can travel through the spyglass together."

"Let's try," he said, taking Skye's hand.

"You wouldn't cope," she said in a last-ditch attempt to persuade him to drop it. "It's far too dangerous."

"Fine. I guess I knew it wasn't real anyway. I've just never known you to make so much stuff up. Normally you hate *fiction*," Arthur replied dismissively.

Skye felt like kicking him out of her room, but she was far too angry to take that from Arthur. How dare he! She felt the fizzing behind her eyes that told her she needed to calm down before the power of the ring on her finger took over. She'd fought hard to keep it in check since she'd returned home, but she still couldn't channel the power without losing all control. She'd only ever tried it on Ithilmir where Snudge had paid a druid to help her. The lessons hadn't gone well, and eventually, he'd stormed off and never returned. She daren't think what might happen if she tried it on Earth.

Reluctantly, Skye took a few minutes to stuff some of her regular clothes and to pack everything that she knew she would need on another adventure into Weard's old satchel bag and strapped Burrower to her waist. She grabbed Arthur's hand and made her way over to the spyglass. She made him turn around whilst she quickly changed into a pair of combats and a warm hoodie.

"No matter what happens," she warned him, "do not let go of my hand. When we arrive, don't panic and don't move anywhere. Wait for me to find you if we get separated."

"What will happen if I don't?" Arthur asked. He suddenly sounded less confident.

"You don't want to know," Skye answered. She grabbed his hand, raised her eye to the eyepiece and waited.

A minute later, the room was empty.

The Shadowed Eye

Salismir gasped as he saw the orb resting peacefully inside the wooden crate.

"My lord," he whispered to Jorn the Bandit, "you do know what this is?"

"I have spent a lifetime in these woods, Salismir, worrying about nothing more than the comings and goings of the lords and ladies that keep us fed. I have no interest in what those beyond these trees do. Spare me your wonder and put us all out of misery. Tell us why it is not such a terrible thing that we have wasted an ambush, not on piles of gold and food but instead on some druid's seeing crystal?" Jorn spat back, clearly incensed at what he saw as a wasted opportunity. The other soldiers laughed at Salismir's ticking off.

"Of course, my lord," Salismir stammered. "This

is what my people call the Shadowed Eye, my lord. Those in the north refer to it as Akeldama. It is said to be the embodiment of evil left behind in our world from the beginning of time.

"Lord, there are powerful armies looking for this very thing as we speak. What it is doing in such a remote outpost as this, I couldn't say."

Jorn seemed to calm down with Salismir's words and grabbed the orb from its coffin. He stuffed it into a leather satchel that he slung back over his shoulder and indicated for the rest of their band to pack up ready to leave.

"Thank you for telling me this," he whispered to Salismir as they made their way back into the darkness of the forest. "To the right buyer, maybe this could be as valuable as ten crates of gold." He chuckled to himself quietly as he pushed to the front of the troop and led them quietly back to their village deep within the trees.

As he walked along behind his brothers, Salismir felt his hands start to itch. He couldn't explain why, but the very mention of selling the orb had caused a deep resentment to fall over him. He'd felt this feeling, this itch, before, back in his own village. Whenever he'd felt picked on by the older children or forced to work extra hours on the family farm, he'd feel the rage rise up inside him, and his hands start to itch. It wasn't long before he felt the uncontrollable power start to blur his vision and cause his head to throb before the long, silvery snakes made their way through the veins of his arms and he felt them earth themselves at the tips of his fingers ready to do as he commanded.

He'd never been able to work out how to command them, and the silver lines had found their own way out from his fingers and onto whatever happened to be nearby. What he was feeling now was much stronger. His eyes were aching with the anger that was boiling up inside him.

You are so angry, young hobgoblin! Why so much rage? You know I can be yours, and together we can grow strong!

The voice came from nowhere and seared through Salismir's brain. He dropped to his knees and closed his eyes as tight as he could. Inside his head, a pale green reptilian eye slithered into his vision.

Do not fight me, Salismir. I am your destiny. You have so much power already. You showed that with the barn. And little Suran! She never stood a chance did she, Salismir? Suran! You never told anybody about her, but they knew. They all knew. That's why you had to pay the price for the barn, to even the balance!

"No!" Salismir screamed out loud as the hobgoblins closest to him gathered around and urged him to be quiet. "I didn't. I never could!" The eye was burning bright inside his head, flicking in and out of focus like the tail of a crocodile on a calm river.

Do not lie to me, Salismir!

The voice screamed inside his head. He knew that there could be no way that the others weren't hearing every little secret being laid bare, and yet they only seemed concerned in keeping him quiet until they were further away from the main road. He was immovable on his knees and remained steadfastly bent over in the mud.

I will leave you, for now, my friend. Think of the power that you already have and how much more you could have with me at your side. We could rule the Shadowlands together! We could command an army of the living and the dead and wipe this world clean of all those who oppose us. You could be a god, Salismir! Salismir the Destroyer. Salismir the Infinite. Maybe Salismir the Coward? It is your choice!

Salismir saw the eye flicker and swim away into the distance and felt the force that had held him down leave his body.

"Salismir? Are you all right?" The concerned voice of his lord filtered through his foggy brain.

"I'm sorry, my lord. I am fine. It must be the lack of sleep from being on watch. I will do better next time."

Jorn looked less than amused at Salismir's hasty lie but allowed the matter to drop and urged the group on at double speed to make up for the lost time.

Salismir shook his head as hard as he could as he jogged along to try to shake the memory of the voice loose from his head. Unseen by anyone, a pale scar on the back of Salismir's neck, in the shape of a reptilian eye, faded away to nothing.

Church

Skye and Arthur were ejected from the empty blackness of space and tumbled to a halt halfway across the Glen of Tears in much the same way as Skye had been on her first visit to Ithilmir and, in fact, every visit since.

"That never gets any easier," she told Arthur. "You just have to learn to roll when you land."

Arthur didn't reply. He was too busy turning in a circle, looking at everything around him and moving his mouth soundlessly.

"It's pretty amazing, isn't it?" asked Skye, trying to break the silence.

"Muh," was all that Arthur managed. Skye knew how he was feeling.

"The first time I arrived here, it was dusk, and it looked completely different. Trust me, you don't want to be stuck in these woods at night if you can help it."

Skye's ankle still ached at times and bore a pink scar from her previous encounter with the Glibberig, a hideous worm-like creature she'd been attacked by when she'd first arrived on Ithilmir, and she was eager to avoid any similar misadventures this time around.

Desperate to heed her own advice, Skye gently led Arthur into the surrounding woodland. Every now and then she would stop and pick a berry or two and offer them to him to eat. He took them gratefully but barely said another word. In fact, it wasn't until well after midday that Arthur finally broke his silence and that was simply to ask where they were going.

"Well," began Skye, not sure where to start, "the world we have travelled to is called Ithilmir. We are looking for a village called Kobold, which is the home of the G'Oräk, a tribe of goblins. Don't worry, though," she added, carefully noting his shocked expression. "They are nothing like the goblins we know from storybooks. They are quite lovely and saved my life, as I told you before. Kobold is the main village for the G'Oräk, and their main hall sits just outside of it. That is where I expect we shall be told why I was needed to return here. That is where we shall find out what our adventure is to be."

"*Our* adventure?" asked Arthur, "I thought you

were the hero. Why am I suddenly involved?"

"You wanted to come along to see for yourself, didn't you?" Skye asked sharply.

"Well, yes, but come on, Skye. Swords and stabbing and all that? It's not really me, is it?"

"It wasn't really me either, Arthur, but when you have a Nelapsi staring you in the eye, you soon learn what you can and can't do."

They spent the rest of the day wandering through dense forest stopping only to fill up Skye's water pouch and to eat what little food she found for them. By the time they presented themselves to the guards on the Holden Wall, they had walked through dusk and nightfall was making an appearance. Skye couldn't help but notice that the guards on the gate were a lot more alert and on guard than she had ever seen them before, certainly more so than the night she had been led there by Weard in such a hurry all those moons ago.

"Good evening, Skye," one of the guards offered as he moved his spear from across the Eastern Gate. "We are all glad to hear of your return in these dark days." The goblin nodded towards Arthur. "Prisoner? Or friend?"

"Thank you, Quockerwodger. I trust that you will keep us all safe on the gate tonight. And this is Arthur, a very dear if a little cowardly, friend." Skye winked at Arthur who returned a frown.

"I'll try my best, miss." The goblin smiled. "I'll try my best!"

"Yeah, make sure that we don't get killed, okay?" said Arthur with a laugh, trying to keep up. The goblin didn't respond and instead turned his back.

"Probably best if you let me do the talking, just for now," reassured Skye, taking her friend's hand and leading him swiftly through the gate as he muttered under his breath about the rudeness of the goblins.

"We will see Kobold tomorrow. Tonight, I think we must make for the Great Hall and sleep there. I am sure that Snudge will see us fed and well looked after," Skye said, more to herself than to Arthur. She didn't wait for him to reply but instead took off again into the trees beyond the wall. She knew that Arthur would follow her; he had no other option. Eventually, the trees thinned out to reveal a well-worn dirt track that bore the familiar indentations of cart traffic. Skye knew to follow this until it forked down towards the main village and to take the left road past the meadows.

As she approached the fork in the road, Skye was shocked to discover something new, something that she had never even considered that they would need here. Positioned on the very apex of the fork was a tall gibbet, a metal cage suspended from a wooden pillar designed to hold a prisoner until they died. Inside was a well-weathered skeleton that clearly once belonged to a goblin. Skye shuddered to think who it once was and what they could possibly have done to deserve such a punishment. Then, she thought back to Yop and his betrayal. He could have cost Skye her life, but he had paid the ultimate penalty on top of Liorath's Peak. Maybe it was Elflock. Skye knew that he had been held prisoner at the top of the guard tower, but she hadn't heard anything more for a while. Snudge had always seemed reluctant to talk about him.

Not wanting to look at the foul evil anymore, Skye edged past the gibbet and continued on the lane towards the Great Hall. As she approached, she realised that something even worse waited there. Stood in front of the hall at the foot of the main stairs was a stage erected a dozen feet above the ground. On top was a simple wooden frame supported at both ends and standing above a series of trapdoors set into the stage floor. Above each trapdoor hung a rope ending in a noose. It was a hangman's stage. Why had the G'Oräk suddenly taken to capital punishment, Skye wondered. Something was very seriously wrong. She was glad she had returned. So much had changed since her last visit.

"Are they always this cheerful and welcoming?" asked Arthur sarcastically.

Skye didn't answer choosing instead to press on up the steps and through the open doors at the top. Stepping into the hall, Skye was stunned to see that it was nearly empty. Barely a dozen goblins flitted in and out on business of their own, and the whole atmosphere was eerily quiet. Skye reached out and tried to grab the attention of the nearest goblin as it raced past her.

"Excuse me, I'm looking for Snudge," she asked, but the goblin had raced off into the shadows of the hall.

"He's not here," came a calm voice from behind them.

Spinning around, Skye raced across the floor and threw herself at the goblin, throwing her arms around his neck.

"Snowbroth," she gasped, "where is everyone? What is going on here?"

"We are evacuating the Great Hall and retreating beyond the main village wall. It is not safe here at the moment, Skye, even beyond the Holden Wall. Snudge is waiting for you in the church. He has arranged a council to meet with you and to discuss what must be done. I warn you, Skye, that it is a council of war."

Skye had little time to ask the elderly goblin any questions as he turned on his heels and left as smartly as he had arrived. Skye and Arthur sprinted after him.

It didn't take them long to catch up with Snowbroth. Skye took the time to look over at Arthur. She was surprised to find she was proud of him. She knew how much this must be tearing him up inside. He didn't really care about anything to do with science, but even he would know just how big a deal this was. She could tell he was nervous. He hadn't spoken a word for a long time, something of a record for Arthur. She promised herself that she'd ask the council if they could send him home before whatever was about to happen started. He didn't need to see anything else.

Skye, on the other hand, was worried about what had become of the G'Oräk stronghold. Whenever she had visited before, the goblins had been moving around freely, and Skye could find somebody to talk to day or night. Now, there were no other travellers. They had the tracks to themselves, and it made Skye uneasy, even though she knew that the horrors of the North Wood would struggle to make it past the Holden Wall.

In due course, the trio made it to the gated wall surrounding the village of Kobold. To Skye's surprise, the gate was bolted shut.

"Curfew," explained Snowbroth. "Nobody

is allowed to enter or leave Kobold without first presenting themselves to the council."

"Why?" asked Skye, not understanding how such a peace-loving nation could suddenly turn so defensive.

"It is not my place to say." Snowbroth apologised, "Snudge is expecting you and will explain everything."

Snowbroth wouldn't say any more on the matter despite Skye asking repeatedly. Instead, he reached into a deep pocket in his robe and withdrew a long, rusty key. He inserted it into a hidden keyhole in the gate and turned. With a soft click, the lock slid back and the goblin pushed on the gate until it swung open. Inside the gate, Kobold was much as Skye remembered it. Here, normal life could continue in relative safety, and so traders were shouting their wares from windows and pushing their barrows through the streets thronged with goblins of all ages.

Skye pointed out the church spire to Arthur as it towered high above the rest of the buildings. Despite coming to Ithilmir many times, Skye hadn't really explored Kobold and had never been inside the church. She preferred to stay with Weard in her hut or Snudge in his mansion and often went exploring in the North Wood with them. Because of this and coupled with the fact that her last trip to the village had ended with her being kidnapped by a damaged goblin called Jargogle, finding her way around Kobold still made Skye nervous. She made sure to cling tightly to Snowbroth's robe and made sure that Arthur kept up with her.

She felt responsible for keeping her friend safe even though it had been his decision to come. Skye knew that they would more than likely face battle again on this adventure, and she wasn't looking forward to holding Arthur's hand all the way through it. On the other hand, the thought of him not making it back filled her with such dread that it made her head spin and she had to stop thinking about it in case she fell over.

Their goblin guide led them between buildings and down several tight alleyways until they finally emerged into a crowded square set with heavy stone slabs. Around the edge hung thick golden ropes seemingly to separate the courtyard from the muddy area surrounding it. Inside the ropes, hundreds of goblins were all stood holding their right hand to their left breast and singing in the ancient G'Oräk language. Skye stood and watched, mesmerised by them all singing their own personal prayer. Their faces were all turned towards the tall wooden spire that topped the central tower, and Skye realised there was a silver hand, easily twenty feet across, painted onto the wooden boards.

"They pray for an end to the famine," Snowbroth whispered into her ear. "We should not linger here. They will expect something from us," he finished, urgently.

The elderly goblin grabbed Skye by her hand and led her swiftly towards the stone steps leading up to the main door. Skye quickly reached back and grabbed Arthur, snapping him out of some personal daydream, and dragged him along with them. As they approached the doors, Skye became aware of several of the congregation waking from their prayers and starting to head towards them.

Snowbroth increased their pace, but the goblins quickly caught them up. Skye heard them mumbling, begging for food or water or money. She tried to tell them that she had neither, but as they caught up with her and Arthur, the goblins started pawing at them, reaching into their pockets looking for anything that could be eaten or sold. Snowbroth did his best to fight them off, and Skye took to drawing Burrower to defend herself.

Despite their efforts, the goblins continued their attack, moving slowly like zombies. When they found nothing of interest on their person, they started to get angry. It was then that Skye noticed that Arthur had become separated from them and was surrounded. He was at the centre of a growing mob and fighting back tears as well as goblins.

"We must leave him," Snowbroth shouted over the groans of the crowd. "We must get you safely to Snudge."

"I will not leave him," Skye screamed as shook her arm free of Snowbroth's grasp. "He is my friend. He needs me."

Skye scrambled away before Snowbroth could grab her again and darted into the crowd, drawing Burrower again as she did. She could sense that these goblins weren't evil or malicious. They were clearly just hungry and desperate. She didn't want to hurt them if she could help it, but she knew that she would do whatever was necessary to save her friend. She called out to Arthur and pushed forwards in a new direction when she heard him shout back. The press of goblins around her was stifling and their body heat was exceptional. Skye was sweating and dehydrated but pushed on until she reached the centre of the circle. Arthur was cowering on the ground, and several small goblin children were climbing on his back and grabbing at his hair whilst their parents begged him for help. Arthur was sobbing, and Skye had to fight off his flailing arms as she pulled him to his feet.

"It's me!" she shouted into his ear. "Let's get out of here."

Grabbing hold of Arthur's hand, Skye noticed that one of the attackers had scratched a design into his wrist. It was smudged red with blood, but there was the unmistakable outline of an eye. Putting it to the back of her mind, Skye swung Burrower in front of her causing the goblins at the front of the crowd to part. By swinging the blade back and forth, Skye managed to create a path for them through to the stone steps.

When they reached them, they sprinted up the echoing stone to the ancient, heavy, wooden doors where Snowbroth was waiting to let them in. As they pushed their way into the church, Skye looked back and saw desperate faces chasing them up the steps. Before she could do anything about them, the door slammed shut and they were plunged into darkness.

A Deal

The golden flag atop the tent rippled in the midnight breeze as the flaps slapped against the sides. Inside, angry voices grew louder as each party tried to outdo the other.

In the midst of the argument, Salismir stood in his rightful place to the back of the crowd. He was uncomfortable and his fingers rested lightly on the hilt of his dagger. The entire brotherhood was present under the canvas, but Salismir knew that he was the only one who wasn't pleased to be there.

It hadn't taken Jorn long to find a prospective buyer for Akeldama. In fact, he'd sent word out as soon as they'd returned to their village. Only a few days later, a messenger had arrived looking to arrange the meeting taking place that night. The buyer had wished to remain anonymous, and so his delegation of druids and trusted men had come to conduct the deal on their behalf. Judging by their appearance and weapons and, not least, the fact that they were mostly sand trolls the colour of hardwood, Salismir reckoned them to be from the Rumm Islands or even further west.

The deal that had been agreed to had indeed been very generous with the promise of enough gold to see the Brotherhood of Grield live in luxury for many generations to come. Salismir wanted none of it, though. Since their return to the village, he had not heard the voice again; however, he still felt himself drawn to the orb with a pull unlike any other he'd felt before. He felt as though his brain was on fire whenever he was in its presence and felt a terrible yearning to hold it close and to destroy all those who kept him apart from it.

"How dare you come here to our village and insult us by altering your terms?" shouted Jorn above the voices arguing at cross purposes. "We had a *deal*!" he spat, white foam flecking at the corners of his mouth.

"My lord," the troll opposite him said, one of the few calm voices remaining, "it is not an alteration of terms that we seek, merely a short while in which to verify the heritage of the item in question. You are, after all, asking us to forfeit an awfully large amount of coin based only on your own judgment that this is genuine stone. We have alchemists who can tell us this information—"

"Then you should have brought such an alchemist with you tonight!" gloated Fulop, Jorn's right-hand man. "This kind of insolence will cost you. There are other people interested in her you know. Others who will pay twice as much," he bluffed.

"No, there aren't," replied the troll calmly, calling it. "Firstly, if there were other people offering more money, you would have taken it. You do not strike me as discerning hobgoblins. Secondly, we have taken steps, shall we say, to ensure that no other parties have been made aware of this offer." The troll sat back in his chair and folded his arms.

"Horan? Our messenger—" Jorn stammered in disbelief.

"Is alive and well and only moderately inconvenienced. Should our business be concluded accordingly, then he will be returned to you with most of his important pieces in the correct places." He looked around at the shocked faces and smiled a humourless smirk. "Gentlemen," he sighed, "you are a small tribe in the middle of a forest in the middle of nowhere. Nobody would mourn your absence if you were wiped out this very evening. You consider this item and the gold it will bring you a blessing, but I would argue that you have had not the fortune that you believe but, indeed, the misfortune to stumble upon the most sought-after object this world has ever seen at a time when the major political powers are on the very precipice of all-out war.

"This small, insignificant stone will change all of that. Whoever possesses it will find the armies of the world beating a path to his door and our buyer very much wishes to walk that path.

"Gentlemen, this orb is worth more gold than exists in this world or the next, and yet you will accept the amount we have offered on the terms that we have offered it because, and I want to make this very clear, *you have no other choice.*"

Salismir's fingers gripped the hilt of his dagger hard enough to turn his knuckles blue.

Insignificant stone? You hear how they mock us!

The hobgoblin clapped his hands to his ears in a vain effort to drown out the whining whisper. He'd started at the choice of words himself. He knew it wasn't insignificant. Surely even these heathen trolls could tell just how significant it was and not just as a tool of war.

In their hands, I will be strong. I will move mountains and reduce cities to ash, but it will be nothing compared to the chaos that I will reign down upon this world in your hands. Must I show you yet how great we can be?

A flood of crystal blue light filled Salismir's head and took away his sight. He scrabbled forwards, his hands grappling sightlessly for something to hold him up. Without warning, his vision cleared only it wasn't as he knew it. He was looking out onto the scene in the tent as though through a jug of water. Everything was slightly distorted towards the edges of his vision and took on a bluish hue. He was obviously making a scene as everyone had ceased their arguing and were staring dumbfounded in his direction.

"The eye," muttered one of the noisiest trolls now cowering on his knees. "It is the Shadowed Eye! The mark is on him!"

Salismir turned to Jorn's dressing mirror propped against the far wall. A bright green eye glowed in the middle of his forehead as though carved from his skin to reveal a burning emerald below. Every one of the delegates was on their knees, many muttering repeated prayers under their breath.

Now watch what we could become!

With a suddenness that caught Salismir off guard, a

force flowed from inside his head, and coursed quickly through his arms, burning his veins as it went. His fingers jerked forward no longer under his control, and Salismir felt the magic earth itself in the closest living thing it could find. The troll opposite him screamed as ropes of blue light ripped into his flesh and his body tore itself apart. Blood splattered against the white canvas, and the poor troll's bloodcurdling scream filled the tent. When his suffering finally ended, what was left of him fell to the floor.

Every creature in the tent, troll and hobgoblin alike, fell to their knees and begged for mercy. Salismir was in no mood to grant it, though.

Use me!

Salismir turned his gaze on each of the trolls gathered at his feet. Each one pleaded to be spared as the blue light filled their vision and cast twisting shadows against the walls like a warped shadow puppet theatre. One troll even grabbed up his sword hoping to put an end to the murder, but still Salismir continued with cold abandon reducing each one to a pile of nothingness. Eventually, his gaze fell upon Jorn. He stumbled, lost for a moment in a sea of madness.

Not yet, he may be useful to us.

Salismir blinked and lowered his hands to his side.

As quickly as it had arrived, the power flooded away like a tide leaving the shore. And just like the tide, the power had left its mark this time. Salismir glanced back towards the mirror as an angry red welt rose on his forehead, a permanent reminder of the touch of the Shadowed Eye.

Council Of War

It took Skye and Arthur a while to adjust to the darkness, but when they did, it took their breath away. Arthur had once visited Salisbury Cathedral against his will and had been struck by how vast and beautiful it had been. This was something else entirely.

They were stood in a small porch that was lined with wooden panels from floor to ceiling. The porch opened out onto the main church floor, and his view was uninterrupted all the way to the far altar. Arthur knew that if he were to shout out as loud as he could, the goblins engaged in prayer in front of the ornate shrine would not be disturbed.

Extending above them both, the vaulted ceilings rose to giddying heights, and yet they still were nothing compared to the height of the bell tower that they had seen on their approach through the village. That rose just beyond the porch and was simply an empty square tower with wooden steps hammered into the walls. This gave an amazing view all the way to the bell itself – seemingly a mere dot in the distance – and made Arthur feel dizzy just looking up at it.

Whilst Skye reacquainted herself with her friends and gave the goblin that he had seen on Earth a big hug, Arthur took himself off to have a look at what else the church offered and to calm down from his ordeal. The walls of the church were all built from solid white stone and were punctuated at regular intervals by ornate stained glass windows. As the sunlight streamed through them, they cast iridescent rainbows across the flagstones. The church felt old and the air was still. Arthur noted the specs of dust caught mid-air in the bands of light cast as if fingers from the saints themselves.

Here and there were stone statues laid on top of marble boxes. Each one was engraved with the name and honours of the deceased goblin inside. Each one told a different story of bravery or wisdom or often both, but they were all, in their way, simple affairs compared to the majesty of their surroundings. In fact, the most ornate sarcophagus was laid to rest in a small corner at the rear of the church, hidden behind a blue velvet curtain. It was only by the merest chance that Arthur stumbled upon it. He had to brush away a collection of cobwebs and dust before he could read the engraving upon the cold marble. Underneath, it read:

Kobold San

A leader of goblins beyond all reckoning. Wherever we tread, he will guide us with the Hand of Wisdom.

"We do not expect humans to understand our ways," a voice said softly from behind him, "but you would do well to remember that what was once the Hand of Wisdom, we now call the Hand of Peace. Names change throughout the years and from one telling to the next, but the idea, the idea cannot be changed. Whether it be wisdom, knowledge, charity or, indeed, peace, the ideals of the G'Oräk have never wavered.

"It is this ideal, this moral, which you saw emblazoned upon our church roof and that to which all of the goblins outside were praying. Do you think they are praying for peace? Wisdom? Charity?"

Arthur turned slowly, not wanting to alarm whoever it was who was addressing him. He didn't know what to say, so he waited quietly for the goblin to continue.

"They pray for help, Arthur. In whatever form that comes. It is up to us to deliver it, should it be possible.

I wonder, are you a man of peace?"

"I don't like to fight if that's what you mean," he said to the goblin who stood in front of him, looking at him with piercing eyes.

"That is good," the goblin replied. "We are all very good friends of Skye here, and she has told us much about you, Arthur, and so we are a friend to you as well. At this moment in time, we are looking for all the friends that we can find, as will you be by the time your adventure is over."

"About the adventure—" Arthur began but was cut short by the ringing of the giant bell in the tower. Inside the church, the sound seemed amplified and echoed through Arthur's skull. He clasped his hands to his ears and waited for the sound to die away. As he looked around, he saw Skye had done the same, but the goblin just stood there with an infuriating grin on his face, watching Arthur's reaction with amusement.

"We are to begin our council, it seems," stated the goblin with a smile and a clap of his hands as the bell finally tolled its last chime.

Arthur ran over to Skye and grabbed her shoulder as she made her way to follow the other goblins.

"What is this all about, Skye?" he asked, "I'm not sure I can take this."

"I don't know," Skye answered, honestly, "But it's

not good. The G'Oräk are not normally like this. They are normally relaxed and hospitable. I don't like the feel of it. We must go to this meeting of the council and see what we can do to help."

Before he could protest, Skye raced away to catch up with the other goblins. Not wanting to be left alone, Arthur made up his mind and followed her, catching up with the group just as they disappeared through a small door next to the main altar. They were led into a small antechamber set out with a large round table surrounded by small stools. Arthur and Skye each took a stool along with a dozen other goblins, including the one who had addressed Arthur earlier and who now took a seat at the head of the table.

"Welcome again to the council of war," the goblin who had so recently startled Arthur began before looking directly at him. "For those of you who do not yet know, I am Snudge, leader of the free G'Oräk and head of this council." Snudge took a moment to look at Skye and continued, "We are extremely fortunate today to have our saviour, our hero and, perhaps most importantly, our friend, Skye here with us."

The other goblins said their thanks to Skye and many bowed their appreciation. Arthur noticed that Skye appeared to know most of them and, not for the first time since they had arrived, felt a huge pride in his friend. Back home she was awkward and preferred her own company, but here she was confident and was a hero. Here, she had friends. No wonder she missed it.

"Thank you all," Skye said, addressing the table as she stood. "I would like to say that I am pleased to be here, but having walked along the track I am saddened by what I have seen by the roadside. Why are there goblins strung up into the trees and left to die?"

Snudge looked sadly at Skye and lowered his head, "All will become clear shortly, I promise. Will you do me the favour of allowing me to explain the situation as it stands today before I describe what has gone before?"

Here was the leader of a village asking Skye for permission to speak, Arthur was impressed.

"Of course," Skye answered, sitting back down. "Please tell me everything."

"Some of you may know parts of what I am about to tell you," Snudge started, "but none of you know it all. So I beg you to listen and listen carefully. The last time Skye was sat around a table like this, we were resisting those who urged us to fight and were planning a theft. Today, alas, we are not. You are all aware of the terrible attack on our walls recently; indeed, some of you lost loved ones in the short battle that took place. We were lucky that the rebels who attacked us were disorganised and few in number. We shall not be so lucky a second time. Today, we sit here planning for war."

Conversation erupted around the table as each goblin demanded to know more from Snudge or to question those around them as to what this could mean. As Skye had seen him do before, Snudge just sat back and waited for calm. He gestured to a goblin who was stood in the shadows to bring water to the table and soon each of them had a full glass in front of them. Finally, order was restored and Snudge was able to continue.

"There are some amongst us who would argue with me that had we courted war in the first instance, we would not be here today. To them, I would ask whether they have ever had to weigh the lives of a few against the lives of the many. Should I have risked killing thousands then to save thousands now, or was I right to risk a few to save many more now? We will never know and that is the price of leadership."

Snudge got to his feet and looked each goblin square in the eyes as he continued, "Do not think for one second, that I do not worry over each decision I make. Whether it is the wise decision or the correct decision. Often they are not the same."

The goblin leader sighed and drank from his glass.

Before continuing, he pulled a pipe from the recesses of his robe and struck a match to light it. Once it was burning to his satisfaction, he settled back into his chair and continued his story.

"I do not want war. We have lived for many centuries under a banner marked with the silver hand, the Hand of Peace. Our young guest here has reminded me of why we do this. I was following him with interest as he poked and prodded at our ancestors. I was surprised when he disappeared into a corner and stumbled upon the altar of our first leader, Kobold San. Few bother to look at his stone anymore, myself included, but the message there reminded me of why we seek peace. He will guide us with his Hand of Wisdom, the epitaph reads. Ask yourself, has any wisdom ever sought war?"

"Begging your pardon," spoke a goblin sat opposite Arthur, "but why are we here to discuss war if none of us want it?"

"Indeed, Brack," Snudge answered. "None of us want war, but we have no choice. As you know, we have been searching for Akeldama since Skye removed the Dark Queen from her seat of power, and this has meant that I have many eyes and ears out in the Wandering Place and beyond. They see and hear things and they feed these things back to me.

"I am led to believe that when Skye destroyed the

Dark Queen, whatever remained of her evil soul took exile in a small harbour town called Soulaman which lies to the west of Athancor and serves as a place for ships to restock before heading into the Glass Sea. There are monsters lurking in the waters there that would make anything you have seen before look like mice, and sailors do not sail there lightly and without full supplies.

"I believe that the dark force is laying low on the outskirts of the town, raising an army ready for another attack on the North. It is imperative that we destroy it before it grows too strong. Unfortunately, many of the queen's allies are heading south to join whatever army exists before they are destroyed by the wandering mercenaries that seek Akeldama. Some, though, have remained in the north and are attacking villages and towns. They are all heavily armed and number in the hundreds. Most do not stand a chance."

"Is that the reason for the curfew here?" Arthur asked, before realising that he was interrupting.

"Indeed, Arthur, I must protect my people as best I can.

"Unfortunately, we do not have endless supplies, and so we are all on strict rations until we can send a convoy out to the farmsteads to locate more food. For all we know, they may have been burned to the ground.

Many goblins are not happy with our situation. They would sooner return to their lands outside the gate and face the risks that brings. I have told them all that they are free to leave as they choose, but it appears many are not as brave as their words.

"There is no doubt that by the time we reach the growing army in the south, its number will be into the tens of thousands. We know that there are bands of orcs and men rallying as we speak along with larger groups of Nelapsi, a night-loving race that prefer to feast on carrion than kill for themselves if they can help it, and goblins. It appears that they have trained a band of orc to ride Wyvern again. It has been many generations since last the Wyvern Riders took to the sky. It does not look good, my friends. For now, the guard on the Holden Wall has been strengthened, but it would still not withstand a dedicated attack."

As everyone digested the news, Snudge requested for food to be brought to the table, and they were soon dining on scraps of cold meat and vegetables.

"I am sorry there isn't more," the leader said, "but rationing must apply to us all equally."

Whilst they ate, Snudge continued his story over an empty plate, choosing not to eat himself.

"As I said, none of us are sure if the Dark Queen has indeed risen again or whether this is some new evil rising to fill the void left in her absence. Whatever it is, it may not be the only threat," he started, causing the diners to glance up in alarm.

"I have word of a new force rising in the east on the Dragon Isle. I do not know yet whether they will be a force for good or evil, or whether they may prove of no consequence either way. We will be monitoring them closely, though. This may be a coincidence but, in my experience, coincidences are few and far between.

"I have sent out calls to the leaders of our closest tribes, to Karad Nur who leads an army of goblins from Fenkur across the Silver River and to Porat, the Elder who leads the Grundals, a band of gnomes, from the city of Tor. I have sent word of my intention to take an army to meet the growing darkness and to defeat it whilst it is still weak. So far, I have had no reply, but I am hopeful they will see sense."

"How many soldiers will that give us?" asked Snowbroth.

"If we take every last creature of fighting age, plus the Felmir that we know will join us? Maybe three thousand. Four at the outside."

"Against an army of many tens of thousands? How can we win?"

"We cannot, not without luck and surprise. I am hopeful that we will be able to recruit more soldiers on the way. If we do not, then should we cower away and await our end at the hand of whatever darkness beats a path to our doors?"

Nobody dared to reply, so Snudge continued: "Remember, this is not a choice I relish making, but it is one that falls to me to make. It will take us a week or so to ready an army, during which time the darkness will continue to grow in strength and may choose to progress north. I anticipate that the first target will be to take Hurathi. It was once a great town nestled in the curves of the gently flowing Long River. For many years it traded on the barges that travelled to and from Coraka and even out into Sunport. Trade has been slow for the last few years though and the town has grown weak under the rule of a greedy council. It will be an easy target and will provide a strong base.

"Beyond that, and if this is the resurrection of the Dark Queen, then Liorath's Peak would be a logical target. I am sending a group of you to take and defend the peak against any who try to take it. It must not fall. Is that understood?"

The table nodded its agreement before Skye broke the silence. "Who will you send to defend Liorath's Peak?"

"My most trusted people. Skye, and you, Arthur,

since you are here, I would ask that you lead the small group that I can spare and see them safely to the peak. I will send you with goblins that you know and trust, those you have fought with before. Is that acceptable?"

"Thank you," Skye said. "I will do my best."

"But of course." Snudge smiled. "You always have. Our good friend Geldrig will be joining us soon from Lörieas. I hear that their town is mostly rebuilt now, and they are once again doing a fair trade on the Silver River.

"Whilst you defend the tower, we will ready the army here and will travel south as soon as we are able. We will pass to the west of Liorath's Peak and send riders to replenish your numbers if needed and to bring you to us at Carak Tak.

"We will need you, Skye, and all of your fellowship, for the Battle at Athancor."

"What about the goblins on the corner? Why do you need such cruel punishments?"

Snudge looked Skye in the eye, all humour lost from his face, and said, "Do you remember Elflock, Skye?"

Skye remembered the traitorous goblin well and said so. She reminded Snudge that she had almost died at his hand twice, once when she was kidnapped and once when Yop had betrayed her whilst doing Elflock's bidding.

"Was that him in the cage?" she asked after explaining herself.

"No, though he did perish in the gibbet. Unfortunately, those who supported Elflock didn't go away when he died. There is still a small section of goblins who would wish to topple me and guide the G'Oräk to the Dark Queen's side. What once started as a group seeking war is now, ironically, a group seeking to avoid war and to roll over and surrender. The problem with radical groups, Skye, is that they always want to cause chaos.

"The gibbet serves the role of removing those from our ranks who would otherwise be dangerous and also serves as a reminder to those who are considering joining their ranks."

"Surely it isn't a government's job to just kill anybody who disagrees with them?" asked Skye in shock.

"Skye, I admire your ideological views, but we are entering into a state of war. We need to be united. We cannot afford to have people amongst us who would wish to sell us to the darkness. Can you imagine where we would be now if Yop had succeeded in killing you and the Dark Queen had kept hold of Akeldama?" Snudge allowed Skye time for the thought to sink in. "It cannot be allowed, Skye. Every G'Oräk is duty bound to protect the others. Is that clear?"

"Yes, Snudge," Skye answered sullenly.

"Every G'Oräk, Skye. Remember that."

Attack

Salismir blinked open his eyes. *It is time…* Through the gap in his tent door, he could see that it was still dark but that some of the brotherhood were awake and sat around a smouldering fire. *Not yet midnight then*, he thought. Jorn had made it clear that all fires were to be damped down before midnight and all men asleep. He needed his men fresh for their raids on the carriages.

You know what must be done. You know where I am hidden. Find me, release me and we will ride together on the waves of darkness.

The guards around the fire never saw Salismir sneak up behind them. He left them where he killed them and damped down the fire. He couldn't afford shadows. Tonight's work needed the darkness that reflected the very act itself.

You are close, so very close. He is asleep. Killing him will be easy...

Salismir hummed quietly to himself to drown out the voice.

On his forehead, the eye burned in the darkness.

It took several days to ready the goblins to leave, but Skye and Arthur were called upon several times each day to consult on the plans for the coming journey. They would all take a boat as far as the Wyvern's Wing before breaking off into their groups. As discussed, Skye, Arthur, Geldrig and Brack were to head to Liorath's Peak to secure it against any invaders. Snudge was confident that it would be deserted, and so he was sending the foursome ahead of a group of a dozen or so warriors who would join them within a week. Once Liorath's Peak was secured, the four were to head on to Carak Tak to wait for the G'Oräk army.

Snowbroth, Curglaff and Weard would leave the others behind on the river and travel to Lörieas to try to persuade their Council of Elders to support Snudge in the coming war. Whilst Geldrig argued that he should be allowed to take part in the discussions with his own people, Snudge argued that he was better served protecting the two humans on their important journey. The fact that they would be joined by Brack particularly delighted Skye. She had formed something of a soft spot for the minstrel and often missed his tuneful voice when she was back on Earth.

In time, everyone was agreed on their course of action. With a strange sense of déjà vu, Skye once again found herself in a small boat heading along the Silver River. Once again, Curglaff took control, but all the time he was teaching Geldrig how to steer the boat and read the river. As soon as they reached Lörieas and those charged with recruiting more fighting men had left the boat, Geldrig would be in charge of getting the rest of them as far as Hillmoss. There they would set out on foot towards Liorath's Peak, hopefully avoiding the need to enter the Wandering Place if at all possible.

Skye lay back in the boat and let the summer sun warm her skin. She found herself much more amenable to adventure when the weather was on their side and, all in all, she considered things could be a lot worse. The river was flowing quickly carrying the boat along with the help of the meltwater in the mountains that fed into it much further upstream and they were soon approaching the Wyvern's Wing. It was still before lunchtime, but they all agreed that an early lunch would help see them through the afternoon. So, nervously remembering their last visit to the inn, they were soon enjoying a welcome if simple meal of vegetable stew and bread.

Geldrig insisted that they set up camp for the night before approaching Lörieas the next day. He argued that he didn't want to start his stewardship of the boat at dusk. Reluctantly Snowbroth agreed, and so they spent an enjoyable if uncomfortable night under the stars at the base of the Wizened Peak mountains.

The next morning, the four who were to remain bid farewell to the rest of the group and Geldrig took control of the boat. The river had widened over the last few miles and so meandered along at a more manageable pace, but all sense of enjoyment had gone from the adventure. None of the four dared to speak the words to each other, but there was no escaping the fact that they were now well and truly on their own.

There it was. How dare he leave such a precious thing out in the open for anyone to grab. It was so beautiful even in the darkness. It glowed with a power that couldn't be seen by those who had no power themselves. But Salismir had power, didn't he? Oh, how he knew he had power now! *But the power I will have will be tenfold!* he reassured himself.

Salismir snaked across the muddy floor of his

leader's tent towards the orb that lay nestled on a bed of sawdust. He'd never imagined that it would be this easy; he'd expected more of a fight. He was relieved, though. He knew that if Jorn had tried to hide it, if he'd had to get that information out of him, then he would have stopped at nothing to do so.

In the distance, a wild dog crowed to the half-moon, but Salismir paid it no attention. His palms were sweating and his tongue was too big for his mouth, but it didn't matter. Once he held the Shadowed Eye, he would never be nervous again. He would be unstoppable.

Do not falter. You are close. Release me!

The voice hissed inside his head. It trembled, excited, passionate. There was none of the cold calmness that it had used to lure Salismir away in the first place.

There were noises behind Salismir, but he was too far gone to care. His shaking hands reached out to take the orb, to take the power that was rightfully his. He stopped suddenly, his hands inches away, as a pinpoint of cold steel pressed into the base of his skull.

"Stop, Salismir. You think I don't see how you covet my treasure? You think I don't sleep with one eye open at all times?" Jorn sneered as he pushed the tip harder into his skin. A bead of dark red formed against the blade and ran down towards the hilt.

"It doesn't belong to you!" Salismir spat, craning to see over his shoulder, not even bothering to lie about his presence in the leader's chambers. "You leave the most valuable weapon *in the world* here for anyone to steal, and you expect us to trust you?"

"Do you think I am such a fool? Do you think that I am so hidden away as to not know what this was the moment I set eyes on it? I doubt many of the other brotherhood knew at first. But you and I? We knew what it was immediately, didn't we? We who covet power recognise it when we see it, don't we?

"I know what the Dark Queen nearly achieved with this thing, and I know what happened to her in the end. Destroyed, her soul sent into exile, not even allowed to roam the Shadowlands. This thing," he pushed the blade forwards jarring Salismir's head in the direction of the stone, "is nothing but a curse on those who behold it. Power is nothing without control, and this *thing* is nothing but power. It has all of the control. Look at how it has controlled you! I want nothing to do with it. And so, yes, I will sell it for what coin I can get.

"It would appear that it already has its talons into you, though. So much so that you would steal from your own family to take it? Do you have no shame,

Salismir? Maybe I should have let those who sought to burn you all those years ago get on with their job?"

Salismir rocked against the anger in Jorn's voice. He'd barely listened to the words, but some of the message had seeped into his scarred mind. Tears rolled down his face and dried on his cheeks, the fear and excitement that had driven him on, driven him into this tent, had started to leave him, and he suddenly felt very alone and at sea.

"My lord—" he began, his head bowed against his chest. He felt Jorn lower his sword slightly, though he still felt its presence against his back.

"Do not apologise to me, *traitor!*" Jorn spat, raising the sword once again to Salismir's neck. "There is nothing you can say to atone for this. Once again, I am going to be the one who saves your life, though, gods help me, you don't deserve it. I should kill you right here in my chambers for this. Not one hobgoblin out there would begrudge me that.

"But I shan't, and quite a few may begrudge me *that* when it comes to it. You are not acting of your own mind, Salismir. I can see that clearly. Your eyes are glowing; *all three of them*, I might add. You will leave here tonight, alone and unarmed, and you will leave these woods. You will never set foot east of the Fountain of Tears again. If you do, I will not be so generous.

"I'm sorry, Salismir, but it can be no other way."

Jorn reached forwards with his free hand and removed Salismir's knife from its sheath. He tossed it behind him onto his bed without once lowering his own sword.

Do it!

Salismir felt the power flooding back along with the voice in his head. He felt the anger rise up inside him and burn against the back of his eyes. He lowered his hands.

"No, my lord, I am the one who is sorry."

Before Jorn could react, Salismir lunged forwards and grabbed up Akeldama. He spun on his heels and brought the heavy stone round into the side of his leader's head. Jorn fell to the ground, his eyes open with surprise. He didn't get back up.

Make sure!

Over and again, Salismir brought the heavy orb down onto his leader. He only stopped once he collapsed, breathless and racked with dry sobs against the man he once loved as a father. Outside he could hear the other hobgoblins rising from their tents in response to the noisy attack. Salismir grabbed up his knife from the bed and scrambled underneath the canvas wall of the tent and headed out into the darkness.

Hillmoss

Over the course of the next day and as mile after mile of the Silver River slipped languidly past, the towering mountains in the distance and the dark forests that practically invaded the banks of the river on its western side gave way to splendid valleys and thriving vineyards.

"Rivergold," announced Brack as the yellowing crops grew too bright to look at.

"It looks beautiful. A bit like France or the Netherlands back home, don't you think?" asked Arthur who was much better travelled than Skye.

Brack continued his introduction to the area, ignoring Arthur's interruption. "It's the farming heartland of the north. When Snudge feels that it is safe enough to send out scouts, he will no doubt send them to the valleys of the Rivergold to bargain for whatever they can spare. Their grapes make the best wine, their apples the best cider and their corn the best bread. For now, they have remained untouched by war and long may it continue. If this war goes on for very long, this may be the only source of food from Kobold to Kanthor."

The goblin shivered as if to shake off such a horrible thought. Skye deeply regretted the haste that they were being forced to make on their journey. She desperately wanted to sample some of the glorious food that he had described and even just to sit and relax on the sunny hills.

Instead, they satisfied themselves with drinking in the view and gulping down the fresh air and made promises to each other to return once peace had returned, when they would have time to fully enjoy it unburdened by their quest.

Hillmoss was alive with noise as Geldrig bumped their boat against a wooden pier just before dusk. Having made most of its livelihood as a bustling market town on the main river, the people of Hillmoss were used to conducting their business at all hours of the day and, so long as there was a boat arriving or departing, the stalls hummed with life.

Everything was on offer as Skye, Arthur and Brack made their way from merchant to merchant: fresh seafood brought along the river from its mouth at the ocean; crops grown on the sunshine-blessed farms of the Rivergold and meats and cheeses from the best animals in the north. Every seller seemed fluent in whatever lingo the buyers were haggling in, and gold and silver was flowing from pocket to hand in a blur.

"How on Earth do they know what they are buying? Or how much they're spending?" mused Arthur as they stopped at a small shack that was selling dried herbs from wicker baskets. Brack had mentioned that he wanted to pick up some healing herbs for the journey and was currently engaged in a shouting match with the proprietor of the stall, a skinny troll seemingly carved out of marble.

Having left Geldrig behind trying to sell the boat and with instructions to find them all rooms for the night, Skye felt very exposed out in the open. She was growing more aware of the presence of Akeldama on her finger the closer they got to Liorath's Peak. Back home, she was able to wear her mother's ring without really thinking about what the shiny black stone used to be part of. But back on Ithilmir, it had started to itch and burn and she was sure she could hear it trying to talk to her in her sleep.

She hadn't mentioned it to anyone before. She doubted they'd believe her anyway, and she was already fed up with Arthur thinking she was ready for the madhouse. Even though it wasn't part of Akeldama anymore, Skye still felt that it contained a lot of the dark power that it once had. On days when she was very angry, she could feel the familiar fizzing sensation behind her eyes and the tingling in her arms. It was still a valuable and powerful weapon, and she didn't want to draw attention to it in such a public place. Instead, she thrust her hand into her pocket and tried to forget about it.

They'd said hasty goodbyes to Geldrig, so eager were they to sample to the market, and left him with a vague idea that they'd meet him underneath the enormous clock tower that dominated the centre of the market square at sundown. Skye could see the last of the sun disappearing behind the clock tower and turned to Brack to urge him along in his conversation. As it happened, he was just handing over several small silver coins to the disgruntled merchant.

"We should get going," he said happily. "It's nearly sundown."

"Yes!" snapped Skye. "We could all see that. We'd be well on our way by now if it wasn't for your little argument!"

"Oh, that wasn't an argument. I just made it clear to the lovely gentleman that we were not going to be paying his frankly ridiculous prices and that, if he didn't agree to our offer, he may find that the Office of Trading Standards pay him a visit!"

"Trading standards?" said Arthur in disbelief.

"Yes. Weard mentioned them after one of her visits to Earth. A wonderful idea, she'd said. Anyway, he didn't know what the devil I was talking about, but it seemed to work. I paid him barely a fraction of what he was charging originally."

Skye had been walking along in silence whilst Brack bragged about his victory. *No wonder he looked so cheerful,* she thought. Something was playing on her mind, and she opened the paper bag that the goblin had given her to hold.

"Brack?"

"Hmm?" he said, not really paying her much attention.

"You know the bag he gave you is empty, right?"

"That little—" He snatched the bag from Skye's hands and tore it open. Nothing fell out. "Why the thieving little *takrek*!" he spat and turned back towards the stall, all cheerfulness lost.

"Not now." Skye chuckled as she grabbed him by his shoulders and dragged him towards the clock tower. Behind them, Arthur stifled his own amusement at the goblin's misfortune. "We must go and find Geldrig.

You know how he'll be worrying about us."

As they walked towards the tower, Skye and Arthur continued to remind Brack of his betrayal. Skye was pleased to see Arthur laughing for the first time since they'd arrived on Ithilmir. She'd noticed earlier that the scratch on his hand, the red eye, had started to fade already, a few more days and it would be gone. She was glad, she hadn't like seeing it, even if she couldn't place her finger on why. She still felt a terrible burden to make sure that he stayed safe. She'd only meant to bring him here to show him that she wasn't going crazy. She'd never meant for him to get dragged into a war.

"There you are," grumbled Geldrig in his deep voice as he stepped out from the shadows at the base of the darkened tower. "I thought you'd managed to get yourself kidnapped again," he muttered at Skye with a half-smile. "It wouldn't have surprised me."

"I'll have you know," mocked Brack, "I am quite the knight in shining armour and would never let a hair on her head be harmed. I am more devious and devilish than you know."

"Didn't you just get ripped off by a troll?" teased Arthur to the goblin's dismay. Skye nearly choked, and even Geldrig managed to chuckle to himself as Arthur re-told the story for the hundredth time.

Geldrig led them quietly down meandering back alleys until they popped out into a small courtyard that fronted onto a small yet hospitable-looking cottage. The Felmir had managed to persuade the owners to rent them the stable for the night and had bought from them four strong-looking horses to lead them across the grasslands the following day.

The owners of the cottage turned out to be an elderly pair of tree trolls. They had left Landragog, they said, many years ago and moved to Hillmoss to retire in the sun and away from trees. The idea of a tree troll wishing to leave the forest behind was considered unimaginable to most of their family and friends, and so they had lived alone since they arrived. They said they were glad for the company. Skye, in turn, thanked them for their generous hospitality and in particular for their excellent meal of meat and potatoes.

Arthur was obviously exhausted from the day's work on the river and he was soon asleep once they'd made their way to the comfortable stable. Geldrig and Brack had soon followed him, but Skye found that she couldn't get to sleep no matter how hard she tried. In the end, she climbed up the ladder in the corner of the stable and made her way out onto the roof. In the distance, she could see the lights in the marketplace marking out the streets and alleyways where the traders were still buying and selling. If she tried, she could still hear them arguing between themselves. Or maybe they were just all sharing the story of the troll who'd managed to outsmart a goblin. She laughed to herself as the thought struck her.

As the night grew darker, Skye made her way back down into the stable and slipped into a fitful sleep. The next day would mark the beginning of her adventure. For the moment, they had found nice place to sleep and nobody was trying to kill them. That wouldn't last.

Skye turned over in her sleep and gripped Burrower tightly to her chest.

Weard shivered as she set foot into the marble city of Lörieas for the first time since they had fought the Nelapsi what seemed like a lifetime ago. The city was once again thriving. Where last the healer had seen only crumbled walls and empty streets, she now saw a bustling marketplace and gleaming houses once again finished in ornate marble. Pillars and exquisite busts adorned the front of the more expensive properties and businesses had set up along the main thoroughfare. The sound of a blacksmith hammering steel mixed easily with the sound of children learning drifting from the windows of the schoolhouse. Further into the town and overlooking the river stood a brand-new theatre occupying the space where the town hall had once stood.

"It's beautiful," she whispered to Snowbroth who was similarly taken with the resurgence of the Felmir who lived here. Curglaff had wandered off on his own and was taken with an ornate statue in a small square off the main road. He called the other two over hastily and pointed to the script that had been engraved on the base.

"For Brabble, who helped return this city to glory," read Weard with a tear in her eye.

"How did they know?" asked Curglaff. "We buried him before we left."

"Geldrig returned," answered Snowbroth flatly. "No doubt Snudge is aware of it. Anyway, it's true. It's nice that what he sacrificed amounted to more than a petty end to a petty fight."

Weard nodded, and the three set off down the road towards the centre of the town. As they walked, Weard looked around at the people going about their new lives in a city that was just finding its feet in the world. It wasn't just Felmir who were wandering the streets, she was pleased to notice. Gone were the ideals that had driven other races from the town to the ultimate demise of those who chose to remain. Instead, all seemed welcome.

"We have worked hard, but there is still much to do," said a voice from behind, apparently reading her mind. The voice was clean and crisp but thickly laden with charm.

The three goblins turned around and looked into the large face of a man used to a plate filled with rich food.

"Mayor?" asked Snowbroth hopefully.

"Close, but alas I am not!" the tall man smirked at the goblin. "I am Faldoric, one of his assistants. I am, I suppose, his messenger. He has been expecting you for a while, Snowbroth. Am I to assume that you are Weard, the healer of whom we have heard so much, and Curglaff, the only goblin to ever sail on the open ocean?"

The two goblins indicated that they were as described but said nothing more. They hadn't anticipated their arrival being foretold, and it had thrown them off guard.

"Do not worry," Faldoric calmed them. "There is no spy amongst you. Snudge sent a message to us a week or so past telling us to expect your arrival. He also had the grace to inform us of your errand, and it is to that end that I must now take you to see the mayor. If you would be so kind as to follow me." The mayor's second-in-command headed off towards a squat but wide building in the distance without waiting to see if the goblins would follow.

With nothing else to do and knowing that what they had set out to achieve had already been decided one way or another, they followed Faldoric towards the town hall.

Return To Liorath's Peak

The horses that the old tree trolls had sold them turned out to be splendid white beasts almost taller than Geldrig and who seemed to take no issue with being loaded up with equipment and rider together. It wasn't long after an early breakfast that the foursome found themselves heading out along the main thoroughfare through Hillmoss.

They had chosen to keep their true destination a secret from their hosts – Skye had enough experience with spies to know not to trust kindly strangers – and instead had told them that they were heading towards the small town of Salabah which they knew to be in the shadow of Liorath's Peak.

Jol and Pesh, as the two tree trolls had introduced themselves, had instructed them to keep to the main road out of Hillmoss as it continued as a well-beaten track all the way south to Carak Tak and would take them past Salabah in due course. Many thanks had been said, and it was with genuine sadness that they had mounted up and left. Skye doubted that they would find such generosity again before the war was over and said as much to Arthur.

"What the hell have you dragged me into?" he muttered to her in a simple reply. She'd been asking herself the same question.

It didn't take long before Hillmoss was a speck on the horizon and even the tall clock tower had merged into the distance. The weather was nice and warm, and so they took their time and saved their horses' energy. Despite the weather, Skye couldn't help but feel a chill inside her as they drew closer to Liorath's Peak. She still had flashbacks and nightmares at home where she would scream as the Dark Queen, with her own mother's face, turned into view and bore down upon her cursing her for sending her back to whichever darkness she had risen from. Her mother had talked about paying for her to see a therapist for her "night terrors," but Skye doubted it would help. She could hardly tell her the truth, after all.

As promised, the road to Salabah was well worn and they passed several carts heading in the opposite direction as they meandered across the countryside.

All of the way, the Wandering Place was just visible in the north as a line of cracked and twisted desert on the horizon. Even in such a warm spring, the land was ravaged beyond growth and the hedgerows and copses that were such a feature of the landscape up close seemed to cut off abruptly rather than spread out into such a desolate environment. All of the carters proved to be very friendly and some even offered them water and small pieces of food to help them on their journey.

All the while, Skye's ring seemed to buzz against her finger, and she felt it start to burn and rub against her skin. Once, she took it off and placed it in a small pocket in her jacket, but the worry of it falling out and becoming lost soon took over and she hurriedly worked it back on.

Despite the track being well worn, it didn't take a direct route to Salabah. So the group found themselves outside in the wilderness when their shadows started to grow long ahead of them. Geldrig led them to a small copse, and Brack managed to light a small fire for them to sit and camp around. Despite the imminent war and the danger of their destination, they were all still relaxed and didn't put up too many protests when Brack started to fill the night air with another of his beautiful songs.

In Malagao's folly,

Where the dragons grow merry,

I met a young goblin by the name of Felglin.

He'd fought twenty dragons,

Slain more than a dozen,

But couldn't remember which way was his home!

So I told him I'd help him,

If only he'd promise,

To give me the weapon that'd slain all his foe!

By the end of the last verse, Skye and Geldrig were laughing along with Brack whilst Arthur just sat there with his mouth open. Skye had forgotten that Arthur's idea of good music was anything in the charts by the latest grumpy solo artist. He wasn't used to music containing so much passion and soul. To his credit and Skye's amazement, he immediately stood up and gave Brack a genuine round of applause.

Once again, they were back on the road a little after dawn the next morning. They were eager to arrive at Liorath's Peak with as much of Eye day left to scout out the surrounding area, before making their ascent to the top.

Skye was secretly hoping that she could remember

the place where she had climbed up before. She'd found it entirely by luck the last time she had been here and wasn't certain she'd be so lucky again. She hadn't voiced her concerns when Snudge had asked her the question back at his house; instead, she'd reassured him that she'd definitely know where it was again.

"Is that it? Is that where we are heading?" asked Arthur, suddenly grabbing Skye's arm and pointing towards the south. They'd been travelling for a few hours, and they'd all drifted into their own private thoughts as they often did when riding for long distances. Skye was quite startled by Arthur's intrusion.

"Yes," answered Skye flatly. "That is Liorath's Peak."

"It's spooky!" said Arthur nervously. "It's a bit like those scary vampire castles that you see in old black and white movies. I almost expect thunder and lightning as we get closer."

Skye had to fight back the urge to knock her best friend from his horse. How could he be so crass, so unthinking? She fought back the urge and reminded herself that he didn't know, not *really* know, what it had been like and he was seeing all of this for the first time. She knew how nervous she was, and she knew what to expect. She'd have to cut Arthur a lot of slack in the coming days. Best to start now.

"When we get closer, it's more like a giant rock.

I wouldn't say it's spooky, but there is certainly a darkness that lives there. I can feel it now as we get closer. The power is still strong here."

"I agree," interrupted Geldrig. "Even though the Dark Queen has long gone, evil still calls this place home. We would do well to watch our step from this point on. I am worried that the tower may not be as deserted as Snudge's little spies have told him."

Arthur shivered at the news, but Skye and Brack just sat and stared at the peak in the distance. So far they'd continued along the track, but that now veered far to the south, and so they were forced to leave the comfort of a well-worn road and head out onto the uneven, rock-strewn grassland that made up the rest of the distance.

They found that the closer they approached the slower they pushed their horses as though trying to delay the inevitable, but eventually they arrived at the woodland to the far south of Liorath's Peak that formed a barrier between the tower itself and the towering mountain range that extended to the east and that disappeared into the Gloom; the dark forest that Skye, Brack and Geldrig knew all too well had once concealed a marauding band of orcs.

In the shadow of the tower, all of the heat from the air disappeared. Before long, they had taken out their cloaks and covers from their bags and were wearing them tight over their shoulders. Arthur was struggling more than the others, and Skye felt worried for the first time that there was a very real chance that her best friend might not make it back. The fact that he was shivering with uncontrollable nerves was making matters worse for him, and so Skye took him to one side to try to reassure him whilst Brack and Geldrig tethered the horses beyond the edge of the woodland and made an effort to scout the foot of the wall.

"How are you feeling?" Skye asked when she was sure they were out of earshot.

"I don't know, Skye. None of this seems real, you know? I keep expecting to wake up."

"I know." The truth was, she knew more than words could ever say. She'd felt exactly the same the first time she'd set out from the safety of Snudge's mansion. "There's nothing I can say that will make this any easier. It's a rubbish situation that you don't deserve to be in." She looked over at Arthur and lifted his chin with her hand. "I'm sorry. I really am."

Arthur sat quietly and stared into her eyes. For the briefest moment, Skye felt butterflies in her stomach, almost nerves but not quite. She held his gaze until her eyes watered until, suddenly, Arthur's face broke into an awkward smile and he playfully tapped her on the shoulder. "You'd better be. If I die here, you've got to tell my mum!"

Skye couldn't help but laugh. Arthur always had that ability. She turned to walk back to the others and was surprised when Arthur grabbed her and spun her into a tight hug.

"Thank you for keeping me alive," he whispered softly, just loud enough for her to hear.

"You're welcome," she replied, shocked. Arthur had never hugged her before. Not one to let an opportunity to get one up on her friend pass her by, Skye spun out of the hug and drew Burrower. "Better teach you how to use that thing so that you can return the favour."

Arthur smiled and drew his own blade. "I think I'll be fine," he said through a wheeze as he lunged at Skye.

"I'm not so sure!" She barely had to move as she parried his sword easily and knocked him to the ground with her shoulder. She couldn't help but revel in his defeat, this was the first time she'd ever been better than him at sport.

Over the next few hours, Skye tried to remember everything that Brabble had taught her when she had first been given Burrower. It seemed like such a long time ago. She fought back tears and reflected on how much she suddenly missed her friend again.

She tried her best to teach Arthur the basic rules; keep your balance, crouch, watch their sword not their eyes, and some of the more basic moves. In the end, she knew too well that, when an enemy was trying to gouge out your eye, you didn't remember all of the little tricks and moves that you'd been taught. You stabbed and hit and bit and tried to do whatever you could to kill them before they killed you. Unfortunately, that was a lot harder to teach.

Skye was under no illusion that she was nearly as good a teacher as Brabble had been, but by the time their friends returned she felt a little bit more confident that Arthur was more likely to injure an enemy than a friend. At least knew which end of the sword should point towards them.

Their friends returned with good news. reporting that Snudge's advice did, in fact, seem to be true, at least for the area surrounding the tower. Arthur, for his part, apologised for his nerves so far and promised to do everything that he could to help their cause from here on in.

Brack and Geldrig bore bad news as well. Despite searching the tower, they hadn't been able to find any way to the top. They were, they told her, relying entirely on Skye to ensure that their journey so far hadn't been wasted. Skye reminded them that it had taken her a long time to find it last time but that she was sure she could find it again. In fact, it took Skye less than an hour to find the place where she had last climbed the crumbling rock face.

"It's all about how you see it," she told the others as they rounded a corner to find Skye already several feet up the stone ladder. "I couldn't see it last time until I took a few steps back from the face of the rock and the shadows fell just right."

Arthur had to smile at the smugness with which Skye delivered the news to her friends and again felt very proud of his friend who, back home, wouldn't dare talk to her own family with such self-assuredness.

As soon as they had all reached the rocky outcrop and Skye had found the crack in the wall that would allow them entry, the memories came flooding back to her. She swiftly led them through the winding passageways and empty corridors that she knew would lead to the platform at the top of the tower. She made sure to point out the room that had held Akeldama and took the opportunity to retell that part of her adventure at Arthur's request. Buoyed on by a sense of confidence in Snudge's information, the group finally made it to the gateway that led out onto the tower. Congratulating themselves on a job well done, they burst out into the open and pulled up short.

A band of scrawny, twisted goblins turned away from a struggling fire and grabbed up their swords.

The darkness of the forest was claustrophobic and crowded in around Salismir. Tall evergreens towered high into the sky above him whilst roots and rocks threatened to break his ankles with every step. In the distance, a horn sounded and was answered across the forest by a second. Soon more took up the call, and Salismir found himself surrounded by a wall of noise.

Salismir knew their tactics well. He knew how they would fan out to cover the ground and how that would leave gaps that a clever hobgoblin could sneak through.

He'd been running for what felt like hours already, although he knew by the movement of the moon that it had been less than half an hour since he'd fled Jorn's tent. It hadn't taken the rest of the brotherhood long to work out what had happened. They had been reluctant to enter their leader's tent without his permission, and so it had taken them longer than it should have to find him dead inside. Once they had and Salismir's absence had been noted, the horns had been sounded and the hunt had begun.

Overhead, the night was cloudless and a thin frost was starting to settle on the leaves of the trees to add a hellish oily quality to the stones over which he had to scramble. Salismir knew his way through these woods as well as anyone, but in his panic, he had lost his bearings and was now aimlessly pushing through the sharp branches in any direction that he could. It didn't matter though, he reassured himself. Right now, *where* didn't matter. All that mattered was that he was running *away*.

He paused against a stout tree to regain his composure. Small creatures raced away in the undergrowth as he gulped down a lungful of air. His lungs were on fire, and each icy breath seemed to be shorter than the last. The half-moon hung behind him, so that meant he was heading west. That was good, the Fountain of Tears couldn't be far away. Salismir knew the caves that surrounded the towering waterfall better than anyone in the brotherhood.

Getting to higher ground was key. There were hills in the forest that offered a decent view of the surrounding area; if only he could find his way to one of them.

On he ran, taking care not to divert his course as best he could. Sometimes he'd stagger to a halt inches from a vertical drop or loose scree hill and he'd have to double back to work his way around. Other times, he'd scramble to a halt as a giant beast was silhouetted against the moonlight streaming through the trees. Cautiously, he'd edge forwards only to realise that it was a fallen tree or pile of stones that had fallen in such a way as to trick his panicked mind. Scattered through the undergrowth, luminescent fungi formed a glowing runway that threatened to lead him off track.

A few miles behind him, his pursuers were fanning out as expected. They'd seen what Salismir had done to their leader, and so they were moving with caution, none of them wanting to end up in a similar state. Though Jorn had always been their leader, the Brotherhood of Grield were not democratic by nature, and he knew each of them would be weighing up the odds of themselves taking over from the dead hobgoblin. Dead men didn't rise to power, and so their attack moved forwards slowly through the night. The power of Akeldama had touched some of the others as well. As slowly as they moved, they knew that they couldn't allow Salismir to escape.

Salismir felt a second wave of energy and was soon back on his heels, trying to put as much ground as possible between himself and the others before he found a place to hide. He'd considered doubling back on himself, to allow them to pass by him and on into the night, but he couldn't risk it. He needed to keep moving. Every so often his feet would splash through small pools of water, but he never seemed able to find the river that led to the waterfall. As he ran, he felt sure that the echoing sounds of the horns were getting farther away each time they rang out, but the trees muffled all noise. Many times, Salismir found himself spinning around looking for the source of a cracking branch or snarling dog that seemed only feet away.

Suddenly, he heard the sound he'd been listening out for. The roar of a thousand tears falling from the eyes of the gods, as his mother had once described it. He knew that he was close to the waterfall. He stopped and allowed the sounds to filter through, but he couldn't work out which direction they were coming from. The trees were too dense around him. They bounced sounds around their hollow trunks until it sounded as though it came from all directions at once. He gave up and propped himself against a fallen ash.

Far behind but getting quickly closer, the voices of the other hobgoblins were shouting out his name. It wouldn't be long now, he knew, before they caught him, and they wouldn't show the mercy that Jorn had tried to show him. He couldn't kill them all even with Akeldama's power. He pulled the stone from under his robe and held it in his hands. It felt cold, even in the frosty air.

He tucked it back under his robe and set off again at a slow jog. His legs ached and his back was sore, but he knew he had to keep going for as long as he could. Without warning, the ground gave way underneath him, and he sank to his ankles in soft mud. Another step forward and his feet were soaked with the icy water of a fast-flowing river. Suddenly, Salismir knew where he was. He set off against the flow making sure to keep his feet wet at all times. The water froze his blood, and he felt his toes go numb, but still he pushed on.

The roar of the waterfall grew louder, and the sound of the horns fell away to the south. Within minutes, he found himself standing at the base of a waterfall that towered hundreds of feet above him. After the long fall, the water was a mist by the time it fell into the river below. Salismir was able to make his way through it and into the caves that opened up in the darkness beyond. He breathed a sigh of relief and made his way a hundred yards into the darkness before collecting some dry wood and lighting a small fire.

Far away in the distance, the sound of horns disappeared into the night.

Taken

"Shrunken!" bellowed Geldrig above the rising noise of the disturbed creatures. Skye shivered. She knew the ancient and diseased race of goblins well. She remembered Snudge telling her how they'd turned from the light many generations ago, no doubt they were here with one purpose. Skye and Brack drew their swords and stood shoulder to shoulder with the Felmir. Arthur stood, rooted to the spot.

"Arthur!" hissed Skye grabbing him by his shoulder and shaking him until he looked at her. "Grab your sword. This is the real thing. This is no time to freeze!"

Arthur's hands were shaking as he fumbled with his scabbard and managed to pull his sword free and hold it in front of his face. The tip danced through the air as he struggled to focus on every enemy all at once. His eyes were glazed over, and his pupils stared at some point in the distance. He was muttering under his breath.

Skye remembered doing the same thing when she'd fought her first battle against the Nelapsi in the fallen city of Lörieas and noted that it didn't get any easier no matter how many times you stepped up and drew your sword. Her nerves may have hardened and her hands didn't shake quite as much anymore, but her heart still raced and her stomach still knotted itself. She recognised that these were good things though. Gondrag, Geldrig's deceased brother, had once told her that the day you enter a fight and you aren't nervous is the day you don't live to tell the tale.

The Shrunken had them surrounded. Whilst Skye and her friends had been organising themselves to get ready for the fight, several of the hideous half-goblins had crept behind them and cut off their exit from the tower. Their only way down was to fight their way through the two dozen armed creatures barring their way. The beasts were communicating between themselves in a low hiss, but Skye couldn't make out many of their words and couldn't understand those that she did. Their body position gave them away, though. Skye could sense that they were nervous. There was something, some magic, that was holding them at bay. Whatever it was, Skye prayed that it lasted long enough for them to come up with a plan.

"What are they doing?" Geldrig hissed from the corner of his mouth.

"They daren't attack," whispered Brack. "They are scared. I can understand some of what they are saying as Goblin from long ago. They keep talking about a shadowed look, shadowed—"

"Shadowed Eye?" asked Geldrig urgently.

"Could be. Like I said, it's an ancient language from long before our race grew diseased and turned into these hideous beings. What is the Shadowed Eye?"

"I heard it long ago. It is a reference to the dark stone, to Akeldama. What are they saying about it?"

Brack looked stumped for moment before continuing nervously. "I-I-I don't know. I must be rustier than I thought at this. It doesn't make any sense."

"What do you mean?" asked Skye, not liking where she suspected that the conversation was heading.

"They say that they can sense it, the Shadowed Eye. That it must be close." He paused and shook his head. "Like I said, I must be mistaken."

Panicking but moving slowly so as to avoid suspicion, Skye removed her mother's ring, the very ring that contained a large chunk of Akeldama, of the

Shadowed Eye, and pushed it deep into her pocket. She couldn't tell them what she had in her possession. In her heart, she knew that she could trust all three of her companions and most of those back with Snudge, but she'd been blindsided by Yop's betrayal, hadn't seen it coming at all. Besides, whilst they knew nothing then, should they be captured, there would be no point in torturing them for information. If they knew what she had, anything at all, then they were in more danger than they already were. She couldn't put them in that position. Instead, she hid the ring away and prepared to fight.

The Shrunken appeared to have reached a decision as well. They were finally levelling their weapons in front of them in a position to attack and their chatter took on a new urgency.

For a while, the two forces stood at an impasse, neither prepared to make the first move, until suddenly and from behind them a loud scream echoed around the fallen walls that still stood atop the tower and caused Skye and her friends to spin round ready to defend themselves from the attacking hordes. Too late, they realised that the enemies behind them were still holding their ground. Before they knew it, those on whom they had turned their backs had leapt across the open tower and were lunging and hacking with their blades.

Skye turned back just in time to parry a downward chop and deflect the blade to her left. She punched the wretched creature in the face with her free hand and took a swift step back. She felt Geldrig and Brack move into a defensive square. Each defender had their back to the rest so that they were all facing out to the points of the compass preventing attack to the rear. She responded in kind and grabbed hold of Arthur's shirt to drag him into position as well. She was pleased to see that he appeared to have mustered some fighting courage as he blindly swung his blade in a brutal figure eight. He was indiscriminate, and twice she had to duck to avoid falling to her best friend's unfortunate excitement.

There was no blood on his blade yet, but his enthusiasm was certainly causing those intent on attacking him to rethink their strategy. Skye, Brack and Geldrig had no such luxury, and Shrunken were falling upon them as quickly as they could dispatch their friends. Fighting in such tight quarters had its disadvantage, and the skin of the Shrunken was unusually thick, even for a race descended from goblins. Most of those that they were managing to strike with their blades were simply retreating with small wounds and allowing others to fill the breach.

A loud whoop behind her caused Skye to spin towards Arthur. He was covered in dark blood, and it took her a sickening second to realise that it wasn't his. In fact, it was spraying from the freshly exposed neck of the Shrunken kneeling in front of her friend, its head hanging from its neck by the thinnest shred of skin and its eyes staring vacantly into the distance. In the second he took to celebrate, Skye saw another creature step in and strike Arthur on the side of his head. Luckily his head only made contact with the flat of the blade, but it was enough to knock Arthur from his feet and leave him reeling on the ground. In slow motion, Skye saw the half-goblin step forward with its sword raised ready to strike down into Arthur's back. Her arm acted without consulting her brain and threw her sword across the seemingly endless gulf between them. Skye watched as the point of the blade struck home just below the ribcage.

Before she had time to step forward and retrieve Burrower, Skye felt hands grabbing at her back and found herself dragged onto the cold stone. Instead of the raining blades that she'd expected, she felt the rough skin of the Shrunken binding her hands behind her back with a thick rope. She screamed for help as she was dragged away but saw her friends fighting hard to keep the remaining enemies at bay. Her back screamed out in agony as her captors dragged her across the rough ground towards the tower exit. She was at least able to see the rest of the attackers leave her friends behind, all of them still standing. Before long, she felt a canvas bag bundled over her head and everything went black.

Betrayed

"Hello, guests!" announced the well-dressed, broad Felmir that greeted Weard and her companions as they entered the mayor's chambers. He was dressed in a flowing black robe with the hood pulled down over his shoulders and a thick bronze chain that hung low around his neck. From the chain hung an ornate portcullis cast from rose gold. "I am Isi, the mayor of Lörieas and the leader of the people, or what remain of us anyway. We have been expecting you for a while now. I trust that your journey along the Silver River was uneventful?"

"Calm waters and nobody trying to kill us. We could ask for no more," grumbled Curglaff to the mayor.

"Excellent indeed! I assume you must be Weard?" the mayor addressed the healer who bowed.

"And Snowbroth?" Again the goblin bowed to his name.

"And…" The mayor faltered at the last.

"Curglaff, sir."

"Ah but of course!" The mayor exclaimed as he wrapped his arms around the elderly goblin's shoulders in a hug. "I have heard much about all of you from out friend Geldrig. He had many tales to tell when he returned." The mayor's face took on a darker complexion, "Such a shame about his brother, of course. And the dreaded stone orb. That would have been quite the catch for the G'Oräk. Quite the power to Snudge's arm."

"What are you implying?" questioned Weard growing angry at the half-hidden accusations.

"Nothing, of course!" Isi clapped his hands together as if to signal the conversation was at a close. "I'm sure his intentions were entirely honourable, as are mine! But where are my manners? We must eat. You must be exhausted and quite famished."

"With all due respect, sir," Snowbroth started, "Snudge trusted us—"

"Do not worry about your little war, Snowbroth. It is all in hand! For now, let us eat and rest. Later, perhaps, we can discuss *politics*."

The Felmir placed his arms around the shoulders

of Weard and Curglaff and led the trio through a pair of heavy chestnut doors inlaid with fine engravings. In the centre of each door, a prone dragon was carved from lighter wood and stood watch over the doorway. Weard stared at them curiously as she passed and brushed her fingers across the smooth grain but soon found herself pulled into the room beyond by Isi's strong arms on her back.

The large room was dominated by a heavy table designed to seat at least two dozen men. The entire table top was covered with a heady banquet of food and drink. Thick wheels of cheese took centre stage next to plates of ripe and exotic fruit. Bottles of strong mead were being opened by Faldoric, and the sweet smell of fermenting apples filled the room. Many other servants were on hand to assist wherever they were needed.

It was hard for the goblins to focus on their mission – the mayor had been right about their hunger – and so they followed Isi around the table helping themselves to extravagant morsels. Weard couldn't help but think back to the poor folk in Kobold, held hostage by their own fear, who couldn't even put bread on their table thanks to Snudge's curfew, but she didn't know when she might eat again and so put it from her mind and ate her fill.

The mayor spoke about little of importance throughout the meal and infuriated Snowbroth by insisting on only making small talk about such trivial matters as the weather and the influx of refugees from the south. Weard held her tongue. She remembered where the divisive attitude of the people of Lörieas had got them before.

When the meal was finally over, Weard decided to try again with the mayor. "Mayor, time really is of the essence for us, and we would really appreciate whatever time you can spare us to talk about Snudge's request."

The mayor sighed and placed his hands on the table.

"Listen, I respect Snudge and the G'Oräk. The gods know our city wouldn't be here if it wasn't for your adventures with the human girl. You've seen the statue to Brabble by the city walls? We are grateful for what you all did.

"But that is past now. There is no threat from the Dark Queen anymore—"

"We believe that there is a new threat," interrupted Weard. She had moved over to the open window to escape the stuffy air of the room.

"There is always a new threat somewhere or other, Weard. Snudge knows this as well as any of us."

"We were attacked in our own homes. They

breached the Holden Wall," stated Snowbroth matter-of-factly.

Isi paused to consider this new information before continuing, "That is…unfortunate. Nevertheless, our position remains the same. We lost many men and women – good Felmir – when our city was sacked. We simply cannot spare the men for the task that Snudge would have us do."

"Mayor—" Curglaff tried before being interrupted again by the mayor.

"I have said my piece. It cannot be done."

"Cannot? Or cannot unless the price is right?" asked Weard as she stared at the fluttering banners that hung on tall poles in front of the town hall. "The standard for Lörieas is a gold portcullis on an azure background, is it not? Semper Secura? Forever secure?"

"What is your point?" said the mayor, growing agitated. Snowbroth and Curglaff looked at their companion in confusion.

"The dragons engraved on the doors to this room. I knew I'd seen them before but couldn't place where. They are the same dragons that are emblazoned in red on the golden banners hung alongside those of Lörieas on this very building." The healer paused and turned back to face the group. "Before we left out from Kobold, Snudge met with us all and talked of a rising army in the east out of the Dragon Isle. The Army of Enlightenment, an army of dark elves under the rule of Emperor Ki. The same emperor who has long sought power in the west and has had word, I'm sure, of Akeldama's appearance at Liorath's Peak."

The other goblins turned on the mayor now who was backing towards the big double doors that presented the only exit from the room.

"How much did he pay you?" spat Snowbroth angrily. "How cheaply did you sell your soul?"

The mayor reached the doors and swung them open. On the other side stood a dozen towering dark elves, each over six feet tall and dressed head to toe in golden robes. Each one was embroidered with a prone red dragon across the breast and topped with a pointed hood that was pulled up over their heads. On their faces, the elves wore masks made of bone white porcelain painted with dark black eyes but otherwise featureless.

"Listen," began Isi as he put the guards between himself and the goblins, "we don't want a war. We really don't have the soldiers. The empire does, though. They are ready to fight. Persuade Snudge to join the emperor. The end result will be the same. He can join the emperor as he claims his rightful place in the west. It really is the best way. He'll still get his war."

"You are a *rahul!* A coward!" screamed Weard across the guards. "Snudge will have you hung for this. You wait until he hears of your betrayal."

"I really am sorry that you couldn't see sense, my friends. I really am." The mayor nodded to the guards who advanced on the trio. Weard and Curglaff drew their swords, but Snowbroth beckoned them to lower them again.

"Now is not the time to fight. We cannot kill them all, and I don't relish dying before Snudge gets to hear of this betrayal."

The goblins reluctantly sheathed their swords and allowed the guards to tie their hands behind their backs and march them from the room and out into the city. A shrouded carriage was waiting for them, and they were bundled unceremoniously into the back. Once inside, the curtains were drawn and the trio were plunged into a fusty darkness.

"Hello, friends." The voice in the darkness was high-pitched and lilting, as though the speaker were singing a lullaby. "I speak for Emperor Ki. Welcome to the Army of Enlightenment."

Reprieve

"Skye!" Arthur screamed as he woke from another nightmare. He shook himself and crawled out from his small canvas tent into the cold night air. They were still camped on the top of Liorath's Peak awaiting the reinforcements that Snudge had promised them.

It had been two nights since Skye had been taken and Arthur had been woken by a nightmare each time he'd fallen asleep. He found himself reliving the moment over and over. He'd tried to run after the horrible creatures as they'd carried her away, but he'd been dizzy from the blow to his head and Geldrig had held him back. As soon as the animals had captured Skye, they'd stopped fighting and retreated from the tower. Arthur had begged the others to let him go after her, but they refused no matter how much he called them cowards or hammered at them with his fists. His eyes were still swollen from crying.

"Skye knew that our aim was to take the tower and to hold it against all comers. She would want us to stay and do our job. She understood that more than most," Geldrig had said when Arthur had tearfully begged him to follow the Shrunken.

Brack had confirmed the same. "When she fought the Dark Queen, she threw her life into danger so many times to help protect the greater cause. She knew what needed to be done and she will know the same now," the goblin had argued. "I promise you, Arthur. When the time comes, we will go after her and rescue her if we can."

That first night they'd watched from the top of the tower as the Shrunken cart slowly wound itself across the plains below before veering off into the dark forest known as the Gloom.

"They'll be taking her to Alastor, the main city of the Shrunken, hidden deep within the Gloom," Geldrig had said flatly as they watched their friend disappear into the darkness.

The air was crisply cold this high up. Arthur rubbed his hands together in a vain attempt to keep them warm. He knew he wouldn't be able to get back to sleep, and so he wandered over to the north edge of the tower and shook Brack awake. He didn't comment on the fact that the goblin was supposed to be keeping watch. Instead, he ushered him off to bed and promised to wake Geldrig when the time came for him to take over. Once Brack was safely out of the way, Arthur settled himself down against the hard rocks and stared into the empty darkness beyond the tower hoping to see the welcome relief of the G'Oräk soldiers.

The next morning brought better news for all three. Geldrig had ventured out early to hunt for breakfast and had spotted the promised soldiers leaving the Wandering Place. He estimated that they would arrive by noon and so it proved, with the leader of the goblins arriving atop the tower a little after they'd finished a lunch of stewed rabbit. Brack had clambered down to the foot of the tower to show the soldiers where the ladder was and soon after the platform was busy with tents being erected and campfires being struck.

The captain in charge of the goblins was a short, stocky G'Oräk who introduced himself as Stolt and a trusted friend of Snudge. Brack claimed to have heard many things about him, and so they welcomed him with open arms and asked for information from Snudge.

"He says to continue with your quest as per his

instructions. You are to ride to Carak Tak today and parlay with the local lords. A goblin named Jango, one of the lords, is expecting you and will greet you at the city gates. Like all of us, they are aware of the growing dangers and their city is under a strict curfew. If you leave now, you should make it before sundown tomorrow at a steady pace." Stolt turned in his seat and glanced around the growing campsite. "There were four of you? Where is Skye?"

"She was taken!" babbled Arthur, bursting into tears. "When we arrived, the Shrunken things were already here. They were horrible. We fought them, but they took her!" he wailed. Stolt grabbed a passing soldier and instructed him to bring Arthur something to drink.

"That is unfortunate indeed. Was she alive?"

"Yes, when they took her. They were a band of Shrunken. They were weakened but many. They must have been here a while. We think they took her to Alastor. We saw them disappear into the Gloom before we lost sight of them." Brack spoke with a calmness that infuriated Arthur.

"We could have stopped them if we'd tried! You told us to stand and watch!"

"And what would have happened if they killed you all, Arthur?" asked Stolt. "We would have arrived to find a bloodbath and no idea where Skye was. As it stands, we may be able to send some of our men to try to bargain for her release. Did they know who she was? How important she is to us?"

"Maybe, maybe not. They only seemed interested in taking Skye. Once they'd grabbed her, they left us alone," answered Brack. "They didn't attack her though, not properly. It seems that they intended to capture her from the moment they saw her."

"Then we may be in luck!" Stolt clapped his hands together cheerfully. "If they wanted to kill her, they'd have done so here or as they transported her. No, I rather think they plan to ransom her off. That means she will still be alive."

"So we can go and rescue her?" asked Arthur hopefully.

"Not you. You have business elsewhere. You must carry on to Carak Tak with Brack and Geldrig. They will need you before long, Arthur, I'm sure. You say that the Shrunken attacked the rest of you at first? The fact that you are still standing must mean that you are at least half-decent with that sword that you carry. You may spill more blood on this adventure yet, Arthur!

"You must continue on. It's what Skye would want."

"So people keep telling me, but none of you know

her like I do. She's brave and strong and amazing, but she won't cope out there. I need to save her. I want to save her. Promise me we'll save her."

The captain looked for a moment as though he was about to argue before his face softened. "You have my word. I will do everything I can to bring Skye back to us."

Within the hour, the three companions had been fed and found mounts. Their own horses, a gift from the tree trolls, were nowhere to be found in the woodland. With a subdued farewell, they guided their steeds out of the shadows of Liorath's Peak and into the open breeze at the foot of the Scirion Mountains.

The air was warmer out of the shadows, and Arthur was optimistic that Carak Tak would provide the answers that Snudge needed for his army. He'd left Stolt promising to send some of his men to try to rescue Skye as soon as they could, but, for now, he'd have to put her out of his mind and get on with the task at hand. After all, as he'd been told, it was what she would have wanted.

Horongor

Salismir wasn't happy. It had taken him the better part of two days to find a safe place to cross the river and in the end, had been forced to travel farther south than he had explored before. Just as he was sure his legs could take no more, he had ended up beyond the peninsula town of Hurathi where he had hoped to rest and consider his next course of action.

Instead, he'd spent the evenings cold and exposed in the forest with his mind constantly torturing him. He'd wake with a start convinced that he'd heard horns sounding in the distance or he'd throw himself behind trees and bushes to avoid the imagined creatures hunting him in the shadows.

All of the time the Shadowed Eye was tormenting him with its rasping voice inside his head guiding him one way and then another, all whilst reminding him of the greatness that they would achieve together. He'd been persuaded by the voice to practice controlling his new-found power at least twice a day. He was getting better each time, and it scared him. He could still feel the energy burning through his head, searing the back of his eyes and coursing through his fingers, only now he could dam it, stop it from exploding until he wanted it to. He'd learnt to focus so intently that time slowed to treacle, and he found he could start to move amongst the trees unnoticed by the animals that scurried about around him.

Perhaps most worryingly of all, he'd thought one day, was how easy he found it to tame the power to such an extent that he could unleash it in one devastating ball of energy that would rip apart anything that stood in his way, regardless of whether it was tree, stone or beast. He was scared by how much he enjoyed the feeling of power. Of being in total control.

Over time, he'd been forced to leave the forest and consider his next move. He'd emerged from the trees to the south of Hurathi and on the edge of a largely empty savanna. He hadn't enjoyed the feeling of being so exposed as he'd ventured out into the grassland and had scurried with his body close to the ground for as much of it as he could until, after a few days of aimless wandering, he'd spotted a city on the horizon. He'd headed towards it, uncertain of what he'd find there but in desperate need of food, water and a restful night's sleep. Unfortunately, when he finally dragged himself tired and weak through the hanging city gates, he found himself inside the walls of Horongor, otherwise known as the Burnt Fort.

The fort was something of a legend to the hobgoblins that Salismir had grown up with before his exile. According to their tales, it had once been a proud and productive hobgoblin city that had been home to a thousand families, including the shanty towns that had sprung up outside the walls. Over time, the mayors of the town had become more and more corrupt and had taken to overcharging and under-delivering on their deals with the surrounding states.

As is often the case, they had more enemies than friends, and the innocent civilians that called Horongor their home were forced out into the surrounding woodlands. Legend had it that the mayors hung on within the walls to the very end, determined to bring back the glory days. They even refused to leave their homes as the fort was burnt down around them. Salismir had been told that their screams of despair could still be heard whenever the wind blew through the wreckage.

All that Salismir could hear as he made his way through the ruined buildings and overgrown roads was the sound of carrion birds in the sky and mosquitoes in the air. There were vegetables growing in the gardens of former manors that had since been allowed to go to seed and grow with abandon. A well in the middle of the main road still produced fresh, cold water. Herds of once-farmed beast roamed in the wilderness beyond the walls. Salismir had noticed them as he'd approached.

It wasn't perfect, Salismir knew that much, but it would do for now.

You could bring it back to its former glory.

It seemed more and more like the stone could read his mind. Salismir tried to distract himself and set about finding a building that wasn't as open to the elements as the rest. It didn't work, though. The voice in his head just shouted louder.

You could be the saviour of your people! All you need to do is use the power that I can give you. Why fight me? Those people drove your family from their homes and into the forest. They killed your family and friends, and you can avenge them. You can make your people whole again. Destroy those who sought to destroy you.

Salismir shuddered but knew that it was true. He could do it. He could do it all. He would be a hero to his people. Maybe his mother and father would forgive him if he did this. Maybe he'd be allowed back into the village a hero instead of a traitor.

For now, he'd settle for finding somewhere to sleep where he wouldn't be spotted.

Carak Tak

The journey to Carak Tak passed without event. Shortly after noon on the second day, Arthur, Geldrig and Brack tethered their horses on the outskirts of the walled town. The white stone walls towered high above them and were capped with regular turrets. Normally, these would be unmanned, Arthur had been told, but he saw well-armoured archers pacing back and forth, their heads appearing between the crenellations.

The gateway to the city lay on the north wall. It took the trio a while to walk around to it on foot. As they approached, they saw a solid gateway built into the stone wall with well-fitted stones edging the doorway and topped with an ornate capstone engraved with the snarling face of a goblin. At the foot of the gateway was a wooden gatehouse outside of which were stood two goblins, one clearly a guard and the other much better dressed. The more fashionable of the two made his way towards Arthur and his friends as they approached. His arms were spread wide with welcome.

"Greetings, friends. I am sorry that we must meet under such trying circumstances. Normally our hospitality would be so much more…welcoming. But, you know how it is." The goblin gestured to the guards patrolling the tall walls. "My name is Jango, and I am an ambassador to the Lords of Carak Tak. I shall take you to meet them shortly, but first, I'm afraid, I must take your weapons."

Jango saw the look in Geldrig's eyes and interrupted the Felmir before he had chance to argue. "Please do not refuse, Geldrig. We both know what you are here for and what it is you seek. I am on your side. I hope – indeed pray – that my lords will see sense and join Snudge in battle. However, I have my orders and so do you. Your orders do not, I believe, include the slaughter of the residents of Carak Tak and so, today, be sensible and do as you are asked."

Geldrig still looked angry at the request but begrudgingly handed over his sword along with a dagger that he drew from his ankle. Brack and Arthur both handed over their swords, and all three watched as Jango handed them to a guard who locked them away, inside a metal safe inside the gatehouse.

"Now that the ugly business is out of the way, shall we head into the city?" Without waiting for a response, Jango gestured to the waiting guard who shouted up to the archers on top of the wall. One of them disappeared for a moment before a loud grinding sound indicated that something was happening. It took a few minutes for the gate to swing slowly open, but as soon as the doors were wide enough apart, Jango slipped through and bid the others to follow.

Arthur hadn't known what to expect from Carak Tak, but it was different to anything he'd considered. The original walls had been built around a tall hill on top of which sat a vast complex, almost a city within a city. Leading up to a large citadel were cobblestoned streets that rose with the hillside, meaning that each building was slightly higher than the one before it.

Like the walls to the city, all of the buildings within Carak Tak had been built out of bright white stone. The roofs were all flat and had been turned into lush gardens. Each one was overhung with flowering vines and fruit bushes. Tomato plants scrambled down the front of houses and tall fruit trees had taken root on even the tallest of rooftops. Despite the city looking so full of life, the streets were practically empty.

Every now and then a cart would rattle along the cobblestones pulled along by a single small horse, but the streets remained silent for the rest of their journey to the inner sanctum. Once, Arthur found himself drawn away from the group and into the mouth of an alleyway that ran between two tall houses. On the walls in the darkness, a picture of an eye had been scrawled using red paint. Beneath it were written the words "The Shadow Rises."

At the top of the steep street, they presented themselves to the keeper of the door to the inner citadel. After a brief exchange between Jango and the guard, they were quickly ushered through and into a vast but shadowy room lined on all four walls with towering bookshelves. Ladders allowed access to the higher shelves, and goblins were quietly scurrying around grabbing books and dropping them quietly into velvet lined baskets that hung from their arms.

"The Library of All Knowledge." The voice came from the shadows in the corner of the room. Out of the darkness stepped an elderly goblin dressed in a white gown but mainly covered by its enormous beard that reached beyond its feet. "We are the Keepers of Knowledge. We ensure that all knowledge in the goblin world is recorded and remembered for all eternity. My name is Malficia the Seventh, and I am to speak to you on behalf of the lords today."

"The honour is ours, my lord. My name is Geldrig. Though I am no goblin, I have heard much about your library."

"Thank you, Geldrig, and I've heard much about you." Malficia stepped closer to the group and whispered quietly enough as to not be heard by the goblins running backwards and forwards on errands of their own. "We must not discuss matters here, though. There are ears everywhere, and not everyone in this library is true to our cause. Follow me!"

The goblin turned and made his way to a small doorway on the far side of the room that led onto an antechamber set up as a small office. Malficia sat down at a large wooden desk and indicated for the others to take a seat on a well-padded bench against the wall.

"What is this place?" asked Arthur when they were finally out of earshot. "Why do you record everything?"

"Mainly we write down what has happened and why. We don't tend to interest ourselves in the comings and goings of ordinary folk. It's partly so that we don't repeat the same mistakes generation after generation." The goblin chuckled. "But mostly because we always have. It is something that I am very proud to be part of, you understand?" he added defensively. "But the problem with any written history is that it is so one-sided. I live in hope that one day there will be nothing more to record, at least no more accounts of war and betrayal.

"Alas, that seems unlikely with things as they currently are. I am aware that Snudge has sent you to try to recruit the soldiers of Carak Tak to join his army on their march south. You can have them. They will fight for you. I have spoken with the lords, and they are in agreement. We only have half a thousand men, but they are strong and there are a group of berserkers within them."

"Berserkers?" asked Arthur.

"The soldiers of Carak Tak were known throughout history as being some of the best that goblins could offer. We were known for our berserkers, a group of soldiers that trained on their own in the Orcwood to the south of the town. They were sent away at birth and didn't return until they were fully grown.

"Within the Orcwood, they were trained by dark shaman in the arts of dark magic, but mostly they were taught to brew the potion known as Agrimora, a combination of herbs and berries from the darkest parts of the forest. The act of drinking the potion is believed to transport the warriors to the Shadowlands where they are able to visit their own soul. There they may make a deal with Faileas, a mighty dragon built of ice and shadows that guards the gates to Mithrostan. If they make a deal, they may leave their life-force behind temporarily and return to the land of the living without fear of dying in battle.

"As part of their deal with Faileas, they must also leave behind a part of themselves, part of what makes them weaker in battle. They must leave behind their fear. When the warriors awake from their drug-induced comas, they are said to be empty shells of their former self, focused only on killing. It is said that they may only return to the Shadowlands and retrieve their life-force after they have slain an enemy.

"Not all that was once a part of them returns, and they will never be whole again. In time, berserkers simply disappeared inside themselves, their minds forever lost to wander the Shadowlands searching for their own souls. It is believed that Faileas collects their souls to feed his own desires.

"Berserkers are deadly warriors in battle, Arthur, and I am sure that Snudge will be grateful to have them fighting alongside him."

"Thank you indeed," whispered Brack in awe. "I have long heard about the legendary berserkers of Carak Tak, but the chance to fight alongside them is truly an honour. I will send word of your generosity to Snudge at once."

"You are welcome indeed, little goblin. We must all do what we can in these dark times. There are darker shadows to come yet, I am sure."

"Is that what the graffiti means?" asked Arthur.

"Graffiti?" Malficia seemed suddenly unsure of himself.

"I saw it in an alleyway on our way here. They had drawn an eye and written the words 'The Shadow Rises' beneath it."

"That is the Order of the Shadowed Eye. There are rumours that a dark item has once again been found in the south. An evil stone orb that many call the Shadowed Eye. It was thought lost. Indeed, it was thought that your very adventures had rendered it lost to the world, but alas it is not so."

"Akeldama?" spluttered Brack. "It has been found?"

"It would appear so. It was captured by a band of vagabond hobgoblins as it left the town of Soulaman south of the Long River. What it was doing in Soulaman is not yet known, but we suspect that this is where what remained of the Dark Queen fled when she was destroyed by the human. It is possible that she sent out her spies to retrieve the orb. She would perhaps have been able to feel where it was lying hidden. It is unlikely that she could borrow its power for as long as she did without it leaving a mark.

"Either way, for some reason she sent it away from her place of hiding, and the cart that carried it was ambushed by the Brotherhood of Grield, a band of hobgoblins who enjoy a somewhat lawless existence within the woodlands bordering the river. According to my own spies, one of the Brotherhood fell under the spell of the Shadowed Eye and slaughtered his friends before fleeing. We do not know where he or the orb are hiding now.

"The Order of the Shadowed Eye are a group, a cult, of goblins who believe that the orb being found again is a sign that we should embrace the darkness and that goblins should rise to power on a sea of bloodshed. They believe that goblins are the one true race and that all others are inferior. They are led by a goblin called Elfmir. He is the illegitimate son of your very own Elflock and is carrying on his father's work.

"For now, the Order is small and inconsequential, but these things have a habit of growing quickly if left unchecked. Anybody found to be a member of the Order within the walls of Carak Tak is executed without trial. We do not have time for traitors to breed amongst us."

"This is troubling news indeed," sighed Geldrig. "Snudge will need to hear of this immediately."

"Be my guest. Our messenger birds are at your

disposal. However, I would be surprised if Snudge isn't already aware of this particular piece of information. I am not the only one with little birds flitting around the woodlands."

"Nevertheless, I feel we must head to your tower and send a message," urged Brack. "If Akeldama truly has been found, then the balance of the world as we know it has shifted once again."

Traitors

Snudge paced back and forth across the gravel path beneath the towering wooden structure. His unshod feet kicked the stones as he walked in anger and seethed in his rage. When he spoke, he spat and frothed at the corners of his mouth.

"What do you have to say for yourselves, you *rahul*?"

The four men in front of Snudge remained silent. They were stood on a wooden platform a dozen feet above the ground with their hands tied behind their backs and hemp nooses around their necks. On each of their wrists was a dark tattoo in the shape of an eye, a symbol of their devotion to the Order of the Shadowed Eye, that seemed to glow in the failing light of dusk.

"You have starved your own families!" Snudge

spat. "You have denied them food and water due to your stupid beliefs! Do you not know what we gave up to destroy the Dark Queen last time around? And now, here you all are, plotting your dark schemes to resurrect the very evil that gave her that power? What would your families think of you? What would they think of their sons as traitors to goblins everywhere?"

The goblins bowed their heads at the G'Oräk leader's words. Their families hadn't turned up to watch them hang. Many others had. Snudge wanted to make sure that word spread about what would happen to those in league with the Order of the Shadowed Eye.

"We didn't even do anything! We just joined up!" wailed one of the goblins.

Snudge sprinted up the wooden steps to the top of the platform and stood face to face with the goblin, incredulous at what he was hearing. Snudge noticed that the traitor had lost control of his bladder.

"You did nothing?" he hissed. "Nothing? You stand here today, about to die, and tell me you did nothing? Did not the Order attack our very own village just a few months ago? Did they slaughter dozens of innocent goblins in their beds and burn dozens more in their homes? My *sister* and her children were in one of those houses. They never stood a chance!" Snudge was screaming in the goblin's face, his own face creasing with pain.

"We hadn't joined then—" the goblin started before Snudge slapped him across the chin with a stinging blow.

"You joined them since! You knew what they were and what they did and you *still* joined them."

A guard skidded to a halt on the gravel and snapped Snudge out of his argument with a loud cough. "My lord," he began nervously, "I have word from Carak Tak. From Brack, sir."

Snudge growled at the repentant goblin and made his way down to read the message. After he had finished digesting the information, he tore the paper into small pieces and let them drift away on the breeze. Then he made his way back to the top of the platform slowly and took a small pleasure in watching the accused goblins cower away from him. He took a deep breath and turned to face the watching crowd.

"My dearest goblins, whilst I stand here today your leader, I am addressing you now as your protector as well as your friend. I have led the G'Oräk with honour for many years now, and I trust that you all understand that I have always aimed to do what is best for the goblins under my command.

"It is with grave regret that I can confirm that Akeldama, that most evil of weapons, has indeed surfaced again in the south." Snudge waited patiently for the crowd to silence itself again before continuing. "We must never forget what this weapon is capable of and that it cannot be controlled by any goblin, orc, elf, human or otherwise. It seeks only to destroy this world and everything on it. Anybody who believes otherwise is a bloody fool at best and a danger to us all at worst.

"It also pains me to say that Skye, our brave saviour and defeater of the Dark Queen has been captured atop Liorath's Peak by a small group of Shrunken. We believe that she is still alive but, as of this moment, we cannot count on her to save us this time.

"We are not alone, though. Our good friend Brack, along with Geldrig and Skye's friend Arthur, have persuaded the lords of Carak Tak to join our own army in an attack on the south. I am yet to receive information from Weard and our envoy to Lörieas. That does not bode well.

"Because of all of this information and a great deal besides, we have no option but to muster our army and drive south to meet this growing evil before it has chance to kill us in the north. We will leave for Carak Tak within the month."

"What would you have us do?" the voice from the crowd was small but defiant.

"Fight, if you are able. Help to arm the rest if

you're not. I do not ask this lightly. There will come a time in history when this war is spoken of and the names of the heroes will be sung around campfires and whispered in bedtime stories.

"You will not be amongst those names, there will be no medals and no great riches but you will all, each and every one of you, be a hero to me. What is more, you will be fighting to save everything that you hold dear and if that, if your kin and tribe are not enough of a reason, then there is nothing I can say here that will turn you into a warrior.

"On this day, the day on which you decide to fight, from now until the end of time, there will be goblins the world over who will look to the stars and say a prayer for those who chose to stand up and be counted. They will consider themselves lucky to live in a free world, free from tyranny and evil, thanks to you."

There were no more questions from the crowd, but Snudge could see the heads of the more elderly goblins nodding in agreement. He knew he would have every goblin of fighting age at his disposal, the elders would see to it.

"I will ask that all goblins able to fight surrender themselves to our captains by noon tomorrow. Make no mistake friends, many of us will not be returning.

Say your goodbyes and prepare your steads. Come armed and ready to fight. We will change the course of history, one way or another."

Snudge took another deep breath and turned to face those from the Order of the Shadowed Eye.

"As you have heard, our situation is grave indeed. However, we do have a chance to succeed and to rid Ithilmir of the evil of Akeldama for good. It is a small chance, but it would be even smaller if I allowed *rahul* like yourself to undermine our efforts. Let this be a message to all who think that they can sacrifice good goblins for their own ends." He turned and signalled to the hooded goblin at the side of the platform who nodded and pulled a thick wooden level. The crack of the rope tightening echoed around the silent crowd.

The G'Oräk leader stood and stared into the eyes of each traitor as they wriggled on their ropes until they sighed and went limp. Tears streaming down his cheeks, he made his way from the crowd and didn't stop walking until he was inside his front door where he collapsed into a chair and sobbed.

Eternis Mortus

The Darkwood lay silent. Damphir had been forced to leave his dragon at the entrance to the forest. It had baulked at the idea of entering such a soulless place. The sorcerer had no such hesitations, but he had been sad to see the great beast fly off into the sky. He'd be able to call it back if he needed it. That was one of the greatest feats of his mind. He'd been able to bend the wild beasts to his will since he was a small boy roaming the mountains of the Orctooth Range.

The seer had been born to a family of Nelapsi but had quickly outgrown their small-minded desire for destruction. He'd learnt from an early age that he was more powerful than any of them could even imagine, and he'd set out on his own as soon as he could. As a race, the Nelapsi had always been evil creatures of the night that feasted on the blood of others. He reflected that, once, there had been love of a sort in his family. He'd been close to his father, and even to his mother until one night when he hadn't been close enough to save him.

After that, he'd learned never to love or to care for anything or anyone. He'd been betrayed that night for the last time and he'd left soon after. There had been no emotional goodbye. He had simply decided one night that he wanted to leave and he had never looked back.

He was headed towards a lost village that he had heard about whilst in the Solar. When he'd arrived at the edge of the Darkwood, Damphir had found that the trees were impenetrable, and so he'd been forced to fashion a small raft from fallen branches and set off along the slow winding river that ran deep into the heart of the forest. The water was nothing more than liquid mud, and only the occasional ripple belied the fact that there was life underneath the surface. Every now and then, something heavy would push off from the bank and float out into the current.

Where the river narrowed, the branches of the trees overhead reached out and grasped each other forming bridges across the water. Small creatures scurried back and forth always just out of sight. Birds whistled in the distance, but a lazy silence followed Damphir like a shadow.

The river flowed slowly but surely further into the gloom and the only action the seer had to take was to push away the occasional vine that hung like rope as thick as his arm. Some of the trees had been taken over by creeping vines until the tree itself had died and rotted away leaving only the creepers standing like a stone web.

Onward he pushed ever searching for a sign of the lost village of Fankilmir. The story he had been told spoke of a tribe of elves who had turned allegiance and set out to seek the dark stone, the Shadowed Eye. They'd heard rumours of an evil orb in the south and had left the realm of Kanthor, the realm of their kin, and made their way further south towards the realm of Hurusan. There they had found the army of men who legend said were not of this world. They had been born of a queen sent to Ithilmir from another land that lay beyond the stars.

The elves of Kanthor were the purest of their kind and were not used to the evil of man. From the moment the small tribe had entered Hurusan, they were lost. They turned to drinking and fighting. Soon their thirst for the power that they sought consumed them. As they slipped further into sin, they bestowed upon themselves the name of Azrul, the Fallen Ones. They searched far and wide for the Shadowed Eye and eventually made their way to Alastor where they befriended the Shrunken.

Whilst in Alastor, the elves learnt the history of the stone and took upon themselves the beliefs of the Shrunken. They forsook the religion of the elves and turned instead to the darkness of Akeldama, the one true god of the Shrunken and after whom the Shadowed Eye was named. It wasn't long before the elves grew restless. They yearned for the stone like none other before, and they now had word that a dark queen was rising to power in the west guided by the very orb that they sought.

They were weak - far too weak to take on the army that she commanded. They wanted to grow their strength, and so they settled in the Darkwood. There they grew their cult and built a small village to honour the god Akeldama. Over time, their leaders started to brew the potions that the Shrunken had taught them to use to see the future, but the ingredients grew tainted in the Darkwood. They were twisted and stained by the evil that lurked within the shadows, and the potions only served to drive the elves into a paranoid craze. They turned on one another and killed their friends as they slept.

In the end, the village lay dead with only the stone statues and a temple to Akeldama remaining. The elves were buried in a small cemetery on the edge of the village at the foot of the temple; forever in the shadow of the evil that drove them to madness. It was towards this cemetery that Damphir was heading. If the legend was true, then what awaited him there was worth the journey through this foetid swamp.

As the ramshackle raft made its way lazily along, the trees started to thin slightly on the northern bank. A small emerald bird flitted across the glassy water and perched on the prow, a rare jewel in an otherwise murky world. The bird ruffled its feathers and stared at the seer. Damphir considered taking over its mind and having it scour the forest for the lost village from above but thought better of it. A large mind like a dragon was easy and slow, the flitting mind of a small bird could travel beyond his reach before he had chance to return to his own mind. He knew his limits.

He sat and watched the bird for a short while before it dropped suddenly from the boat and plunged into the dark water. It emerged less than a minute later and landed back on its perch, this time with a small silvery fish in its beak. It tilted its head this way and that all the time staring Damphir directly in the eye.

Whilst he watched, it hopped over to the Nelapsi

and dropped the fish at his feet before darting off across the water and disappearing into the trees. Damphir followed its path and was startled to see the outline of a hut beyond the tree line.

Excitedly, he steered the raft towards the bank and moored it to a tree with a thick vine that he snatched from a branch overhead. Making sure to take his bearings as best he could, he darted off between the trees.

Up close, the hut was rotten and half collapsed but had clearly once been the home to a small family. There were several pallets that would once have made serviceable beds and an area had been set out for a cooking fire. Metal pots and weapons had been left to rust against the walls though some of the better knives had kept a half-sharp edge. If legend were true, then the items in this hut would be a century old.

Dotted around the hut were clay offerings to the many gods of the Azrul, but the largest were reserved for Akeldama. To the Azrul their most revered god took on the form of a large cat with the snarling head of a wolf and the wings of a phoenix. Many of the statues depicted scenes of sacrifice; the Shrunken were keen to sacrifice those who were seen as a betrayal to their values and often killed their own in the name of Akeldama. It was said that the darkness of the sacrifice would be absorbed by the stone to protect the priest's soul from being tarnished.

In their constant search of darkness, the Azrul had continued the practice of sacrifice when they had moved to Fankilmir.

Damphir ventured out of the hut and into the shadow of the large stepped pyramid that had been the venue for so many of their murderous offerings. Even though they had been untrodden for years, the stone steps still glistened with the stains of blood that ran in thick rivers from the very top of the pyramid. As Damphir approached, he felt the skulls of the decapitated victims crunch under his feet. The Azrul were a slight race of elves not much taller than a goblin and with fair features. Stripped of their flesh, they were weaker still, and their skulls looked delicate like those of a small rodent.

The steps were steep and shallow, and the early morning air was hot and humid as Damphir started his ascent, but he pushed on relentlessly. By the time he was halfway to the top, he was aching and sweat dripped from his brow. As he turned and surveyed his surroundings, he was surprised to see that he had broken above the canopy and had a panoramic view of the entire Darkwood. He took the time to wander around the entire perimeter of the pyramid and found that the cemetery that he had sought lay at the base of the eastern steps. Smiling, he pushed forwards and climbed to the summit on his hands and knees.

The view from the top was even more encapsulating that it had been further down, but Damphir hadn't travelled all of this way for the view. The stone platform was empty except for a solid stone bench on to which were attached several flaking leather straps, presumably to hold the sacrifice in place, and a tall metal lectern that held court over the cemetery below. Despite the years, the metal still gleamed in the rising sunlight and was already hot to the touch. It would be perfect for what Damphir had in mind.

He stepped up to the stand as a priest about to lead his subjects in prayer and removed the heavy, leather-bound tome from his robe. He placed it reverentially onto the stand and the words *Eternis Mortus* blazed in the light. The Eternal Dead. The seer was familiar with every page of the book and knew every word. He'd made it his life's work to learn it all. It had taken a long life. Nelapsi were long-lived creatures anyway, but Damphir had found that by consuming the life-force of others – not the weak and humbled creatures that the rest of his tribe insisted on hunting, but the strong and powerful druids and shaman that embraced the darkness themselves – he could not only take on something of their power but also some of their life.

Damphir had been born long before the Azrul had settled in Fankilmir. In fact, he'd been born long before those first elves had deserted their homes in Kanthor. Damphir was over two centuries old, but he was starting to feel the cold fingers of time catching up with him. The power of Akeldama, of the Shadowed Eye, would enable him to live forever.

It seemed only fair that if he were to live forever, then those who served him were offered the same choice.

He didn't need the words, not now, not after all this time. It didn't matter, though. Damphir opened the book to the page that he knew held the magic that he needed. It was well thumbed and torn along the edges. Some of the ink had smudged on the page, and many of the words had faded to nothing. It didn't matter. It was time. He breathed slowly and held the page down against a gust of wind. He closed his eyes. He could feel the power already, and he hadn't even said the words. He held his breath and listened. He could hear the animals in the forest below, hear the sounds slowly drifting away as his mind focused and he channelled the energy that he had first discovered all of those years ago in his small village.

He thought about how he'd learnt to control it, to

bend it to his will. He thought about the night that he'd left. They'd tried to stop him, his mother and the village shaman. They'd been strong, too strong to fight and so he'd stepped inside his head and concentrated. That's all he'd ever needed to do, concentrate.

He'd felt the energy burn inside him, and he'd felt the doors into their heads float away like mist on a breeze. He'd stepped through and entered their minds. It had seemed so easy. He'd taken what he'd needed and left them with nothing. When he'd opened his eyes, they were all dead.

He remembered feeling nothing as he looked down on the murdered, soulless bodies of his family.

His voice sounded out across the forest, far louder than any single voice had the right to be. The spell flowed easily, appearing as wisps in the air before racing into nothingness. As the final words left his lips, Damphir slammed the book shut and opened his eyes. He looked towards the foot of the pyramid and smiled.

The dirt that covered the cemetery was moving and shifting like an ocean in a storm. The simple wooden gravestones collapsed into the ground. Dirt fell into empty graves, and the Azrul rose to their feet ready to fight to the death; a second death, for their new god.

Alastor

Skye had no idea where she was. After being dragged to the foot of Liorath's Peak, she'd been bundled into the back of a cart and hadn't been moved since. Underneath her, she could feel the rattle of the cart as it bounced over a bumpy track. Every now and then, it would jolt hard enough to cause her to bounce on the hard wooden floor. Her back was tender and sore, but there was no movement in the ropes around her wrists.

Once a day, her captors poured water over the sack that covered her face. She'd manage to suck a little of it into her mouth, but her thirst was becoming all-consuming. Her head was throbbing, and her limbs ached and felt weak. Even if she could somehow escape, she wasn't sure that she'd be able to support her own weight to run away.

They'd been travelling for what felt like days, but in truth, she knew that she had no idea how long it had been. Day and night were one and the same under the hood, and the cart never stopped its slow, methodical pace. She doubted they ever got above walking speed, but she knew that they must have travelled dozens of miles. She'd been nicked on her calf by one of the Shrunken blades as she'd tried to fight them off and the wound was starting to feel hot and itchy.

Other than the pain, her only company were the Shrunken, the half-goblins that had taken her. They were open with their conversation around her, making no effort to disguise what they were saying. It didn't matter, though. Skye couldn't understand a word of their language.

On what Skye reckoned was the fourth or possibly fifth day, her hood was wrenched from her head. Even though dusk was rapidly approaching over the horizon, Skye blinked and turned her head away from the unfamiliar light. Tall trees were all around her casting lengthening shadows in twisted and mysterious patterns. The trees looked like a sickness had descended upon them. The leaves were twisted and rotted as they grew. Dark, odorous fungi grew from every crevice. Skye had seen these trees once before; before the orcs threw themselves from the darkness and into battle. She was in the Gloom.

"Welcome to your new home." One of the Shrunken screeched in Skye's face as its sharp claws dug into her cheeks and dragged her face upwards. Overhead loomed a monstrous stone tower, the top lost amongst the storm clouds that hung permanently over the forest. Dark-eyed crows rested on iron rods that thrust out from the mortar like bony spines. Tall stone walls spread out from the sides of the tower like the wings of the carrion that hovered overhead hopeful of an easy meal.

Skye could feel the darkness almost as strongly as when she'd faced the Dark Queen. Bile rose in her throat, and she had to fight back the urge to be sick. A long stone ramp rose out of the sodden soil in front of the cart and snaked its way towards the heavy stone door that marked the entrance to the citadel. The cart started to move again, pulled along by a cowering foursome of wretched goblins that were being mercilessly whipped by the Shrunken. Skye felt sorry for them but could do little to change their fate.

It took the group nearly an hour to make their way to the stone entrance, but as they approached, Skye was able to make out the faded writing carved into the block stones above the arch. She could just make out the name of the city, Alastor, followed by the city motto.

All hope dies.

"Hello, little Felmir!"

The croaking voice woke Skye from her sleep, and she found that her hood had been removed. She wished that it hadn't. She'd been pulled to her knees and was face to face with a hideous monster. It looked like most of the other Shrunken, but the face was knitted with a network of cuts and scars, many of which hadn't healed and which oozed a viscous white pus. One eye was made of glass and stared past Skye's shoulder, but the remaining one glared into her soul with undisguised hatred.

"My soldiers tell me that they found you and your friends hunting around the tower for Akeldama?" the voice continued loudly. "That stone is rightfully ours. My ancestors dug it from the very ground underneath us. They found it and protected it, and then your ancestors stole it from us!" The creature was screaming, and Skye found herself trying to cover her face against the spittle spraying from its mouth.

"I thought the Nelapsi stole it from you?" Skye

asked without thinking, remembering the history lessons she'd been given when she had first met Snudge.

"Hah!" The creature started to cough and choke with laughter. One of the soldiers behind him offered him a glass of filthy water that he took and swallowed in one gulp. "That's what the Felmir and the goblins have always said. They said that we had become evil, that we had been turned by the stone. One night, our guards caught a group of men and goblins scaling the walls of the tower. They picked them off where they could, but one managed to grab the orb and escape.

"My soldiers tell me that they were close to finding the stone when you attacked them—"

"They attacked us!" Skye screamed in defiance. "We were not looking for the stone. We were looking to stop the tower falling to the Dark Queen's forces again."

"The Dark Queen is dead."

"So we have heard." Skye was not going to be drawn into giving away any more information than she needed to. She definitely wasn't going to tell them that she wasn't a Felmir. She was confident that the Felmir looked enough like humans to pass as one if needed.

"I believe that you had found the stone within the tower. My soldiers tell me that an aura of darkness surrounded you when they attacked, as though something was protecting you. Did you find Akeldama little one?" The creature spoke calmly, but his words were still clipped. Skye sensed he was only suppressing his anger for the time being.

"No," she lied, "I haven't seen the stone."

"No matter." The half-goblin grinned. "You are my slave now. If those filthy Felmir have what I want, then they may get you back in one piece. Or at least, most you back." He laughed loudly, and once again had to be offered water to calm his cough. "On the other hand, if they don't have what I want, then what use are you to me? Take her away and place her in the base of the tower. We'll see just how highly her people value her!"

Skye screamed as another hood was placed over her head and she was dragged away by her heels. Her head throbbed as it cracked against hard steps as she descended further and further underground. Semi-conscious, she felt herself thrown to the floor and heard a large, heavy door slam shut behind her.

The loud rattle of a bolt being slid shut was the last thing she heard before blacking out.

The Dead Rise

Damphir couldn't believe his luck. Even in his darkest dreams, he could never have imagined how powerful the Azrul had once been. The army wasn't the biggest – there were little more than a few thousand resurrected souls in all – but they were strong and made even stronger in death.

The march to the Burnt Fort had been swift and relentless. Damphir rode out in front atop his dragon, skimming low to the ground to avoid attracting attention. He knew that his army was strong and could defeat most mortal armies, but there would be time for that later. For now, there was only one thing that he desired.

It had never been the lure of an army of the dead that had drawn him so irreversibly to the story of the Azrul. It had always been the idea of Akeldama, the orb. Just the thought of the power that it was said to bestow upon its owner made him feel younger again. And now it was within his grasp. The beasts of the wild spoke to Damphir in the darkness of the night, and they all spoke one name. One name that had succeeded where so many others had failed.

Salismir, they whispered in the shadows. *The Burnt Fort.*

Damphir knew the area well. He had sheltered in the fort as a child during his exile. Even if the rumours where true and the hobgoblin held the town alone, it would be wise to proceed with caution. The lands to the south of the Burnt Fort were wide and open, and an approaching army would be seen many miles before they were able to launch an attack. Much better to approach from the north in the long shadows of the Orcwood.

There were risks involved heading north as well. The walled city of Eragor was heavily fortified and held an army of elves, the last remnants of the realm of Kanthor. Damphir knew the only option was to head west out of the Darkwood and travel north along the lower branches of the Silver River. This they had done a few days before, and already they were breaking cover and heading back east towards the darkness of the Orcwood. The pounding of the Azrul feet against the dry earth echoed for miles, but they were under strictest orders to march without chants or songs. As best he could, he wanted their arrival at the Burnt Fort to be a surprise.

At the request of the Azrul leaders, he'd conceded that a small show of force might be in order, and the standard bearers held their flags high. Strong winds picked them up and pulled them tight. The ornate double dragon's head motif was picked out in silver against the pure black fabric and showed the strength that Damphir felt inside. Underneath his body, he could feel the muscles of his beast flexing and rolling as he guided it this way and that. The Azrul would march day and night if he ordered them to, but he and the dragon needed to rest, and so at the entrance to the Orcwood he ordered his soldiers to set up their camps and rest. They lit no fires. Their dead eyes needed no light to see by.

When the sun rose the following morning, its light seemed to disappear where it fell on the thick, tangled trees of the Orcwood. None of them were in leaf, but so twisted and matted together were their branches that it made no difference. Once Damphir and his army stepped under the canopy, they were plunged into darkness. The dark mage muttered under his breath, and a small ball of blue flame spread over his hand like a glove. When he raised it high, it cast a shallow pool of light in front of him and he used this to pick a path through the undergrowth.

Roots seemed to reach out and grab at his ankles and many of the Azrul tripped and stumbled to the ground. He had known the forest would be too tight for his dragon and had sent it on ahead. Every so often, he would hear the creaking of the big leather wings as it circled overhead, possibly hunting, possibly seeking its master.

For three days, Damphir led his army of the dead through the maze of wooden corpses. At the end of each day, he refused to sleep and pushed on harder despite his growing weariness and hunger. There was nothing in the forest that he dared to eat. Even the mushrooms and plants that he knew to be edible looked weak and poisoned by the foetid atmosphere. He was glad when they finally broke through the outskirts of the south-eastern corner of the forest and were able to breathe relatively fresh air again, though there was still something of the misty vapours in the air until they were well away from the shadows of the trees.

Overhead the clouds darkened and it started to rain. Heavy raindrops beat out a rhythm against the metal armour of the Azrul. The air moved as the giant dragon circled and came to a halt next to their leader. Damphir climbed onto the beast's back and smiled. The gods were clearly smiling on him today. This darkness would conceal their march until they were hammering down the outer gates of the fort.

Under the shield of darkness, Damphir ordered his men back into their ranks, each unit fifty men wide. He urged his dragon forward on foot as there was no need to ruin their surprise by being seen flying through the air. With their spears and standards thrusting into the sky, his men looked like a spiked snake slithering through the scrubland towards a black dot on the horizon that Damphir knew to be the fort.

When he had last passed this way, back when it had been known by the proud name of Horongor, the town had been alive and thronged with busy hobgoblins. Chimneys smoked at all hours, and the sounds of industry could be heard for miles. That's when the cursed name that it now lived under was first used. So great were the fires and so high the flames in the smithies that buildings were often burnt with all of those working within. To work in Horongor was to be burnt. But still the workers piled in, proud of what they were producing, and still the flames ate them alive.

Now the fort lay dormant. Not dead but asleep like

a giant waiting to be prodded into wakefulness. Not by him, though. He had bigger plans. Maybe later but for now he simply needed what was harboured inside.

Under the cover of the dark clouds, Damphir led his army to the edge of the high wooden fences that ringed Horongor. It was nearly nightfall. As hard as it was to stop this close to his quarry, he knew that he needed to rest and that any action would be better in daylight. It didn't matter anymore. He was here. He could sense the orb was close, almost like a magnet drawing him into the town. It would wait. It would have to. He sent the dragon away into the night. He'd call it again when he needed it. Then he found a sheltered nook against the wooden fence and pulled a thick woollen blanket around his shoulders. The Azrul closest to him would keep guard whilst he slept and the rest would form a ring around the fort as he had instructed.

Damphir closed his eyes and allowed Akeldama to draw him in. The voice floated into his head like a mist and filled every corner until it was all he could hear and all he could think about. At first, it was muffled and distant but familiar all the same. It formed a song whose tune he recognised but with words that evaded his memory. And then it burst into clarity and struck at nerves rusted through centuries of neglect. It pierced his heart like threads of broken glass and tore into his soul in a way that he had had only experienced once before. It was a song from his childhood, from his mother's knee. It was a song that suddenly he knew all too well. His lips moved of their own accord and he picked up the tune as it started over again.

> *Sleep my angel and peace will bring thee,*
> *Through this long night.*
> *Safety and comfort, I will give thee,*
> *Through this long night.*
> *Tho' our enemies are slowly creeping,*
> *Lay your head and fall to sleeping.*
> *I my loved ones' watch am keeping,*
> *Through this long night.*

The voice was suffocating. It drowned out all his attempts to silence it. He felt his throat tighten as once again he was a child being embraced by his mother. He remembered the scene well, hunkered down in the basement of the temple whilst the orcs rampaged through his village. All the women had gathered together with their young and had sang together as much to drown out the horrible noises from overhead as to comfort the children.

My love protects thee, all around thee,
Through this long night.
Peaceful slumber comes to greet thee,
Through this long night.
Here the sleeping hours are comfort,
Through this long night.
I my loved ones' watch am keeping,
Through this long night.

Now he could smell his mother's scent in his nose and feel the softness of her cloak against his skin. He remembered pushing against her, begging to go out and fight with his father. His father had been his hero, his rock. He'd taught him to control the anger that had plagued his childhood and to harness it ready for when he needed it. He could remember the pain of not knowing what was happening out there. And then, eventually, the sounds had died away and silence had settled heavily.

The devastation when at last they'd emerged from the dark cellar had been complete. Bodies littered the ground and the buildings had been burned to hollow shells. And there was his father, dead at the doorway to the temple. So close to where they'd been hiding and yet seemingly so far away. He'd been punctured by a dozen arrows, and the look of surprised pain on his face would stay with Damphir forever.

It filled his mind, and still the voice sang on, each word hammering home the loss that had driven him this far. He'd never forgiven his mother for not letting him fight alongside his father. In his mind, she'd been responsible for the utter devastation. That's why she'd had to die come the end. It was the only way to be rid of his demons, at least until now.

Hear, the mourning bell is ringing,
Loud through the night.
Feel our lost ones smile upon us,
Through this dark night.
Turned to dust but not forsaken,
Power granted thee to waken,
Undone their last journey taken,
Saved this long night.

Damphir had never heard that verse before, and it filled him with rage. He knew who was singing and knew what it was trying to do to him. He pushed back in the way he always had and felt the familiar burning edge in his mind, like serrated steel cutting deep, as the power started to grow. Before it had time to reach its peak, he felt whatever was invading his mind retreat beyond his reach. He could still hear the voice, but now it was scared, or cautious at least.

You try to fight me? It should have been a scream in a gale, but it arrived like a whisper from a loved one, full of warmth but disappointment. *We will be unbeatable together. We will rule this world and bring it to its knees!*

A calm washed over Damphir and he felt himself regain his composure. "You tried to force me to my knees with your cheap parlour tricks and memory games. I wonder if you made the same promises to poor Salismir before he brought you here."

He is not a believer! He only wanted me for my power. You have the burning belief inside you. I can feel it.

"You are wrong. I have always believed in whatever I needed to in order to succeed. I have worshipped more gods than I care to count and cursed more still. You are right, though. We will be great together. You are wrong if you think that you will be in charge. I learnt long ago not to let anything else control me, back when my father taught me to control my rage. I will not bow down to you now, Akeldama. I will tame you, and you will bend the knee to me."

I only want what is best for this wretched world. If you are the one to lead, then I will follow willingly. You know where to find me.

A vision of a tall wooden tower flashed bright for a second, and Damphir woke with a startled grunt.

Daylight was breaking on the horizon, and the chill had left the air. He rose to his feet and made his way round to the main entrance gate into Horongor. He ordered the Azrul soldiers to stand their ground no matter what happened and not to allow a soul in or out of the fort. Then he drew himself up and rang the large brass bell that had been hung next to the gate for visitors seeking entrance to the town. It rang loudly before falling to the ground.

"You are not who I was expecting. Unless who I see is not entirely true?" said Salismir from behind the gate. He was small, even for a hobgoblin, and his voice was thin and made weak with hunger, but Damphir heard him well enough through the wooden gates.

"I am entirely as I seem, Salismir. Maybe who you were expecting was not the person you should have been most concerned with. Surely you understand that the treasure you so covet is coveted equally by many more than just Queen Camarina?" answered Damphir loudly enough to hear his voice carry away in the wind.

"You cannot have it!" Salismir sounded like a wounded animal. Damphir wondered just how long the poor hobgoblin had been under the control of Akeldama. He had felt the strength of the orb himself and had no difficulty imagining the damage it could do to a weaker mind. "I have done terrible things to keep it, and I will do more if I need to. You have no idea how powerful it has made me!" There was a desperation in Salismir's voice.

"Look around me, my friend. Do you see my army?"

"I will kill them all! I've done worse, and to people I cared about!"

"You are free to kill them at will. It didn't stop them last time."

Salismir paused as he tried to work out what this meant. Damphir filled the silence. "You may have heard of the terrifying army of the Azrul. They waged war across these lands and brought death wherever they trod. After years of this, they were wiped out by a sickening plague that ravaged their minds. They were greedy and they died. And now I have brought them back to fight once more. This time for me. There will be no greed, no grand plan to conquer the world one city at a time. I did this without the power of Akeldama at my side. Let that be a lesson to you, Salismir, in how powerful I already am.

"Open this gate now, and you may live in my shadow. Choose to fight me, and you will die. Betray me and you will die. At this point, you may relish the release of death, but I think there is a little of you left yet. Make the wise choice, Salismir. You cannot win today."

For a few long moments, there was no sound but the creaking of the wooden fort in the wind. Damphir smiled at the sound of the thick bolts being slid open and stepped forward to embrace the broken hobgoblin as soon as the gates swung inward. He could almost sense the relief flooding out of Salismir at being released from the burden that Akeldama had become. He almost expected him to make a break for freedom. He wouldn't have blamed him even as he had his soldiers cut him down. Instead, he fell to his kneed and pledged his undying loyalty to Damphir.

"I appreciate your gesture, Salismir. However, there are far more pressing matters to attend to. I do believe that Akeldama is hidden away in the church tower?"

"How did you know?" Salismir seemed to forget his fear for a moment.

"It spoke to me in the night. I'm sure that you are familiar with its ways. Please go fetch it for me and do not delay. Remember our agreement. Now is no time to test my forgiveness."

The hobgoblin scuttled away in the direction of the church, and Damphir followed him inside the wooden walls. Most of the buildings had fallen into disrepair, but there were still a few that stood strong against the elements. The roads had disappeared in a mat of weeds and grass, and the skulls that were mounted above the gate as a warning to attackers had long been picked clean. A darkness lay on Horongor that had nothing to do with the people that had left it to rot. Maybe it was centuries of living in the shadow of the Orcwood or maybe it was the presence of Akeldama within its walls. Whatever it was, Damphir could feel it in his bones and, like all darkness, he could feel it reinvigorating him.

Dungeon

The air in the dungeons underneath Alastor was so hot and foetid that even the walls seemed to sweat. Skye tossed and turned on her patch of bare earth trying to find a position that was comfortable to sleep in. At least her hands had been untied whilst she was unconscious. She'd balled up her shirt for a pillow, but that simply left her arms open to attack from the insects that buzzed in through the small, barred windows high in the walls and tried to feast on her arms and ankles.

Skye had lost track of how long she'd been underground. She'd discovered fairly quickly that she wasn't alone. There were at least a dozen other miserable souls caged in with her, mostly goblins, but there were also a pair of Shrunken that lived alone in a dark corner and refused to speak to any of the others.

After the first few days, the goblins had approached Skye and started to talk to her about why they had taken her. She'd decided to stick with the story that she was a kidnapped Felmir being held for ransom. She'd noticed straightaway that the goblins all bore tattoos of an eye on their wrist. Once she'd worked out which goblins were more talkative than the others, she approached them to find out more about it.

"I don't recognise the symbol on your wrists. Is that your tribe?" she asked when she was alone with two of the group.

The oldest of the two goblins seemed reluctant to talk and dismissed her question off-hand, but the younger seemed more eager. He seemed proud of the mark and jumped in to talk to Skye just as soon as his partner had wandered back over to the rest of the group.

"It's the sign of the Order of the Shadowed Eye," he explained eagerly. "It's why we're in here." The goblin gestured to the dungeons. "There are those goblins amongst us who believe that enough is enough. We've sat idly by for long enough whilst other races rise to power and take our lands and freedoms away from us." He was starting to get riled up, and Skye found herself backing away as he started to wave his arms around in front of him. "Did you know that in the south goblins are kept as slaves by the elves? Even in the north, in the North Wood under the order of the heathen Snudge, goblins are routinely killed just because they dare to question his authority. We want our place in history, and we are determined to take it by force if needed."

"Force?" asked Skye. "What is the Shadowed Eye?"

"There is a legend that before time began a stone orb was forged and imbibed with all the dark powers of the world—"

"You mean Akeldama?" interrupted Skye.

"You dare to use the Shrunken name for it? Here, underneath their halls? You are very brave little Felmir. They say that it can hear its name being uttered, you know.

"Anyway, the Shadowed Eye was considered lost for thousands of years before a glorious queen rose to power in the south not too long ago. She harnessed the power of the Eye and very nearly brought balance to our world. Unfortunately, she was betrayed and her soul was cast away, too damaged for the Shadowlands and too weak to rise again without the power of the stone."

Skye struggled to hold back her anger as she listened to the goblin relive her battle with the Dark Queen in every way except for the facts that mattered. How dare he stand here in front of her and dishonour what she went through? She took a deep breath. It wouldn't achieve anything if she blew her cover now. She allowed the goblin to continue.

"After her destruction, the stone was cast from the top of Liorath's Peak and was thought once again lost from the world. Even though the queen's soul was left to wander the Shadowlands, her agents of war remained true to her cause and searched day and night for the missing orb until, in time, a nameless dark sorcerer journeyed to the Shadowlands and sought help amongst the spirits. They spoke to him and told him where the stone could be found and, sure enough, he found it buried at the bottom of a dark pool far to the south of Liorath's Peak.

"Immediately he raced to the only place that he knew he would be safe. He'd spent many years training in dark magic in a system of caves just north of Soulaman, and it was there that he fled. He carried the orb alone and in total secrecy. Some say that the stone spoke to him and sent him crazy with lust for its dark power, but as soon as he arrived, he summoned the soul of the Dark Queen back from the Shadowlands and resurrected her. For his services, she had him killed, such is the darkness it brings about.

"It is said that she is still weak, nothing more than a shapeless spirit held in this world only by the dark cowl that she wears around her and she is still tied to the power of the Eye. Without it, she will wither away and disappear once again."

"And it is to this queen that you pledge your allegiance? That is what the tattoo is about?" spat Skye, unable to hide her disgust.

"Of course not. She showed us what can be achieved with the power of the Shadowed Eye, but we cannot forgive her for the war she waged on goblins during her rise to power. No, our allegiance is to the Eye itself."

"You plan to take it from her? To steal Akeldama from the Dark Queen?"

The goblin sat back and smiled smugly at Skye. "We don't need to. Somebody has already stolen it from her. Right now, the Eye is in the possession of a single hobgoblin somewhere south of the Orcwood. The Order of the Shadowed Eye has agents in all of the goblin armies seeking out the true location of that which we seek.

"We will find it, Felmir, and the goblins will rise to power on a tide of darkness."

Skye shuddered despite the heat and backed away into the corner.

A New Sword

Arthur had taken to spending an hour each morning staring out beyond the turrets on top of the tallest towers in Carak Tak. Snudge had promised him that he would bring the G'Oräk army to meet them, but the likelihood of that happening seemed to grow smaller with each long day. Brack had sent word to the goblin leader as soon as he had been able. His message had been short but urgent.

Come quickly, he'd urged. *It has been found. Skye has been taken.* Brack tried his hardest not to show how worried he was growing, but Arthur saw it in the goblin's eyes. That message had been sent nearly a week before, and they still had no word back.

During these daily breaks from his new friends, Arthur could almost convince himself that the world was at peace, such was the silence. A grey, early-morning sun was rising on the horizon and filled the valleys of the Scirion Mountains in the distance with a golden glow. To the south and west, this fork of the Silver River came to the end of its journey south. A foetid swampland in the distance, bordered with ancient mangroves and tall bull-rushes, buzzed with life, but the rest of the plains seemed empty.

The air felt heavy and humid and the clouds promised thunder at any moment. The only noise was the soft chirrup of the crickets in the long grass at the foot of the tower. Arthur pressed his palms to his eyes and said a quiet prayer to whoever was listening. He longed more than anything to see Snudge leading a vast army of goblins over the hills to the north, but he nurtured this yearning as a defence against what he really wanted most, to see Skye to know that she was alive and well.

Another few days passed before Arthur's daily vigils bore any good news. It was an unusually cold morning, and Arthur was huddled under a heavy blanket and nestled down between two stone crenellations trying to shelter himself from the wind when a golden dove, the same bird that Brack had used to send his message all that time ago, landed on the ground, at his feet.

Attached to its ankle was a scrap of paper that bore Snudge's seal. Overcome with excitement, Arthur carefully unravelled it and rushed the dove to the small goblin that tended to the messenger birds. Then, happy that the dove would recover from its arduous journey, he hurried down into Carak Tak and to the keep where he knew Geldrig and Brack would be meeting with Jango, Malficia and the other Keepers of Knowledge.

The large wooden door was ajar when he arrived, but he still took the courtesy of knocking. He'd raced in once before and had interrupted the sacred prayers of the Keepers. His rudeness had earned him a shift on the night guard, and he never wanted to experience the cold and utter darkness of a Carak Tak midnight again.

Geldrig called out that it was safe to enter, and Arthur pushed the door open as softly as he could in his excitement. Even though he had no idea whether the message was positive or not, having any contact at all was invigorating.

"What does it say?" he asked breathlessly. Geldrig seemed to take an age to read the note, and Arthur grew restless. He cursed himself for not reading it before handing it over.

"Snudge is a day's ride away. He has brought the G'Oräk army with him and picked up more en route, around two-thousand goblins in total. He urges us to prepare to leave. He will not be staying for long."

The rest of the day passed in a blur for Arthur. Horses, weapons and armour had to be readied, and the entire Carak Tak army seemed to be passing through the keep at once. In the end, Arthur took himself away and spent the afternoon huddled on top of the tower with his eyes fixed firmly north for any sign of their salvation. He felt his eyes growing heavy and jolted awake when a hand grabbed his shoulder.

"Do not fear, Arthur. It is only me, Malficia. I have something for you. Come with me." The old goblin pulled Arthur to his feet and led him back down into the tower. Huge candles were blazing in nooks in the walls and hurt Arthur's eyes after the growing darkness outside. At the bottom of a curved set of steps, Malficia produced a mess of keys and slotted one into a small crack in an otherwise unremarkable section of wall.

To Arthur's surprise, a glow appeared and marked the outline of a door. With a soft push, the section of wall swung open and into a small room beyond. The room was dark except for a small candle that burned on a silver platter on top of a long, thin glass case. Inside the case, the candlelight reflected off the most beautiful sword that Arthur had ever seen.

It looked to be forged of copper and inlaid with gold, but even Arthur knew it wouldn't be strong enough. This was some entirely different metal, but it cried out to be held. Arthur could never imagine striking an enemy with it. It seemed sacrilege to put a thing of such beauty to such barbaric measures.

"This is Siorraidh. It belonged to a long-forgotten but successful Elven queen named Buidhe. She lived a thousand years ago when the elves still stood tall and proud and held court with the highest races in Ithilmir. Sadly, they no longer venture this far north. They were driven from their lands a long time ago by a twisted version of themselves, but that story must wait for now.

"Buidhe was the first queen to take her place in battle alongside her soldiers. She was said to be a thing of beauty, porcelain features with the yellowest hair and darkest eyes, but she vowed to never take a king. She often spoke of a curse in her bloodline and said that it would be an act of greatest cruelty to pass that curse on to a child. Without a king to fight alongside her army, she saw it as her duty to lead her soldiers into battle. She really was brave for she allowed the strong women of their city to fight alongside the men and it is often told that they fought with more valour and often with more aggression.

"Beautiful and brave as she was, she wasn't as strong as she would have liked and would often grow tired in battle trying to wield the heavy long-swords that were customary for mounted knights to carry into battle. She was lethal with a bow but needed something to defend herself with when that failed. There was a blacksmith in the hills outside her town who was said to be able to forge anything, and so she had him smuggled into her castle one night and set him to task smelting and working the strongest metals he could find."

Arthur looked down at the sword again. He could just imagine the fine, spidery lines of gold flowing in molten rivers across the copper-coloured metal. It would have been something to see.

"He made Siorraidh?" Arthur asked.

"Not at first. The first swords that he made were strong, perhaps stronger than any other sword made before, but they were still too heavy for Queen Buidhe to lift. She soon grew impatient with his failures and gave him an ultimatum; make the lightest, strongest sword ever forged or lose his head. The blacksmith feared for his life and so he begged the queen to grant him some time to travel the world and find such a material. She granted him a single year and not a day more.

"For a while, it looked like the blacksmith had fled into the shadows and would never be seen again. But, with three days to spare, he staggered back through the gates with a wooden crate filled with strange ores. He wouldn't speak to anyone or reveal where he had found them, and he spent the last three days of his time forging them into the sword that you see before you."

Siorraidh seemed to glow as Malficia spoke. Arthur hoped that it couldn't hear them talking about it.

"With only seconds to spare, the blacksmith presented Queen Buidhe with his final attempt. She lifted it and weighed it in her hands. 'There is no weight to it at all!' she exclaimed, much to his delight. 'But, I must test its strength. Can something this beautiful, this light, take a life?' The books tell us that at this point she pointed to a courtier who was suspected of being in league with her rivals and ordered him to his knees. As he knelt there before her, begging for his life, she swung Siorraidh over her shoulder and took his head. Before his body fell to the ground, the blood on the sword had disappeared as if by magic."

Malficia carefully lifted the candle from the glass case and placed it onto the floor. Even in the darkness, Siorraidh seemed to shine. The goblin raised the hinged lid of the glass case and pulled out the sword. He handed it to Arthur who took it slowly, his hands shaking. The legend was true. It felt like he was holding nothing heavier than a stick.

"Queen Buidhe fought many battles with this sword, and she never suffered a wound. She used to say that whenever an enemy struck the sword would be there to block the attack, whether she saw it coming or not. That's why she named it Siorraidh. It is the Elvish word for eternity. She believed that she could never die whilst she possessed this sword, and it very nearly proved true. Alas, even the most magical of swords cannot defeat death and old age. Eventually, she passed into history, but Siorraidh found its way to us and has been in this room ever since. Only a few Keepers know that it is here, and only I have the key."

"It's beautiful," Arthur said, and he meant it. He offered it back to the goblin.

"It is a gift to you, Arthur. Skye has Burrower. Now you have Siorraidh. May it bring you the same luck that it brought Queen Buidhe."

Arthur didn't know what to say. His old sword had been blunt and rusty, but it had served him well on Liorath's Peak. This was something special.

Malficia continued his speech whilst Arthur turned the sword over and over in his hands. "We now know that it is forged from metals so rare that they have never been seen since. The blacksmith travelled to Mithrostan in the heart of the Shadowlands. It is called the City of Souls for a reason. No living creature has ever set foot within its walls and been allowed to leave. Somehow, the blacksmith managed to travel to the city and leave with some of its most precious ores. Nobody knows how he did it, but he was never the same again. Soon after he forged Siorraidh, he disappeared. Some believe he made a deal with Faileas and returned to pay whatever price he had agreed. Others say he went mad with grief at the thought of the perfection that he had created."

"Thank you, I shall treasure it." Arthur was snapped out of his concentration by the thunderous sound of a war horn outside the tower.

"It would appear that Snudge is early!" Malficia had a smile on his face. "Let us go greet your leader."

Escape

Skye knew that she needed to escape. One of the goblins had died overnight, and the corpse lay rotting in the middle of the floor surrounded by a buzzing swarm of flies. It seemed to move in the shadows as maggots crawled across the skin, cracked open after one too many beatings at the hands of the Shrunken.

She had a plan.

Every morning a guard would throw open the door and toss in a basket of old food for the inmates to fight over. The next time the guard came, she knew that she'd have a better chance than ever to escape. The guard would have to drag the dead goblin out of the cell, and that was when she'd make her move.

Sure enough, as soon as the weak sunlight started to filter through the small windows, the voice of the guard screamed through the keyhole in the heavy wooden door.

"All of you horrible lot, line up against the far wall. I want to be able to count you nice and easy." It was the same warning every day, but Skye had hidden herself in a dark corner away from the others. As the key turned the heavy bolt, she made her way silently to the nook behind the door. She had to make sure that the other inmates didn't see her and give her plan away. In her hand, she held a thick metal pole that a previous prisoner had worked loose from the window frame and had left half buried in the mud.

The bolt slid back and the door swung open more quietly than its size would suggest. Skye felt her heart racing in her chest. Her breath came in ragged, short bursts. She knew she'd only get one chance at this. Any hesitation at all and the guard would kill her without a second thought.

She saw the eyes of one of the other goblins widen as he saw her from their line-up. She saw his mouth move to say something just as the guard stepped into the shadows of the dungeon and stood, silhouetted against the torchlight beyond the door. Without thinking, Skye stepped forwards and brought the metal bar round into the base of the guard's skull. She felt the bone give way under the weight of the weapon and snatched the keys from his hands before he crumpled to the floor.

Without looking back, she darted from the dungeon and locked the door shut behind her. It would be hard enough escaping on her own. She couldn't afford to risk it with the others as well. She didn't feel any remorse as she made her way into the brightly lit corridor that led directly away from the dungeons. The Brotherhood of the Shadowed Eye sounded like a dangerous group, and Skye preferred to leave as many locked up as possible.

Outside the door was a guards' desk, on which was a half-eaten breakfast. Skye forced the horrible gruel into her mouth – it was better than the slop they'd been served at least – and rummaged through the rotting sacks propped up against the wall. Her heart skipped a beat when she pulled out her beloved sword, Burrower, and its scabbard. She tied it quickly to her waist and scurried away trying her hardest to stick to the shadows against the walls.

The corridor soon split into two, and Skye veered left along the passage that seemed to be heading upwards. The last thing she wanted was to head farther underground. She had no idea where she was in relation to the main city of Alastor, but she had to hope that she wouldn't emerge in the centre of the tower.

The passageway seemed to go on forever. The only features that gave any sense that Skye was actually moving forwards were the wooden torches hammered into the walls at regular intervals. These burned with a sickly smoke and only added to the heat and overbearing humidity. In her desperation, she tossed her thick woollen cloak aside. It didn't matter. She was still sweating with every step that she took. She knew that she needed water badly. The guards had kept the prisoners dehydrated to keep them weak.

As she turned yet another corner, Skye felt a breeze against her skin. It was only weak, but she could definitely feel it. Like a horse turning its head towards the rain, Skye ran forwards with renewed energy. Burrower rattled in its scabbard, but Skye ignored the noise and pushed on. The torches had given out, and soon she found herself running blindly through complete darkness, but still she didn't stop.

Suddenly the ground gave way underfoot. Skye found herself slipping and sliding down a steep hill carried forwards by the loose stones that rolled and bounced around her. She felt her weak ankle buckle beneath her, and she fell onto her back. When the avalanche stopped, Skye found herself lying on her back looking up at a bright moonlit sky.

She was free.

Not for long though, she thought, *if I lay around waiting.*

Despite the protests from her ankle, Skye pulled herself up to her feet and set off at a pace. Her fall had taken her into the middle of the dark forest that surrounded Alastor, the Gloom. Skye knew too well what these trees contained, but she had no other choice than to push on.

Trees as thick around as a house towered into the sky and broke the moonlight as speckled shadows on the floor. Even though it was still spring, the trees in the Gloom rarely had a full canopy and certainly never blossomed. The branches reached down in the foul air and seemed to snatch at Skye's shirt as she pushed her way through. She regretted throwing away her cloak, even though it was still close and foul the heat of the dungeon was long gone. She shivered in the night air.

As the night wore on, Skye found her progress slowing as she started to move uphill. In the higher areas, the trees thinned out slightly, and she started to hope that she was approaching the edge of the forest. Long strands of old spider webs hung from the trees and stuck to her face. Every now and then, she'd squeal as a sticky rope caught in her mouth, and she'd flail her arms around until she was free.

Abruptly Skye found her way blocked by a deep ravine that seemed to split the forest in two. Too far to jump, there was only one way across. A few hundred yards away a tall oak had been uprooted and lay across the chasm. Small ferns had taken root in the crevices and mosses and lichens had started to blanket the surface. Overall it looked sturdy enough, if a little slippery, and so Skye cautiously climbed onto the trunk by using the root ball as a step ladder. Her head spun as she made the mistake of glancing down. There was no bottom to the darkness beneath her. It took the strength of a low hanging branch to keep her from toppling over the edge before she'd even started to cross over.

Skye forced herself to breathe the cold air into her lungs and tentatively took a step out into the abyss. The trunk was thick enough around for Skye to stand two abreast, but as she looked down, it stretched away into infinity no thicker than the spider webs that had so recently grabbed at her face. She wobbled again but managed to regain her balance and took a few quick steps farther out. She was barely a quarter of the way across, but already she was gasping for breath and her head was spinning. She'd never had a head for heights. She pushed herself on, though. She knew that the Shrunken would notice that she was missing soon, and they'd head out into the forest to capture her. They knew the terrain better than she did and they'd have no problems clambering over fallen trees to get to her.

"You can do this," Skye repeated to herself, a mantra to get to where she needed to be. "You can do this."

A horn blasted through the trees stripping any remaining leaves and shredding Skye's nerves. She spun on her heels and saw a band of Shrunken tearing through the forest at the bottom of the hill. Turning back around, she headed further onto the log throwing all caution to the wind. She didn't have time for slow and steady steps. She started to sprint as fast as she dared, her feet flying in front of each other and barely making contact with the wood. One foot landed more heavily, and she felt the rotten wood give way. The world spun for a second, and Skye watched with awe as the giant tree trunk disappeared into the distance as she fell into the darkness.

With a snap, Skye landed on an enormous spider's web strung across the entire crevice. The rope was sticky to the touch but not nearly as bad as those that had stuck to her face in the forest. It was enough to make it difficult to move. Each time Skye fought against the web, she felt the vibrations travel along the strands. Only they weren't strands of web. Now that she looked closer, Skye realised that they were rope spun from the fibrous vines of the forest. Somebody had made these and set the trap below the fallen tree trunk. Or was it just a safety net?

Overhead the Shrunken were squawking to each other in their rage. Skye heard them disappear into the night far beyond her secret hideout. She had to get out. If she fell from the web, she doubted that there would be another before she finally hit the floor of the canyon. Slowly, she eased herself along the ropes on her hands and knees. When she reached the centre, she heard the first whistle. It was high-pitched and sing-song, almost like a lullaby. Then another joined in and another. Soon Skye was surrounded by whistles in the darkness coming from each side of the giant web.

"Who are you?" she hissed, thinking back to the night she had encountered the Glibberig. "What do you want with me?"

"We want everything!" Again, the voice was high and lilting as though the speaker would much rather be singing than talking. "We know who you are, Skye Thistle!"

Now Skye saw who had her surrounded. Tall, slender elves were slowly walking along the strands of rope like tightrope walkers at a circus. They were dressed in golden robes with a red dragon embroidered across the chest.

"We've been sent to rescue you, saviour!" sang another dark elf from behind Skye. She spun to look at him and nearly lost her footing on the rope.

"Do not fear," whispered yet another. "We mean you no harm. We are to take you to the emperor. He very much wants to see you! He knows what a brave warrior you are."

"He wants you to join us!"

"He wants you to fight for the Army of Enlightenment!"

Skye was surrounded. The elves were almost on top of her. As she reached for Burrower, she found her hands clasped tightly behind her back. Despite their willowy stature, the elves were as strong as iron.

One of them stood directly in front of her as a companion held her arms behind her back. "This is for your own good. We can't risk a fight in such a… precarious…situation." He gestured to the web that surrounded them. In the darkness, Skye still couldn't see just how big it was.

"I…I…," she stammered, unable to find any words. She wondered if she'd ever be free again.

"We are to take you to see the emperor, Skye. Though I'm afraid that you are too valuable to travel openly. You must travel as our slave until you reach Dragorith, at which point you will be taken to see

Emperor Ki. You should be honoured!"

Skye didn't see the point in fighting anymore, and so she allowed herself to be led by the elves to a rope ladder that led back into the forest. Once back on solid ground, she found that they had an ornate chariot waiting amongst the trees. The panels were a dark golden colour, and once again the red dragon was printed across the doors. A single white unicorn was tethered to the front of the carriage and stood growing restless. Steam rose from its back in the cold air, and the horn seemed to Skye to shimmer and move like the very best seashells.

Wordlessly she boarded the carriage and jumped when the door clicked shut behind her. None of the elves had entered with her, but Skye was relieved despite herself to see them jogging alongside when they finally started moving. This carriage was much lighter than the one in which she had arrived and the unicorn far stronger than the poor, beaten goblins.

Soon the trees were whipping past the window and a cold breeze wrapped itself around Skye. She shivered against the biting cold and tried to huddle into herself. She was startled when a thick black blanket was tossed onto her lap. Somehow the elves were managing to keep up with the carriage. Thankful, she smothered herself in the thick wool and tried to sleep. Wherever they were going, she'd need as much energy as possible.

As she fell asleep, she worried about her friends, particularly Arthur. How could he cope here without her to keep him safe? Worried and cold, Skye finally felt the warm embrace of sleep overcome her.

A Dark Visitor

In the weeks that followed Damphir's arrival at Horongor, the frost had barely lifted from the ground. The skies were often clear and blue, but a chill wind kept the fort in its grip at all times. The sorcerer found himself spending most of his time inside the tall, stone spire of the church. The heavy walls and slit windows kept out the worst of the chill, but the sorcerer barely felt it anyway.

Ever since Salismir had brought Akeldama to him, he had spent more and more time alone with his eyes closed, talking at length to the glass orb. He had felt his power grow immeasurably since then, and now he felt like he barely needed his outer body as any more than a vessel to carry his dark soul.

No matter how long he spoke to Akeldama, Damphir knew that the spirit wasn't to be trusted. Its soothing tone and whispered promises were nothing more than a fleeting fog, but the power that it gave him was tangible. He was well aware that all Akeldama craved was power: raw, aimless power. It didn't care if Damphir was destroying worlds or building them up, so long as the power flowed and grew. Damphir had more focused desires. He wanted to rule Ithilmir and where to better to start than here in the north?

He had long known that the kingdom of Crazak D'Ur was the cornerstone of the land. The city was a melting pot of species but had always been under the rule of a Felmir. King Camut Dri had been on the throne for nearly a hundred years, and his army had grown weak as his health had faded. Damphir knew that now was the time to strike, but to capture Crazak D'Ur alone would not be enough.

His enemies further north were still strong, and he'd heard word that, in the south, dark shadows were reaching out into the world once more. Until they were dealt with, Damphir knew his throne would always be made of glass. He'd spoken at length about these issues with Akeldama, and the stone had been less concerned than he had expected. Their combined power, it had assured him, was a match for any army and any queen. The spirit had spoken of a meeting with a shadowed figure on more than one occasion. Whenever he slept,

Damphir had been troubled by visions of a strange twisted shadow crawling across a sheet of broken ice. No matter how hard he concentrated, the vision slipped away like quicksilver whenever the creature lowered its hood.

As for those to the north, there were the goblins to be dealt with and their pesky human who they had allowed to live for reasons that Damphir could never understand. If ever there was a race to be wiped from history, it was humans. They were nothing but a curse on the land, a sick joke by some twisted creator in the far corners of the universe.

There was nothing to be done about either of these threats whilst the deep frosts and sharp chills of winter held the fort in its seemingly eternal embrace. Damphir was out on one of his rare patrols of the empty streets when he heard the heavy iron knocker drop against the city gates with a crack that shattered the cold silence. Before he could react, he saw Salismir scuttle down from the derelict hut that he'd taken as a home and scurry over to unlatch the heavy wooden gates.

"Be still, Salismir," Damphir ordered. "Would you be so hasty to unlock passage to your heart? We have no idea who is out there and what harm they mean us." Damphir was feeling tightly wound and shaken by their endless imprisonment within the high walls of Horongor and found he had no patience for his snivelling servant. He was coming to curse his decision to let the hobgoblin live more with each passing hour. He approached the gate and cupped his hands to his mouth. "Who ventures out in these desperate times and seeks shelter within our walls?" he bellowed.

The answer didn't arrive on the icy wind but echoed in his head. It was like speaking to Akeldama. *You know who I am, Damphir! But I am weak, far too weak to be a threat to you. I am the shadow on the ice. I have tried to speak to you in your sleep, but, alas, I am not strong enough even for that.* The voice was gentle and feminine but at the same time cracked and broken. He had heard a voice like that only once before; when the Azrul had risen from their graves and their general had requested his orders.

"You do not sound like you are alive. Weak would be an improvement." Though Damphir was cautious and even taken aback by such an unexpected visitor, he knew that were he to show even the smallest sign of fear to Salismir, the hobgoblin would slit his throat when he slept.

"I was dead, but now I am not. I am here to be made strong again. I know what you have. I coveted it too, once upon a time. It was stolen from me by the very vermin that crawls at your feet."

Damphir looked across at Salismir. If that little rat had brought unwelcome trouble to his gates, then Damphir would make sure that death was the least of his troubles. He knew who the voice belonged to, though. He knew who Salismir had stolen Akeldama from. "Queen Camarina. I have heard much of you. Especially how you were defeated by a human." The scream of rage was expected but still caused him to blink at the searing pain inside his head.

If it was indeed the Dark Queen, then she could prove to be a powerful ally. Then again, she could prove to be even more useful than that. "Salismir." The hobgoblin jumped at the sound of his name and skidded through the frosted dirt to his master's feet. "Unlock the gate. Let's not leave our guest in the cold any longer."

Salismir pushed the heavy iron latch out of its catch and swung the gate, taking care to duck behind it as it opened.

On cue, the wind picked up and snow started to fall in droves. It swirled around the hooded figure forming a white halo. The hood was pulled far enough forward to cast her entire face in shadow, and the visitor's arms were folded and cloaked in the grey material. She shuffled forwards, and Damphir ordered Salismir out from behind the gate to help steady the hooded figure.

"You are gazing upon the one true queen of Ithilmir, Salismir. You may know her better as the former owner of Akeldama. It is from her that you stole the most valuable treasure on our world." He paused to allow this information to sink in. "Make sure that she is well fed and given warm clothes, and you will do well to suffer any further demands she has of your worthless body. After she is finished, and if there is anything of you left capable, bring her to me in the topmost chamber of the church tower. We have much to discuss."

Damphir left the quaking hobgoblin and the Dark Queen to their own devices and made his way quickly to the tower. Akeldama was rested on a tall, white marble plinth and was covered with a thin black cloth. Damphir had found this was the only way to quiet the orb's voice when he wished for silence in his own head. Now he needed advice. He whipped the cloth back and slumped onto the straw pallet on the floor. He closed his eyes and allowed the whispering voice back into his head.

"Is it her? Is it really the Dark Queen? Or am I being led like a horse to my own death?" he asked.

It is her. I recognise that mind from when she served me. She is a strong woman and would make a powerful ally and yet...I sense you have other plans.

"You are right. As my queen, she would be strong and I even stronger. But there are other ways to harness that power. Darker ways indeed, but I have never been afraid of the darkness. We must play it carefully. She will be suspicious of us. If she wasn't, then her power would be nothing to me."

Before he had time to discuss the matter any further, he was woken by Salismir's familiar, stuttered knock on the chamber door. He bid them to enter and expressed his surprise at how quickly the queen had been delivered to him. He was happy to note that the hobgoblin was sporting several open wounds on his face where the Dark Queen had extracted at least a little revenge.

"Her Majesty would not eat or change her clothing, master. She insisted on speaking with you immediately."

"Then so be it. Leave us alone, Salismir." Damphir noticed Salismir's fixed gaze and unfocused eyes. He slapped him hard around the face, and the hobgoblin cowered to the floor. "If I ever catch you coveting Akeldama again, you will very quickly learn just how tall this tower is. You had your chance and you gave it willingly to me. Do I make myself clear?"

Salismir didn't respond. He covered his head with

his hand and crawled from the room, making sure to shut the door behind him.

"Queen Camarina, to what do I owe this great pleasure? Have you travelled this far to take back Akeldama? I must tell you now that I have no intention of giving it up."

"I have not." This time the queen spoke normally to Damphir though he noticed that her voice was still the same, broken one that had drifted into his mind outside. "I am weak. Skye Thistle destroyed my body and nearly everything I ever was." Damphir could sense how much it cost the queen to admit this weakness.

Do not be fooled, she does not trust you any more than you trust her. He reminded himself.

The queen continued, "My spirit lived on in a few of my more loyal supporters and so part of me was able to survive. I was able to grow, slowly and not without cost, but to the point where I can stand here before you and do this." Damphir had seen, indeed caused, a lot of death and pestilence over his many years, yet even he recoiled as the Dark Queen pulled back the hood on her cloak and revealed her face.

Her mottled skin was stretched tight over broken cheekbones and covered with open and infected sores. She was bald and her mouth was empty of most of her teeth; the ones that remained were yellowed and cracked. She wore a twisted and rusted crown high on her head which bled where the old metal had rubbed. Her green eyes were deeply sunken, but they burned fiercely. Whatever death and disease had been inflicted upon her body hadn't come close to damaging the darkness that burned within her.

"Even in this sorry guise, I can sense the power of the Shadowed Eye like a compass pointing north. I have travelled a long way to beg you to use the power to bring me back to my former strength. As payment for this service, I will kneel beside you and accept that I will never fully control the power I once had. Can you help me?" she whispered coyly.

Damphir knew that he could. He also knew just how much it would be costing her to sacrifice less than total control over the power. He knew that he could never do that and he doubted she would, if she were given the chance.

He could raise her up to her full strength even without the power of Akeldama. After all, he'd done it before. His army of the dead were testament to that. But to share power was to diminish it. Why share what he had when he could so easily take what he wanted from her?

"I can make you more powerful than you have ever been, my queen." He grasped her rotting hand

and placed a gentle kiss on the back. "It is a marriage that you seek? To combine our strengths and destroy worlds?"

"It is," the queen hissed quietly.

"And you will share with me your soul?" Even still so close to nothingness, the mere mention of the word *share* caused the queen to wince. She nodded and stepped forward to embrace her saviour.

In the darkness, the sound of kissing faded into the night.

Dragonfire

Port Escrildor was the northernmost port in Ithilmir and the gateway to the Dragon Isle. When the dark elves shouted through the window that they had finally arrived at their destination, Skye pulled back the curtains of the carriage and shook off the thick, woollen blanket. Looking out of the window, she saw a bustling old city.

The unicorn had drawn to a halt on a long stone wharf that curved away into the distance. Tall wooden buildings towered over the carriage and cast a dark shadow on an otherwise bright afternoon. On the far side of a wide expanse of water stood a broken walled city. Skye could see that the old town had once been great and powerful but had since been left to ruin as the inhabitants favoured the more affluent buildings and bustling marketplaces that stood in front of her. The walls of the medina were broken, in some places down to the ground, and Skye could see into the warren of maze-like streets beyond. Even as she watched, Skye could see people scrambling over them stealing blocks of stone for their own houses.

The door clicked open, and an elf poked his head around tentatively. Skye considered kicking him in the face and making a run for it, but she had no idea where she could go, and she wasn't sure how many dark elves had followed them on their long journey. Instead, she allowed herself to be gently led by her hand onto the stone walkway and round to a group of several elves who were leaning against the wall of a bakery.

The first thing that Skye noticed as she exited the cab was the noise. Fisherman and sailors were shouting to each other across the catch of the day whilst harbour masters guided heavy loads on and off of the tall wooden ships that were tethered to the harbour walls. There were three enormous galleons packed so closely to each other that the dock workers could walk from bow to stern like a long walkway across the water. The sails were all lowered, but Skye could just imagine the force that they would appear to be when fully at mast and gliding across the open ocean.

"We are just in time," said Sang, the tallest of the elves, as he approached Skye and placed his arms around her shoulder and pointed to the middle and grandest of the boats. "We will ride on the *Dragonfire*, the personal trade ship for Emperor Ki."

"I'm not good on boats. I get sick watching the waves. I'm much better if I can go below deck."

The elf smirked a joyless smile. "Oh, that won't be a problem. His Imperial Majesty has deemed you a prize worthy of protecting. Unfortunately, he considers you too recognisable to ride with the other shipmates. Instead, you will ride in the galley with the slaves."

Skye was shocked at this treatment and said as much to her captors. They were indifferent, and the leader continued mocking her with his words.

"Unfortunately, girls would never travel as galley slaves. You wouldn't want to be found to be female down there, Skye." Skye spun around as she heard the sound of blades scraping across metal and saw one of the other nameless elves making a chopping motion with a pair of rusty scissors. "It's for the best, Skye." The elf laughed as Skye's hair fell around her feet. Soon her red hair was cropped close to her head and, with the addition of a well-oiled leather cloak, Skye was ready to pass as a male galley slave.

The dark elves unceremoniously dragged her along the gangplank leading up to the deck of the *Dragonfire* and handed her over to the captain, a burly, one-eyed orc who wore nothing but a cut-off pair of blue shorts and had a body full of tattoos.

"Don't worry about me being no orc," he rasped at Skye. He reeked of a mixture of alcohol and sweat. Skye retched as he grabbed at her wrists. She had to remind herself to act like a man, and so she stood up tall and tried to push the orc away. "Ha ha! We have a feisty one here! Don't worry. He'll soon learn to calm that temper in the galley. The galley knocks the fight out of 'em all in the end."

Skye heard the dark elves giggling as she was dragged below deck by the stinking orc. At the bottom of the rotten steps, a dozen benches had been set up, facing towards the stern. Four slaves were sat on each one, all tied to their bench by their ankles. Their wrists were lashed to the large oar that passed across each of their laps.

The walls were stacked high with barrels marked with foreign symbols and stretched between the support beams were threadbare hammocks. In one corner of the boat, a pile of bodies was piled up and starting to rot. Skye gagged as she looked over at them and the stench caught in the back of her throat.

"They didn't row hard enough." was all the captain offered as way of explanation. Skye tried not to look in their direction.

Skye had read enough about pirates in her time to know how this worked. She didn't put up a fight as she was led to an understaffed bench. She was the third to be attached. She soon realised that unless a fourth joined them soon, they'd be in for a much harder journey than the rest. The captain wasted no time in slamming the iron rings around her ankles and locking the chains to her wrists to keep her in place. There was little give and Skye's legs soon started to cramp and protest at the lack of movement. She couldn't stretch them out in front of her to loosen them up and soon the pain grew too much and she started to sob quietly to herself.

It wasn't long before the captain untied the ship, and Skye heard the crack of the sail taking on the wind up above. The ship jolted as it moved slowly out of the harbour. Skye knew that it wouldn't be long before she would be ordered to work along with the other lost souls below deck.

Sure enough, the order came down that they were in open water, and to row as hard and fast as they could. They were due in Dragorith the next day, and anybody not pulling their weight would end up on the pile in the corner.

Skye had no choice but to row. The others on her bench were all bigger and stronger than her and were heaving the oar back and forth with immense strength. If Skye held on and did nothing, she would be pulled from her seat and her arms from their sockets. When her hands blistered and were too wet with sweat and salt water to grip the wood firmly, it slipped from her grasp and rose hard into her face. She soon had a split lip and a chipped tooth, but had no time to mourn for either. She held on with all her might and tried her hardest to keep up with the other slaves.

The pace was relentless. Stroke after stroke, hour after hour, throughout the afternoon and on into the night they rowed. The captain was desperate to be in Dragorith by dawn, and there was no wind up above to help speed the ship along. The slaves in the galley were the only thing that powered the mighty vessel as it cut through the dark ocean. Cold saltwater blew in through the holes for the oars and soaked Skye's clothes. It wasn't long before she was sodden and cold, but there was no relenting from the pace. The other slaves seemed impervious to the harsh conditions, but as she looked at them, she saw that they had just switched off. Something inside them had broken, and they were nothing more than machines. Row and sleep, that was all they would do for the rest of their lives. There weren't down here as criminals due for release after they'd rowed off a debt; they were owned by the captain of the ship. They were property and, like all property, when they could no longer fulfil their purpose they were cast aside to the scrapheap in the corner.

At first light, just as the sun rose overhead and the harsh light filtered through the cracks in the decking forcing Skye to turn away, the captain pulled open the hatch and yelled down that they had made it to the port just outside Dragorith. Each of the slaves would be allowed to rest until they left for Sunport that evening. Skye noticed that they weren't removed from their shackles, simply left to rest in the damp, foetid air with the rusty chains holding them prisoner. Skye was lucky. As the captain stepped away from the hatch, a dark elf lowered himself carefully down the wet wooden steps and approached Skye with a knowing smile.

"Hello, slave. You have been bought from your master. You are to come and serve the emperor. This is a great honour." This was not an offer and Skye knew it. Even if she had been a slave and not merely undercover, she would have been powerless to protest. It made her sick to think that there were slaves being bought and sold as nothing more than workers to be pushed until they ended up in the pile in the corner. The captain removed her chains and helped her to her feet. She couldn't bear to look into the eyes of the other slaves as she was led away to the upper deck. She realised that she didn't need to worry. When she did turn back and look, they were all looking forlornly at the floor, all hope lost.

Skye had to steady herself as she stepped up onto the top deck. Even though the ship was docked, the motion of the water was still unfamiliar to her after hours of nothing but sitting and rowing. The dark elf had carefully guided her up the steps with his arm around her shoulder and whispered into her ear.

"My name is Yin, and I am an emissary of the emperor. Do not fear us, Skye. I know my friends who rescued you had their fun, but you really must not fear the emperor. He is a great man and a great leader." He looked over Skye's shoulder and motioned with a nod of his head. "Besides, you will not be alone here."

Skye turned and followed his gaze towards a goblin dressed in a familiar silver robe embossed with a silver handprint.

"Weard!" she cried as she raced across the deck and embraced her old friend. "What are you doing here?"

"That story is long and tiresome, my friend," the healer laughed as she pried Skye's arms from around her. Skye noticed the healer quickly thrust a loosely wrapped parcel into her robes as if to keep it hidden but, before Skye could question her further, they were moved along by their hosts. "We must make the short journey up to Dragorith to meet with Emperor Ki," Weard whispered as the dark elves started to prepare to disembark. "I will tell you my tale on the way."

Yin took the pair gently by their arms and led them from the ship. There was another decorated carriage waiting for them. Before long, they were moving at pace through the lush, mountainous countryside of the Dragon Isle.

The Dragon Isle

Nestled amongst the crown of a mountain that rose up from the harbour like a talon tearing through the ground, Dragorith was an enticing sight from the dock. From below, the city was almost lost amongst the clouds, but even from a distance the ivory walls that formed a hexagonal perimeter shimmered with a pearlescent lustre. On each point of the hexagon, a tall circular tower rose even higher into the sky. The crags and peaks of the mountains cradled the city like a precious jewel. It reminded Skye of her mother's ring.

As if to remind visitors of the Dragon Isle's past, an enormous pair of intricately carved marble dragon heads flanked the tall gateway that led from sea level to the city above. As Skye watched from the carriage window, the heads loomed ever closer. She half expected the eyes to blink and a bright red eye to stare into her soul. She rubbed her mother's ring for comfort and felt the reassuring surge of electricity flow through her. She hated how comfortable the power made her, even though she had no idea just how powerful it was. She looked over at Weard who appeared to be staring out of her own window. Skye had never been able to read the healer's thoughts very well, but at that moment she looked nervous.

As the pair had dismounted the *Dragonfire* and waited in the carriage, Weard had told Skye what had happened in Lörieas, including the cowardliness shown by their leaders and her capture by the dark elves of the empire. It appeared that Weard had been treated well. "More as a guest than a prisoner," she said. Curglaff and Snowbroth had been sent home to Snudge with message of Weard's whereabouts and to try to strike a deal between the G'Oräk and the Army of Enlightenment.

"I do not trust them yet," the healer said, turning from her window to face Skye. "They may have the best intentions but, for now, we should treat them as dangerous."

"Why are there so many dragons?" Their carriage had taken them through the tall stone gateway, and they were now slowly progressing along a steep gravel road.

On each side of the narrow road, the ground gave way to a steep drop down to the tumultuous ocean below. There were no fences or barriers to stop a startled horse running its load into the abyss. Every hundred yards or so a stone plinth rose from the rock. On the top of each was set the skull of a dragon, each one the size of a large dog and seeming to snarl at Skye as she passed.

"There are still dragons on Ithilmir. You know this as well as anyone." Skye felt her shoulder and ran her fingers across the rough skin where a dragon scale had embedded itself during a fight with a group of Bogomils what seemed like a lifetime ago. "But the dragons that exist now are mere shadows of their ancestors, tiny and weak compared to the beasts that once ruled the land. These weren't tame beasts of war. They answered to no man and gave no mercy to any who tried to reign them in. The Dragon Isles were home to the biggest and fiercest of all of these monsters, and the city of Dragorith likes to remember its beginnings.

"Legend has it that many hundreds of years ago, before the last of the dragons disappeared, there was an elven city called Esnor. For many years, their city had been held captive in a cage of ice and the people grew desperate. One day their oracle, a man named

Ton, was visited with a vision from their gods. They told him that he would find a new home for his kin, one free from ice and hardship. It would be a city of fire that would rise above the clouds and sit amongst the gods themselves. He would know this place, they told him, when he found a dragon sat amongst the ice keeping watch over the sea.

"Knowing of the legendary dragons of the Dragon Isle, the oracle bid farewell to his people and set sail on the Glass Sea in a small wooden boat barely big enough to stay afloat."

"Why was his city frozen in ice?" interrupted Skye much to Weard's annoyance.

"If you travel far enough south, everything is ice. Beyond the Trolltooth Mountains, you can walk for years and see nothing but ice.

"Eventually the oracle made it to the Dragon Isle, but the seas were unkind and he was cast from his boat before he could land. For days, he was swept along by the current never quite close enough to wade ashore. When the ocean grew bored of toying with the man, it spat him out where the jungle meets the sea on the northern side of the island.

"For many years the oracle searched. He found many dragons but no ice. The island was too warm. He lamented his gods and swore to have his vengeance upon them and his people who had so willingly sent him to this forsaken land.

"Only when he had given up all hope and had resigned himself to death did the oracle start to look for a way home. His boat had been destroyed when he arrived, and he now set about making a new one with wood from the forest that lined the very mountain that we now climb. It is said that one day, whilst collecting wood, the oracle slipped and fell to the ground. As he lay on his back staring up into the sky, he saw that the top of the mountain was capped with ice."

"But there isn't any ice now," Skye interrupted.

"This was a long time ago, Skye. The world has changed a lot since then. Anyway, he immediately set about climbing the sheer faces that lie below the summit and finally he was able to set foot on ice. As he pulled himself over the edge and knelt amongst the clouds, he looked up and saw a beautiful, golden dragon perched on a cliff-edge staring out to sea. As the oracle watched, it opened a pair of wings wider than any longboat and gracefully launched itself out to sea. The oracle wept for he knew that he had found a new home for his people, here amongst the ice and stone at the top of a mountain.

"When at last he stood and looked down upon all that stood below him he knew that not only would this be a new home, it would be a great city. One that would stand firm against its enemies. He immediately declared himself emperor and within years the city of Dragorith was built and remains largely unchanged to this day. It has never fallen to an invading army, and it is said that it never will. The dragons that you see remind us where the city came from. The skulls that stand proudly by the side of the road are of the mighty dragons that fought alongside the Army of Enlightenment before they were driven from this world for good.

"But, alas, that is a story for another time. It would appear that we are nearly here."

Skye looked out of her window again as the carriage slowed to a halt. They had reached the end of the gravel path and stood waiting at another giant stone gateway. The gates were made of thick, solid wood that shone in the morning light. Though they were hundreds of years old, they looked barely older than a day. The polished stone that formed the two thick pillars either side of the door and a tall spike in the centre of the arch glittered and sparkled like fool's gold.

Beyond the gateway, a deep gorge separated them from the city. A thin bridge of ice projected from the earth and thrust out across the opening, blending effortlessly into the rock on the other side of the valley. At the other end of the bridge, a twin gateway welcomed visitors to the great city and was flanked on both sides by thunderous waterfalls that filled the air with sound and spray.

"The oracle wanted the people of Dragorith to always remember where they had come from, and so he had his sorcerers forge a bridge of ice across the abyss. It is magical and strong. It has been here for hundreds of years. I think we needn't worry!" Weard laughed as she saw Skye's expression as they set out onto it.

Sure enough, the frozen bridge held their weight, and they were soon presented to the guards who held the gateway to the city. Skye heard their escorts telling the guards that she and Weard were treasured guests of the emperor and were to be taken to him immediately. Skye was relieved to hear that they weren't yet being treated as enemies, but she still had no idea what they could want with her or how they knew her name. As far as she could tell, Weard was here to discuss joining forces with the G'Oräk, but Skye was quite sure that the goblin could do that without her.

Then there was the matter of the package. Skye was used to Weard having secret conversations with Snudge, and she would never dare to pry, but it was unusual for the healer to keep things so obviously from her. She'd tried to raise the issue whenever there had been a break in the conversation, but Weard had always acted like she hadn't heard and changed the subject to something else. Whatever it was, it worried Skye, though she couldn't work out why.

When they were finally allowed through the tall wooden gates, they entered a long open corridor formed by two enormous walls made from large limestone blocks. The walls rose so high that they appeared to fold inwards to form a tunnel. They were lined almost entirely with a thick climbing plant with small, feathery green leaves. It was in full bloom, and delicate purple flowers hung serenely in the still air. Skye leaned out of her window and plucked one from a hanging vine. Up close, the flower looked like the head of dragon opening its mouth. The stamen formed a long yellow tongue or a lick of flame erupting from deep within the throat.

"That is Dracones Viriditas, a delightfully scented flower used to make some of the most violent poisons imaginable. Imagine not only feeling like your insides were burning but to actually have them burn with a flame that engulfs your body from the inside out." Weard chuckled as Skye threw the flower as far from the window as she could. "Don't worry unduly, little one. The process of turning the flowers into the poison is quite arduous, so I'm told.

"Nonetheless," she reflected, "it's probably best if you wash your hands at the first opportunity."

Skye looked out of the window and watched as the delicate dragon heads floated past. They seemed to snarl in the scattered shadows.

Two Souls

Damphir was overjoyed. He hadn't been this excited for a long time. Even finding the Shadowed Eye hadn't lifted his spirits this high. Once the night was over, there wouldn't be a soul who could touch him. He would ride a wave of darkness across Ithilmir and destroy anything that stood in his way.

He would even wipe out the Shadowlands themselves. He could see it when he closed his eyes, the shadowed souls of his slain enemies, all there ready to be slaughtered again. In his dreams, he went even further, battling the great gatekeeper of Mithrostan, Faileas. He'd sever the snarling head and mount it on his warship. He had to force himself awake when this happened. He knew better than to get ahead of himself.

His would-be bride knelt in front of him, her head bowed and covered by her dark hood. They were stood alone in front of the altar within the church. Overhead, a full moon turned midnight to noon, and the brightly coloured stained glass windows cast iridescent jewels on the flagstones. Akeldama stood on a stone plinth atop the wooden lectern. If he listened hard enough, Damphir could convince himself that he could still hear the sermons of centuries past as strange whispers contained within the old stones.

He'd always liked churches when he was young, until that day in the darkness. Even when he was young, he'd never had much time for religion itself. He'd respected it though, the power of it washing over the congregation like a tidal wave sweeping away their doubts and disobedience. There was something about the sheer force of the belief that soaked into the very bones of the building. It made him feel stronger to bask in the presence of the priests who'd demanded so much servitude from their congregation. They'd even managed to do it without any real magic. Now, he looked around and felt strong. Outside, surrounding the city, were a thousand disciples who would march into battle or steal into the bedchamber of an enemy to cut him down whilst he slept. That was power. That was belief.

Something rustled in the old leaves that had drifted into the church and Damphir sighed inwardly. He would have to do something about his wretched servant and quickly, he was growing too bold. To enter the chapel during such a private moment bore testament to this.

"Salismir." Damphir's voice echoed in the silent building. "I can feel you watching me, waiting for your chance to steal back what is mine. Step out of the shadows, and I shall allow you to live."

The hobgoblin crawled out from behind an old wooden pew and stepped into the candlelight. He hung his head and crouched sheepishly at his master's feet.

"You dare to defy your master's wish at such a time?" The Dark Queen's voice was high and broken, but in the emptiness of the church, it sounded full of malice. Slowly, she pulled back her hood and revealed herself to the hobgoblin. Salismir turned his head away in a mixture of disgust and fear. He pressed himself to the stone floor and started to whimper.

"You are very lucky," Damphir said to Salismir. "You will be part of history tonight. The merging of two souls. The binding of the most powerful forces alive. You will bear witness to the birth of a new darkness."

"Together we will rule Ithilmir and beyond." The Dark Queen was visibly shaking with excitement. Outside, storm clouds veiled the moon and cast the church into darkness. Only the dozen or so guttering candles gave the darkness an edge. As a storm broke overhead, a wild animal called out the start of a hunt. Inside the church, Akeldama started to glow faintly. Damphir led his bride towards the lectern and tried his hardest to shut out the whispers in his head. He didn't need advice at a time like this. He needed to trust his own instincts like he'd always been forced to.

As they approached the stone, the whispers grew louder, but Damphir drew on all of his strength and spoke only to Queen Camarina. Salismir had crawled behind them, unable to resist the urges that burned inside him. "First, I must heal you." He knew his voice was calm and steady, but he could feel his heart racing. He hadn't felt this excited, this *alive*, since he'd first killed all those years ago. It had become a distant memory etched on a long-damaged part of his soul, but now it all flooded back. The screams, the pain, the fear and most importantly of all, the control.

He gently urged the queen to her knees and tenderly stroked her disfigured face. She recoiled at his touch, but he held her shoulder steady and stared into her eyes. He saw them soften briefly before the burning rage returned.

This was the easy part of the ceremony, and Damphir wanted it to be over quickly. He ran his hand across Akeldama, and the glass orb floated into the air and hovered an inch above the lectern. It turned translucent, and a bright blue light shone from within it. The queen gasped as fingers of light reached out and bathed her skin. Salismir scrambled even further away as her knees left the floor and she floated high into the rafters of the church. She spun and turned until she lay on her back cradled by some invisible force high above their heads. Slowly, her dark robes started to disintegrate and turn to dust.

A bright white light engulfed her as the last remains left her body. Damphir turned his head and closed his eyes, but still, the burning dots of light shone brightly in front of him. When he returned his gaze, the light had gone and his queen stood before him once more. She looked young again. Her skin was firm and glowed with a youthful flush, and her hair was wavy and hung long past her waist.

As he watched, it curled and wrapped itself into a tight crown atop her head. An ice-white dress hung from her shoulders and flowed to the floor in a river of silk and crystals. A mink scarf rested on her shoulders and long satin gloves covered her hands past the wrist.

She was beautiful and yet still as cold and hard as a mid-winter frost.

Queen Camarina reached out a gloved hand and took hold of Damphir's. She leaned forward and gave him a soft kiss on the cheek. "Thank you. I am now a queen fit to rule alongside such a mighty king."

Damphir shook himself out of his daydream.

Do not forget that she is using you to get to Akeldama. You know how strong the urge will be within her. The stone served her once. It will cast you aside now if it feels her calling.

Truly she was the most beautiful woman he had ever seen, but he knew that he must not deviate from the plan. He was already in love, he told himself. He loved power and control. He loved the strength that Akeldama gave him. He didn't need anything else. He didn't need to risk being betrayed.

He held onto his queen's hand and looked into her burning eyes. "Do you give me your soul willingly and forever?" His voice was broken and almost a whisper, but in the silence of the church it rang as loud as the tower bells.

"I do." Any weakness was gone from the queen's voice, and her eyes burned with a dark yearning.

"Then we must perform the ritual." Damphir reached into his robes and pulled out the heavy bound book that he had read from many times before, *The Eternal Dead*. He turned immediately to the correct page and set it out on the wooden lectern. The light from Akeldama illuminated the strange symbols and images on the page.

"We will need a blood sacrifice." He spoke solemnly, as though he were asking the gravest of favours.

"Of course." The queen held out her palm. Damphir recognised the urgency in her, the unwavering desire to once again feel that power surging through her veins. He'd known it himself for the longest time, though he hoped he'd never appeared as desperate as she did now. "Not you, my queen. Your blood is too precious, even for this." Salismir had taken the opportunity to sneak closer to Akeldama. Damphir turned and grabbed his collar. "Yours will do."

The hobgoblin tried his hardest to kick and scratch at his captor, but it was no use. Damphir pulled a sharp knife from his belt and sliced at his servant's hand. A tiny trickle of thick blood welled up out of the wound, but Damphir wanted more. "Hold him still."

Queen Camarina reacted swiftly and grabbed both of Salismir's hands. She held them out in front of him and placed them palm up onto the lectern as though she were about to inspect them. Salismir tried to fight, but his strength seemed to drain away and he soon relaxed into a sobbing mess. Not wasting his chance, Damphir hacked down with his knife. The cut was clean and swift, and Salismir fell to the floor screaming and trying in vain to grasp at his bloody stumps. Queen Camarina raised the hobgoblin's hands and bathed Akeldama.

Damphir stowed the knife back in his belt and reached out and took his bride's hands in his. He closed his eyes and spoke the words of the spell that would forever bind their souls. For a second, nothing happened. Then he felt the familiar rush of ice running through his veins as everything that made the queen powerful flowed into him. He risked opening his eyes and saw the look of shock in hers. Even as he watched, she started to age rapidly, her skin wrinkling and bones falling as she withered away to nothingness. Noiselessly, her mouth begged him to stop, to tell her why.

"To share my power is to share my strength. This way, I shall live forever and so, in turn, will you. You will live within me. Your power is now mine. Our souls are bonded and so too is our strength. Nothing can stop me, us, now. Thank you."

With his last words, the queen disappeared into nothingness, but he meant what he had said. He could feel her inside him, still living as a presence on his soul. He'd felt it many times before whenever he had killed or taken on the life force of another, but this was stronger than anything he had ever experienced. An overwhelming sense of indestructibility overcame him.

Damphir grabbed Akeldama and raced over to the door of the church and called for the head of his army. A towering man strode over to him, dressed in a thick black cloak with one eye covered by a black bandage. His face was covered in blistered and rotting skin, and his lips were pulled back in a hideous smile where his flesh had started to tighten after death. His one remaining eye socket was filled with ice-blue fire that spun like endless galaxies.

Damphir held the orb out in front of him and waved his hand over the glass. A weak image flickered into focus of a large armada amassing ready for battle. Hundreds of masts pierced a bright blue sky and golden banners fluttered in the breeze. Suddenly, the vision blurred and swam before refocusing on a young girl, tall and thin with short red hair. She was talking with a goblin and a tall elf wrapped in a golden robe.

"She is the one. She must be killed. She is all that stands between me and greatness." Damphir spoke with an urgency to his general. He'd never seen the girl before, but she had appeared as an urgent memory as soon as he'd absorbed the queen. He knew too well who she was. If she had fought against Akeldama before and won, she mustn't be allowed to do so again. "It must be done soon. I cannot risk her finding me. Is that understood?" The general grunted and nodded.

"Be quick," Damphir ordered. "I shall need you back here before long. War is coming to our gates, and we must be ready to meet it."

Dragorith

Unlike most of the walled cities that Skye had been to on Ithilmir, Dragorith wasn't set out as a working town. Once inside the main walls, the entire city was set out as one large parkland. Lush green grass carpeted the ground and undulated over banks and hills mixing with tall meadows and cosying up to sparkling still ponds. Tall trees dragged the eye up towards the clouds that hung low around the polished walls that framed the everything like a perfect picture hung in a gallery. Though the clouds were low, the sun was able to break through and flood the entire city with a warm morning glow.

Up close, the white walls were all formed from four stories of polished white balconies with beautiful archways. Beyond each balcony was a doorway that led to a place of business. As Skye and Weard were led along a road that skirted around the main parkland, they saw up close that each room was a stall or a workshop or a place for storage.

From a distance, the walls and archways and doors all blended to form a bright, reflective surface. It was only when the shadows shifted that they appeared as if part of an elaborate optical illusion. Skye liked it considerably and found herself relaxing as they progressed past several groups of elves enjoying themselves on the grass.

At the far end of the parkland and dominating the horizon was a tall, broad palace built of similar white stone with vaulted windows set into the front. The whole thing was capped with aged copper. Even though it had tarnished to blue-green, Skye could imagine just how resplendent it would have been when it was new and glowed orange in the bright sunlight.

The road swept gently around to the back of the palace and into shadows before it started to pick up a gentle gradient. When they once again burst into the sunlight, they found themselves level with the tops of the trees and pulling into a semi-circular courtyard.

Yet another set of guards came and dismissed the ones that had formed the escort from the main gate and stepped in to unlock and open the carriage doors. Skye and Weard were beckoned silently, and they carefully stepped from the carriage and into the bright light. They were quickly ushered through the front doors of the palace. Skye felt herself stumble as they were plunged into relative darkness. As her eyes adjusted, she was able to take in the details of the throne room.

The walls were vaulted like a church and towered above her. They were made from serviceable grey stone, but they lost nothing of their impressive stature. The room was long and thin and empty but for a throne that sat at the top of three broad steps. The throne was almost transparent, and it took Skye a short while to realise that it was made of ice carved into two dragons poised on their hind legs, back to back and ready to attack.

"Skye Thistle! It is truly my honour to have you here in Dragorith."

Skye looked at the emperor who was rising from the throne. He was tall, taller than any of the other elves, and slender. Even though he was thin, he looked strong, like a young tree. He had jet black hair that hung past his shoulders and a fringe that flopped in front of his face. A long beard hung to his knees in a single plait as thick as Skye's wrist. His eyes were black and sunken, but his face radiated genuine happiness.

At first, Skye thought that the emperor's skin was almost as dark as his eyes, but as she approached the throne, she saw that it was covered in ornate tattoos. As he smiled and spoke, the patterns seemed to dance across his face like the waves on the ocean. She found herself mesmerised watching each swirl to see where it ended up.

"Please, come and sit!" The emperor motioned to a servant to bring chairs for the guests. Skye and Weard soon found themselves sat in front of their host who had once again taken a seat on his throne. "May I please start by apologising for your treatment so far? We did not mean to startle you in Lörieas. We knew that you would try to persuade them to join Snudge's cause, and we knew that they were too cowardly to do so. They would never let us into their city to speak to you, and so we had to persuade them with the only language that they speak, gold. Once we were in their city, it suited us to play the part of evil overlords looking to defeat the goblins.

"In fact, we were not there for the G'Oräk at all. We were there for you, Skye. I had been informed that you always travelled with your goblin friend here, and so we naturally assumed that you would be with her. It was only by chance that we heard of your capture atop Liorath's Peak and your imprisonment in Alastor."

Weard looked aghast at this news and started to berate Skye for not telling her of her own ordeals.

"Now is not the time for such tales," calmed Emperor Ki. "For now, you must listen.

"As for you, my little human girl, when my soldiers found you wandering alone in the Gloom they were very fortunate indeed. Although many would argue that you were the more fortunate, in fact. The Gloom holds many worse terrors that the orcs that you so bravely fought before."

"How do you know—" Skye started before being waved into silence by their host.

"I have been keeping my eyes and ears open for news of you since your arrival on Ithilmir. I have followed your progress for a long time. I watched as you defeated the queen the first time, and I am well aware of the prophecy and of the course that you feel you must take to fulfil it. I am also aware of the link that exists between your world and ours that has nothing to do with you. Am I correct?" Skye felt her stomach spin and twist as the emperor gave her a knowing look.

How could he know?

"Do not worry, Skye. Your secret is safe with me. There is nothing good to be gained from it. Besides, by now I am sure you realise that it was little more than a shell that the Dark Queen inhabited. There may have been the odd link left between the two, but I am positive that there is no danger there now.

"However, it is to your home that we must now turn. I believe that you have something for me?" This was addressed to Weard who was sat looking confused at the previous conversation. Skye still hadn't told the G'Oräk about the link between the Dark Queen and her mother. She wasn't sure what it meant, and the emperor's words had been somewhat comforting. Weard shook herself and retrieved the tubular package from within her robes. She handed it over to Emperor Ki who unravelled the loose paper. Skye's heart stopped. It was the spyglass. Her way home. Her *only* way home. Why was it here? And then she saw the answer.

"I am so sorry, Skye," Weard sobbed. She tried to put her arm around Skye, but she recoiled in horror. The spyglass was bent and twisted, and the glass had been cracked at both ends. "When the Order of the Shadowed Eye attacked Kobold, they ransacked Snudge's mansion. They destroyed everything! I'm so sorry, Skye. Snudge ordered that I bring it with me. We were hoping that the artisans of Lörieas would be able to fix it, but everything happened so quickly that I didn't get to speak to them.

"The empire is renowned for its Gazers, oracles who stare into the sky to see the future. I was hoping…"

The healer turned longingly to Emperor Ki who shook his head sadly.

"I am sorry. I truly am. This cannot be fixed. The magic is broken along with the spyglass. You cannot use this to return home, Skye."

Skye shook with grief. She felt something break free, and she realised that it was her only link to home. She suddenly wanted to be there more than anything. To hell with this place. Not since she had first arrived on Ithilmir had she been so desperate to leave, and she knew that she couldn't. Her first thought was that she'd never see her family or Arthur again, but then the force of realisation hit her and she fell to her knees. Arthur. He was stuck here as well. He hadn't even wanted to come. She'd brought him out of spite and to prove a point, and now he was stuck here, somewhere, wherever he was.

Slowly, as if creeping up on her in a dark alley, something else struck Skye and she turned and glared at Weard.

"You said that this was broken during the raid on Kobold? You came and found me and *brought me here* knowing full well that I couldn't *return*?" She was seething. "*How could you?*"

Without thinking, Skye reached for her waist and drew Burrower. She waved the sharp point in front of her and approached the goblin who cowered on the floor. Just as she was stepping up, still unsure of what she might do, Emperor Ki stepped calmly in front of her and raised his hands to Skye's shoulders.

"Unless you wish to run me through and start a second war all of your own," he whispered kindly, "put down the sword." Reluctantly, Skye slid Burrower back into its scabbard and took her seat. She couldn't look at the goblin.

"Indeed, the spyglass is broken beyond repair. However, there is another way that you may yet return home and, coincidentally, it is also the reason that I was so eager to bring you to Dragorith."

A Bargain

Skye barely heard what the emperor said. Even if he could return her home, it wouldn't undo the deceit. She hated the fact that she had been brought back to Ithilmir when they knew that she would be trapped. She felt it was the ultimate betrayal after all that she had done for them. What did they need from her? Hadn't she done enough for them already? Sacrificed enough? She knew that there was some link between her and the prophecy, and maybe her mother's ring had something to do with it, but right now she wished she'd never met any of them.

Whilst the others had waited for Skye to calm down and at least consider listening to alternatives, the emperor's servants had brought the original copy of their religious text to the throne room. It had been written by Emperor Ton whilst his new city rose around him and was alleged to be a record of his most revered prophecies and precognitions.

The ledger had been laid closed on a stout wooden table in front of the throne. It was roughly the same size as one of the flagstones that lined the floor and stuffed with loose pieces of paper held together within a thick, battered leather cover. The front was left blank except for a scribbled signature in the lower right corner that identified the author.

Skye begrudgingly sat back down and nodded that she would be prepared to listen to the emperor. She couldn't bring herself to look at Weard.

"As I had started to tell you, Skye, there was a reason for me seeking you out and bringing you to my halls. It has little to do with the spyglass I am afraid, though I must admit that this turn of events does add further weight to my proposal. Before I tell you what it is that you may help me with, I must tell you a little of what is written in this book."

The leather binding on the giant tome creaked as the emperor folded back the cover to reveal the yellowing parchment inside. Skye could see the joy on his face. This was something that he enjoyed doing, and the speed with which he found the required sheets hinted that it was something that he did regularly. Skye noticed that as the emperor spoke he played with the fringe of his hair, flicking it back behind his ears whenever it became too much of a distraction. She noted that he wasn't an old man, barely out of his teens, and yet he spoke with an assuredness that make him appear so much older.

"I know that you are aware of the Spirit Voices that long fought for control over our world and so created the land that you see around you. The prophecies of Emperor Ton speak of a similar battle long ago, but where our beliefs differ from those of the goblins is that we believe only one orb was forged and that both Spirits were contained within it. I know that Snudge has spent a long time searching not only for Akeldama, for the Shadowed Eye, but also for Fréod the sister stone. According to Ton, there is no Fréod to be found. The stone that the Dark Queen found and used to rise to power may well be the only one in existence which makes it all the more powerful and rare.

"More importantly, if Akeldama truly does embody both the good and evil Spirit Voices then that means that it can be used for either purpose. It doesn't have to be used just for evil deeds."

"And you hope to take control of it and use it for good, I assume?" asked Weard sceptically.

"No," the dark elf sighed. "Many hundreds of years ago, during the dynasty of Emperor Wyn, a prophecy was found that spoke of the true masters of the Spirits. It is said that no creature born to this world can ever contain the power of the Spirit Voices. When the Spirits cast themselves down and locked themselves away, they cast a spell so that no creature would ever rule in their name. If any should try, they would be driven mad, and their life and soul forfeit.

"There is a legend, told many thousands of years ago by the elves, that speaks of a lost race, a race of men that once flourished here on Ithilmir. The legend says that the Spirit Voices cast themselves down and rose again from the Shadowlands as mortal beings. Their intention was to monitor the world that they had created, to guide all living things towards the utopia that they desired.

As with all mortal beings, they soon succumbed to their desire for power and their guidance turned to tyranny and all other races were soon forced to bend to their will or be destroyed.

"Eventually, the other races of our world grew tired of the rule of men and rose up to destroy them. In their hubris, the men forgot that they had sacrificed their immortality when they returned from the Shadowlands, and they were swept aside. As payment for their tyranny, the sorcerers of the Nelapsi were called upon to cast down the race of men forever.

Their punishment was swift and brutal; they were cast from our world and scattered beyond the stars. The legend says that they found places to live amongst the other worlds out there, but I have always found it hard to believe. Until recently."

Skye frowned and looked hard at the emperor. "Are you saying that men, humans, began life on Ithilmir and were cast aside and found a home on Earth? My home? There have been humans on Earth for far longer than your legend allows."

The emperor laughed and closed the book carefully. "I have no idea. I doubt it, but who knows? Time is such a wonderful thing, Skye. Remember that a second is only a second because we say that it is. The passage of time may well be different depending on your point of view. Is it not true that whilst you are here time is not passing on your Earth?"

"I suppose."

"And, do you suppose that this still holds true now that you have no way of returning? Are the people there stuck, forever frozen in time? Or will they continue their lives with an empty hole where you used to be?" He raised his hands to quiet Skye's outburst and continued, "I am not saying that either is so, just that we would be foolish to judge what time can and can't be.

"I did not tell you that legend for idle conversation. I am sure that you can see the logical conclusion to our tales."

Skye, who couldn't, said as much. Weard, who had spent the conversation deep in thought, looked far angrier and snapped at the emperor. "I won't have it! That is not a logical conclusion at all. What you are suggesting is stupidity based on fairy tales and rumour."

"And what is wrong with fairy tales and rumour?" asked Emperor Ki who remained annoyingly calm in the face of Weard's indignation.

"They are made up! There is no basis to them and certainly no basis on which to send a young girl to a fate worse than death!"

"Excuse me! You had no issue sending me to my death when it suited you before," shouted Skye spitefully, in order to be heard over the healer's rants. She made sure to address their host. She still had no desire to speak to Weard any more than necessary after her betrayal. "Would somebody mind telling me what this is all about?"

"He plans to have you embrace the power of Akeldama and use it to control an army. He will no doubt tell you that once you have controlled the power, you will be able to use it to travel home." Weard folded her arms in victory and was shocked when Skye turned to emperor.

"And will I be able to?"

"If the race of men were indeed the mortal form of the Spirit Voices, then I see no reason why you would not be able to control the power of the stone. I have told you that the Shadowed Eye is the only true orb and it can be controlled for either good or evil. If this is the case, then you can use it with pure intent and bring an end to this terror that is rising.

"I will not say that you can bring peace, Skye, for there is no such thing. Many of us have set out to achieve peace, and we have always failed because of the simple fact that people fight. Whether they are goblin, elf, troll or men, they will always find a reason to settle a disagreement with the sharp end of a sword. You almost did the very same thing earlier with your good friend Weard."

"She's no friend of mine anymore."

"Do not speak too harshly, little human. Words said in anger cannot be easily unsaid. Their need must have been desperate indeed to bring you back when they knew that they could not return you. They must trust you more than anything else in this world to do such a thing. Do not dismiss flattery as selfishness. There is often a reason for both."

To Skye, the emperor's words were nothing more than platitudes. She had no intention of forgiving the G'Oräk so easily.

"Whatever you decide, Skye, I hope that you will stay the course and continue to help us with our battle. You fought the Dark Queen valiantly, but you didn't destroy her. Her soul found refuge in the south, amongst the caves that surround the city of Soulaman. Even if she is too weak to ever rise again, there will be others who do.

"Unfortunately, she is not the only evil that has risen. A dark sorcerer by the name of Damphir has escaped from the Solar prison in the west. He has travelled to the lost village of Fankilmir in the Darkwood. There are rumours that he has plundered their graveyards and raised an army of the dead. If such a powerful mage comes into possession of the orb, then our world truly is in peril."

"None of this matters anyway," spat Weard, still seething at the elves proposition. "We don't have Akeldama, and so there is no power here for Skye to use."

"That's not entirely true, is it, Skye?" The emperor looked across at her and winked. He held out his hand and Skye reluctantly pressed her mother's ring into his palm. "As I suspected, this is no ordinary black glass, is it?"

Weard looked across at Skye and shook her head.

"I thought you knew," Skye apologised. "When you set it for me, I assumed you knew where it had come from."

"You have been walking around with part of the most powerful weapon of all time *on your finger*? And you dare to call me a betrayer?"

"No harm has been done, Weard. Skye was right not to tell you or anyone else what she had. The power of even this tiny part of the orb is strong indeed, and she could not know which of you would be turned to steal it should you know. Even the most valiant amongst us would be weak in its grip. Skye appears to have worn it with little burden."

"Not quite. I feel the power rushing through me sometimes when I'm angry. I feel like I could destroy anything I want, if only I would let the power out. It scares me, if I'm honest. I have no idea how to control it."

"You will, in time. I was told by the druids at the Druidmotte that you were prone to visions, even before coming into possession of this stone. Is that correct?"

"Yes, I saw the Dark Queen a lot, and the Shadowlands. I haven't had one for a while."

"The druids confided in me that they had great

hopes for you as a seer, somebody who is able to see possible futures and to speak with those who have passed from this life. It is a great honour indeed to be considered so powerful whilst so young. When they heard that I was seeking an audience with you, they dispatched one of their members to come and help train you. I had, of course, informed them of my plan beforehand."

The emperor nodded to a servant who left the room calmly through a small side door.

"I have sent for the druid to come and join us, Skye. I think you would be wise to listen to what they have to say. You will be with us for a while, and so their training may be a useful way to pass the time. We have plans to travel to the mainland soon enough, and I would be honoured if you would join us, though I cannot tell you the details just yet. All will become clear soon enough.

"Ah, and here we have our druid," Emperor Ki finished with a flourish as he rose from his seat and warmly embraced the hooded figure who entered the throne room via the same small door. When the druid pulled back her hood, Skye was delighted to see a familiar face.

"Hello, Skye. I am glad that we get to meet again," gushed Roke the Foreseen, the same druid who had advised Skye so well on the tower at the Druidmotte before she had first set off to fight the Dark Queen. She had helped Skye to form the plan that would eventually lead to victory, however impermanent, on the tower. "I am glad that you were able to vanquish the Dark Queen despite any lingering doubts about your mother."

"I hardly vanquished her. She is still alive and rising to power again," Skye said, almost apologetically.

"No matter. You destroyed her army and the threat that it posed. I am sure that you will be just as successful again. Although, if rumours are true, you may be better equipped to see your own future than I?" The druid embraced Skye and started to lead her from the room. "Come and sit with me in my chambers. We have much to discuss before you leave once again on yet another adventure."

Skye allowed herself to be led from the throne room and left Weard alone and arguing with the emperor about his foolhardy plan. Skye had no idea how she felt about it herself. The chance to return home was obviously a strong reason to go ahead with it, but what if their legend was wrong? What if Akeldama really was the evil orb and to embrace it was to embrace evil? She couldn't risk ending up like the Dark Queen. Hopefully, Roke would be able to guide her again as she had done all those months ago.

Armada

Emperor Ki hadn't exaggerated when he boasted of his large armada. Skye stood on the bridge that linked Dragorith to the harbour road and stared out to sea. The view was stunning, the sun was just rising and the light reflected off the ocean far below with a blinding whiteness. Fighting for space on the calm waves were the boats.

Every war vessel in the area had been summoned, and they were gathering at Dragorith. Already there were thousands of ships, a mix of tall galleons that sat high and proud in the water and smaller, shallow boats more suited for scouting ahead and reporting on enemy numbers. Many were already loaded with cannons and grappling hooks, and those that weren't were being armed by hundreds of men that scurried back and forth like ants. In the distance, yet more boats were arriving, called back from far-flung missions by the messenger birds sent out days before. Even some of the local fishing boats had been caught up and were taking on board whatever arms they could carry.

Each one of the ships, large or small, were flying the flag of the empire. Simmering golden sails hung proudly adorned by the red dragon rearing up ready to attack. Horns were sounding that could be heard even from such a great distance, and the activity increased yet again. Skye knew that they weren't due to leave until the following morning, but she couldn't help but feel nervous. She had never liked travelling on the sea even back home. She'd travelled on a ferry a few times and had managed to avoid being sick, unlike Arthur who threw up as soon as he set foot on a boat. But she hated the feeling of isolation. It was the same as being in an aeroplane. If something went wrong, you were stuck.

"It is good weather for sailing. The wind is in the right direction." Roke had appeared silently alongside Skye and startled her. "Have you searched for your future, Skye? To see what the journey brings?"

When Skye and Roke had been training in the Lost Temple, the druid had taught Skye to channel the power of her mother's ring to see her visions more clearly and with more control. She had referred to it as "searching," and it truly felt like that. The more Skye grew accustomed to letting the power take over, the more she found that she saw everything all at once. It was like a thousand worms slithering into the soil under her feet and knowing that she had to work out which one she wanted and grab hold of the elusive tail before it disappeared. Skye now recognised the Shadowlands as the place where she went for her visions. She felt that the spirits that dwelt there were somehow guiding her.

Sometimes she didn't need to talk to the spirits at all; the message appeared clearly formed in her mind. Often though, she found that there was somebody there waiting for her. Only through conversation with them could she get to the information that she needed. They often spoke in riddles or gave misleading stories that wandered off on tangents or that hid the message in metaphor. She was getting better at interpreting their meaning, but she still wasn't comfortable embracing the power of Akeldama.

Whenever Skye allowed the power to course through her, she felt more alive than she had ever felt in her life, as though a bolt of electricity had woken her from a hazy dream. For the brief moments when the ring was guiding her, everything was clear and she felt like she was able to determine which strands of time were past and present and which ones might represent the future. As soon as she relaxed and let the power fly away, she felt a sadness and an aching urge to drag it back. More than that, she felt anger. The first time after she had fully embraced the power, she had very nearly cut Roke down with Burrower, such was her immediate rage. It was all consuming and it worried her. Skye wasn't sure that she believed that Akeldama was the embodiment of both good and evil. There was too much anger in its magic, she could feel it every time it passed through her veins.

"No, I haven't. I don't want to burden myself with too many futures, and I do not like the way I feel when I step into the Shadowlands. It is cold there, and I feel unwelcome, as though I am an intruder who they only accept because of the power that I bring with me."

"You may well be right, Skye. Not many of us are lucky enough to be able to communicate with those who live in the shadows beyond time. In fact, there has only been one other in all of our history. Would you care to guess who that was?"

Skye didn't need to.

"Your mother often told Fen and the tree trolls that she suffered terrible dreams of a desolate mountainside filled with whispering voices that left her with messages burnt across her memory that she couldn't explain. They haunted her for the entire time that she lived with them here on Ithilmir. It is quite possible that they were visions of the Shadowlands. Of course, you have the power of Akeldama that will help you to better control your visions, but it is also possible that you are just a more natural seer. Either way, I think it is clear that there is more in common between you and your mother than mere parentage. It is as though you are here to finish the journey that she started all those years ago. It would explain why the Dark Queen was so powerful in your mother's form and why you were able to defeat her.

"You may defeat the power that you possess. This is good and natural. It will help to keep you safe. Unfortunately, we are not living in a time of safety. If you are to truly win this war for us and defeat all that we are fighting, then you will need to be very brave, little human. Perhaps braver than even you have ever been. You will need to embrace the power of Akeldama and allow it to guide you to greatness. Just remember that you are the controlling force. You must remain in control at all times. The Dark Queen allowed the power to control her, and all of her innermost fears and desires became real but at a great cost."

Skye reflected that it was easy for the druid to speak like this. She wasn't the one putting her body and mind in peril every time she closed her eyes and allowed the familiar crackle to spread. She said nothing, though.

"Look at all of those ships, Skye. Every one of those captains is loyal to the emperor and would fight to the death for him. There are tens of thousands of elves out there and yet – and this is important, Skye – we could have ten thousand more and still not have a hope against Damphir and his army of the dead. There are words from the west that he controls a dragon. Not a small, waspish thing like the Bogomils, but a dragon of legend, a dragon that would make even the Dragon Islanders weep with fear.

"I fought the dead once before, Skye. Where I was born, out west on the Rumm Islands, magic and superstition were king. Back then the islands were home to a peaceful mix of goblins and elves and even some Felmir, but times were hard. Our village, like many others, had a *mambo*, a mysterious lady would sit alone in her hut and carry out ceremonies to the spirits. Our mambo was a twisted woman who called herself Mesaje, the messenger. We believed that she was a messenger from our god sent to tell us his wishes. That much power should never be given to a mortal being.

"Mesaje was a powerful priestess and could return the dead to roam amongst the living. It was often joked in our village that nobody died until they felt ready. She would say her words over the body of the deceased and dress them in herbs and unguents and hide them away in the swamp. The family were told not to mourn as this would scare the spirit away but instead to celebrate the life of the dead. It was said that if they celebrated hard enough, then three days later the dead would rise again and return to their family stronger than when they were alive."

"That's horrible," shuddered Skye. "Why would you want the dead to be returned?"

"Selfish reasons mostly. To ensure the harvest was gathered perhaps, to make sure that the family didn't go without. But the dead never returned, not truly. Their body often found itself back, but the person was changed. There was nothing in their head anymore. The only person who could control them was Mesaje.

"We were stupid. We so desperately wanted to keep our loved ones with us that we allowed her to bring them back in their hundreds until eventually, we had provided Mesaje with an army of the dead. I watched from our hut as the men tried to fight them on the night they came pouring out of the swamps. There was nothing they could do. No blow sent them back to their graves. I watched as everyone I knew was wiped out by this unholy army and then I fled.

"So, Skye, I know what is coming for us, and I know how little there is that can be done by those lining up below us. You are the saviour. You have proved this over and again, but you will never be as great as you can until you fully embrace the gift that you have been given. Think about it, please."

Roke patted Skye on the back and disappeared back through the large gateway. Skye turned and looked down on everything below her. She removed her mother's ring from her finger and stared at it again. The stone was too dark to reflect much, but what it did reflect seemed twisted and warped by the surface. She closed her eyes and closed her fist around the ring. Being careful to keep her balance, Skye extended her hand out over the edge of the bridge. Below her were thousands of feet of empty air with only the swirling sea to catch anything that fell. Or was dropped.

She had to know. She needed to know just how strong the bond was between her and the stone. She felt it becoming more a part of her each time she used it. She needed to know if she could ever be rid of it. She opened her hand. The pressure of the ring on her palm disappeared, and she opened her eyes and looked down into the abyss. There was nothing. The ring wasn't falling. It simply wasn't there. Feeling a weight in her pocket, Skye tentatively placed her hand against her leg and felt the familiar shape of the ring. She'd expected as much.

Don't ever do that again, Skye! I belong to you and I will make you great, but I will destroy you before you destroy me!

The whisper darted through her mind like a silverfish and only lingered long enough for Skye to know that it had really existed. Terrified, Skye thrust the ring onto her finger and raced back through the gates to find Roke.

News

Snudge was true to his message and wasted little time on greetings and well wishes. Almost at once, he escorted Arthur, Geldrig and Brack out of Carak Tak and away into the throng of the encamped troops. Curglaff and Snowbroth stood guard outside of Snudge's tent and were far more generous with their hugs and backslapping as soon as they saw Arthur and the others alive and well. Snudge ushered them all inside and sat down on the bare earth. Before he could speak, Geldrig asked the goblin what news he had of Akeldama and Skye.

"About as much as you, it seems. Snowbroth and Curglaff have told me of the betrayal at Lörieas. I have to say, it didn't come as a great shock. Whether we like it or not, Isi is right. They do not have the manpower at the minute to fight a war, though they may not have much choice soon. The news of Akeldama is also true. We have word that the Dark Queen returned a while back, albeit in a much weaker form, and was in possession of the dark orb. However, it has been stolen from her and has disappeared once again into the shadows. Unfortunately, so too has she. We lost track of her around Horongor, and she hasn't been seen since."

"We must do something!" Curglaff burst out. "We must head south now and find it. You know very well, Snudge, that our enemies will be."

"It is too dangerous right now. I also have news of an ancient sorcerer by the name of Damphir. He is a Nelapsi from the darkest parts of the Gloom. There are worrying words that he has used his power to raise an army of the dead. The diseased tribe of elves that called themselves the Azrul have once again been seen marching to the south. The last I heard they were headed towards Horongor as well, but beyond that, I have little information. It is possible that they have located Akeldama already or are aware of its whereabouts. If that is the case, then we are ill-equipped to meet them in battle with such small numbers. If Damphir has met with the Dark Queen, then all may be lost already."

"That's coward's talk!" roared Geldrig, jumping to his feet. "You know we can beat them! We beat the

Dark Queen, didn't we?"

"We once counselled Skye on the folly of throwing souls into battle, did we not? Maybe now we should heed our own advice?"

Geldrig looked disappointed but sat back down. He pulled out a whetstone and started to sharpen his sword. The rhythmic whisper of stone on metal was the only sound in the tent for a while.

Eventually, Snudge broke the silence. "I have spoken at length with Emperor Ki, and I am happy that he seeks no control over the western lands of Ithilmir. He, too, has grown concerned about the rise of evil in the south and the whispers of Akeldama once again returning and has set out to defeat it. From what I understand, he had no real intention of taking Weard but was caught off-guard when she and Skye were separated."

"You have heard where Skye is?" It was Arthur's turn to jump to his feet, demanding answers from Snudge.

"Calm down, Arthur, please. Indeed, I have heard. After she was taken from Liorath's Peak, it seems that she was taken to Alastor. What horrors she experienced there we can, for now, only guess at, but somehow, she managed to escape and disappeared into the Gloom. The next time my messengers had word of her, she was aboard the same ship as Weard and heading out to the Dragon Isles to meet with Emperor Ki.

"However, if Damphir truly has raised an army of the dead, then the Dark Queen is the least of our worries. I am unsure what use Skye will be. She is still only a young girl, despite her experiences with us."

"Why did he not simply ask us to join forces?" Geldrig asked. "Rather than try to kidnap Skye."

"As I said, he had intended to do just that at Lörieas, but he hadn't expected Skye and Weard to be travelling separately. They rarely do."

"But she's alive?" Arthur whispered, not sure if he wanted to know the answer.

"The last I heard, they were preparing to head out to sea with the emperor's armada and had set a course for Draconia. I have heard nothing since, but the journey is long and hard and golden doves do not fly well over water. They may have to wait until they reach port before they can send message."

"So what do we do now?" Snowbroth asked. "We can't just sit here waiting for this sorcerer to grow ever stronger."

"No, we cannot. But equally, we are not yet strong enough to fight him. When Emperor Ki arrives in Draconia, we will hear of it and we will make our way to Crazak D'Ur where we will join forces and proceed towards Horongor to besiege Damphir. The emperor rules over one of the largest armies of dark elves in the world. We would be foolish to turn away his support in such dire times." This was directed at Geldrig who had opened his mouth to protest the need for allies.

"For now, we must take on what provisions we can. A siege is intolerable for those trapped inside, but it is hard enough for those of us on the outside. Food and water will be key along with tents, blankets and firewood. We start preparing tomorrow."

"And now?" asked Curglaff. "What do we do for now?"

"Sleep. It will be a long few days at least before we hear from the emperor so we must rest when we can. You may all share my tent. It is warm at least."

Arthur tried hard to get comfortable on the hard floor, but he was still awake when, long after the sun had set, a messenger slipped into the tent and raced over to Snudge who had made no effort to sleep himself. Arthur tried hard but couldn't make out any of the whispered conversation. It didn't matter. As soon as the messenger had left, Snudge struck a match and lit a candle and roused them all to tell them the news.

"I'm afraid I have news. Worse news that I wanted." They were all suddenly awake and listening. "It is as we feared. Akeldama has somehow found its way to Horongor where it has been taken into the possession of Damphir. The most powerful sorcerer to roam these lands is now in control of the darkest magic we've ever seen."

Geldrig and the goblins started to squabble amongst themselves over the best course of action to take, but Snudge soon waved them into silence before continuing with his bleak news. "It is worse even than that. A hooded figure was seen entering the gates of Horongor. We strongly believe that it was the Dark Queen. It seems that she has followed her precious orb to its new owner and has formed an alliance.

"I fear there is no time now to wait for the emperor before making a move, but we are still too weak to tackle this new darkness alone, particularly if the rumours are true. Instead, the six of us will head south whilst the army continues to prepare. We will skirt around the Orcwood and head for Kanthor, the old realm of the elves. It is long abandoned, but there are whispers of some elves returning to reclaim their home. If we are lucky, we will find them willing and able to help."

"And if we are unlucky?" Arthur had no idea what elves were like, but he hadn't liked the tone in Snudge's voice.

"If we are unlucky, then we will be captured, tortured and made into playthings. Elves are beautiful but cruel. If we can win them to our cause, then they will be ferocious and loyal fighters, but you will do well not to trust them until we have an accord."

Arthur shuddered at the thought. "When do we leave?"

"Now. Grab what things you can carry, and we'll head off before sunrise."

It didn't take Arthur long to pack his meagre belongings into a canvas pack which he slung over his shoulder after wrapping two thick cloaks around him to ward off the cold night air. He took Siorraidh and slid it into its ornate sheath which he attached to his belt. It hung almost to the floor, and it banged against his ankle when he walked, but he felt more like a warrior when he wore it at his side. He hadn't had time yet to practise with it, but he knew instinctively that Queen Buidhe had been right. The sword would not let him be harmed.

In less than an hour, Arthur and the others were nothing more than shadows slipping away into the night. Snudge had left word with his commanders that they were to continue preparing for the march on Crazak D'Ur but that they were to remain at Carak Tak until he returned.

"If I'm right," the goblin had muttered to Arthur as they'd left, "we should be back within a week and hopefully by then, Emperor Ki will have docked in Draconia and will be on his way to join us. Make no mistake, this coming war will be the worst in many generations. We will need all the allies that we can muster."

Kraken

The blast of the large war horns echoed around Dragorith and woke Skye from a deep sleep. She'd managed to find Roke the night before, but she had seemed unconcerned by Skye's revelation. She'd tried to convince Skye that she had imagined it, and it was just part of her fear of the ring. She'd gone to bed angry after that and hadn't woken in any better a mood. She quickly threw on her clothes and grabbed up her bag before heading to the outer gate where they were due to meet in an hour.

Skye knew that Weard and Roke would be having breakfast with Emperor Ki, but she had no desire to be sat around them making small talk. She still hadn't spoken to Weard since their meeting with the emperor, and the longer it went on, the more awkward it became.

When she arrived at the outer gate, Skye was annoyed to find that the goblin had apparently skipped breakfast herself and was sat waiting on a small stone bench just to the side of the heavy wooden gates that were still closed after evening curfew. Without saying anything, Skye took a seat next to Weard and sat staring out over the harbour below. Already the ships at the back of the crowded mass were starting to raise their golden sails and make their way out into deeper water.

Skye knew that she and her friends were to sail on the *Dragonfire* along with Emperor Ki and his closest advisers. Looking carefully, she could make out the black sail that differentiated their ship from the others. It was adorned with the emperor's personal crest of a golden dragon curled into a circle with the mouth about to bite the tail. Emperor Ki had said that it represented the immortal nature of his dynasty. He knew that he could not live forever, but the world that he built could. Skye had to admit, it was a beautiful ship. The dark walnut hull shone, and the towering masts seemed to almost reach the bridge on which they were sat.

"Skye, I'm truly sorry," Weard began quietly.

Skye sighed and continued to stare out to sea as she spoke softly to her friend. "When I first arrived on Ithilmir, I was terrified. I had no idea what had happened or where I was, and you took me in and saved my life. You've saved my life many times, in fact. When we took on the Dark Queen, my only motivation, certainly in the beginning, was to get home. I wanted to leave this place and never return.

"But then I felt a sense of duty. Whether I am the one spoken of in the prophecy or not, once I saw what was happening here, I couldn't walk away and leave what I started unfinished. I knew that one day I would be back to finish this."

"If we had seen any other way—" the goblin began before Skye cut her off, indifferent to what she had to say.

"You knew this. I made a promise to return when needed. You could have told me that there would be no way for me to return if I came back. You could have given me the choice. And you know what, as we sit here now, I don't know what choice I would have made. But it would have been my choice to make.

"Whenever I have come to see you, I have known that there is was a risk that I might not return. I knew that and I was prepared to take the risk. But Arthur? He didn't know the risk, he didn't agree to take it and you *didn't give him a chance!*" Skye stood up as she looked angrily at Weard. "Arthur is out there somewhere at risk because of us! I take responsibility for bringing him here. It was foolish and headstrong. If anything happens to him, I will bear that for the rest of my life, but – and this is very important, Weard – you have resigned him to death on this world. He will die here *because of you!* I am not sure that I can ever forgive you and Snudge for that."

Skye turned away from Weard and wandered across to the other side of the bridge. Snow-capped mountains filled the landscape from top to bottom, and a wide, lazy river ran through the valley and down to the ocean behind her. As she stood in thought, the rest of the group arrived on the bridge, noisy and excited after a good breakfast and buoyed by the bright day.

The emperor gave a call to the guards atop the gatehouse and the heavy gates swung open to reveal a dozen chariots ready to ferry them down through the mountains to their waiting ship. By the time they reached the *Dragonfire,* much of the armada had already cast out and were now forming a formidable block a mile or so out to sea. From this distance, it looked like the sky had been painted gold and thousands of red dragons were dancing across the rays of the sun. Skye shivered at Roke's words that even with this many men they would not be able to defeat Damphir.

Skye was amazed at how different it felt to set sail on the top deck compared to the sweaty galley below. She felt a sting of guilt for the hundreds of slaves that she knew were killing themselves below her feet to move the boat out of the harbour. She hoped for a strong wind so that the sails might take up some of the strain and give them a much-needed rest. As soon as they were free from the harbour walls and the risk of crashing into their neighbouring ships had passed, the call to raise the sails went out and the loud crack of the canvas catching the wind along with the jolt as the ship suddenly picked up speed threw Skye to the floor. She dusted herself off and stood to see Emperor Ki standing over her with a strange smile on his face.

"You know, Skye, many of my sailors consider it bad luck to have a woman on board. They wanted me to cast you overboard rather than bring you with us."

"But what about Weard? And Roke? They're girls."

Emperor Ki laughed softly. "Skye, they don't count. They are goblins! Just remember, do not show yourself to be weak amongst my men. I cannot promise that they won't do the job themselves if they think you are putting them at risk." He laughed as he wandered away, but Skye doubted he was entirely joking.

Before they had left Dragorith, Emperor Ki had told the group that they would be sailing for the port city of Draconia where they were hoping to regroup and meet with their allies on the mainland. Weard had sent a message to Snudge, after hearing he had made it to Carak Tak with the G'Oräk army. She had told him where they were headed in the hope that he would be able to join them and arrange an alliance with the emperor.

Skye had noticed that Weard had been in and out of the emperor's chambers a lot during their time in Dragorith and had slowly come round to the idea of an alliance. She didn't know what was being discussed, but it worried Skye that Weard was willing to give over a lot of power with no reassurances of the emperor's aims. She hoped that Snudge would be more cautious with his plans when they finally met.

The first night at sea, Skye slept fitfully. They still had a strong wind behind them, and so the emperor had commanded them to sail on through the night. The motion of the boat rocking on the waves made it hard for Skye to relax. Soon, she found herself drifting off only to be woken suddenly by a suffocating weight on her chest. She opened her eyes and was blinded by a bright white light in front of her. She tried to close her eyes, but they were stuck open. The light burnt hard as she stared ahead. She reached out and tried to claw it away, but her arms felt as though they were moving through treacle.

A loud roar thundered through her ears, which started to ring. The bright light became a circle at the end of a black tunnel that now started to fall upwards. Or was she falling downwards? She couldn't tell, but the circle was rapidly becoming smaller and smaller and further away. Out of nowhere came the voice again, the voice that she'd dreaded hearing again since the bridge.

Use me, Skye. Only I can save you!

Skye felt her mother's ring burning on her finger. The pain was agonising as it stripped the skin and flesh before it finally cut through the bone, and she felt the ring fall away into the darkness.

It is too late now. You must die.

Gasping for breath, she opened her eyes again and found that she had fallen from her hammock and lay on the floor of the galley. The slaves were all sat to attention, ready if they were needed but none of them dared to look her way. She knew that she must have screamed as she dreamt, but they showed no signs of emotion. They really were broken.

Sickened by her dream, Skye made her way up to the top deck which was strangely quiet. The sails were raised but hung limply in a soft breeze. There was no activity at all, no sailors desperately trying to find the wind to get them moving, no shouting or screaming instructions. Nervously, Skye made her way to the back of the deck and to the emperor's quarters. Inside, she heard familiar voices and so knocked politely before letting herself in. She was shocked to see Weard sat at the emperor's table. They were clearly involved in an intense conversation, and they both sat awkwardly waiting for Skye to say her piece.

"There is nobody on deck. I thought you should know. There is no wind, either. We aren't moving anywhere."

The emperor rose from his seat in a panic and strode past Skye. He raced up onto the bridge to ring the heavy brass bell that hung there. Within minutes, the rest of the crew had been woken and mustered, and Emperor Ki was screaming and shouting for them to find the missing sailors who had so recklessly abandoned their posts. After a thorough search of the ship, they were nowhere to be found. Terror started to spread amongst the sailors.

"It is her! It is bad luck having a girl on board. We are cursed!"

Skye stood terrified as a small group of elves broke off and surrounded her. She drew Burrower but knew that she had no chance once they charged. She was determined to die fighting rather than be cast into the freezing water.

"Land!" the cry came from the top of the main mast where one of the elves had claimed for a better view. "Westwards!"

This caused renewed chaos. Skye was left alone as the dark elves busied themselves looking out into the night. There was no breeze at all. The order was given for the galley slaves to drive them towards the island that rose from the waves where the sea touched the stars. Their progress was slow, and it soon became apparent that not only were they becalmed but they were also alone. The rest of the fleet had disappeared into the night as mysteriously as the crew.

Slowly they made their way across the calm ocean until the island rose up before them. From this distance, it appeared more like a rounded rock thrust up from the ocean floor, and it was smaller than they had thought, perhaps no bigger than the ship itself. The surface didn't look like rock or sand. It was more pitted and smooth like the skin of a whale. A sharp ridge ran through the centre of the island, and it looked more organic than it should: like the scales that formed the spine of a lizard.

Skye was convinced that if she looked hard enough, she could see the island rising and falling slowly. She started to feel the ring tingling again. Something wasn't right. She could feel the tension in the air.

Skye was startled out of her observation as the emperor's chief adviser burst out of his chambers and raced across the deck towards them.

"Your Majesty, please, we must retreat. We must turn the ship around now!" The elf was clearly shaken and struggled to get his words out. "Please, we have wandered into the Manumi Straight, the Devil's Sea. That is no island!"

As the messenger finished, he fell to his knees and started to plead in broken sobs, but it was too late. They stood and watched the sea start to boil and froth and slowly the island rose from the sea. A single giant eye a dozen feet wide blinked slowly as a long, conical body reared up out of the waves. The giant beast continued to rise a hundred feet in the air until it blocked out the moon and cast the ship into shadow. An enormous, razor-sharp beak, big enough to bite the ship in two, thrashed open and shut as the monster struggled to breathe in the air. A piercing scream split the night sky and it roared angrily at the trespassers who had dared disturb its sleep.

All at once the entire ship tilted backwards throwing the crew onto their backs. A giant wave rose above them and crashed down onto the deck. Salt water stung Skye's eyes. She choked on mouthfuls of it as she tried to steal a breath underwater. She managed to regain her footing and scrambled to her feet in time to see a thick tentacle rise above them. Pale suckers the size of dinner plates rippled and contracted as they tasted the air. In the darkness, each one shone like a moon pinned to the black canvas of the night.

"Kraken!" The shout seemed to come from everywhere all at once. Suddenly there was only one goal, to cast the small wooden life rafts overboard and try to make it clear of the ship before the kraken dragged them to their doom. The red mist of chaos descended on the crew, and every elf turned to fighting for their own safety. Skye frantically looked around, desperate to see somebody that she knew. Her stomach turned as the ship listed, knocked by another giant tentacle rising from the tempestuous sea. The kraken was squealing with delight at the meal that had wandered into its trap. Those elves that had regained their composure had taken up arms against the beast. Arrows and spears flew through the air, but most fell drastically short of their target. Those that made the distance simply rebounded into the sea, turned back by the thick, leathery skin. The thick tentacles thrashed down onto the deck repeatedly snatching up sailors before throwing them whole into the sharp beak that opened like a gateway to hell.

"Stay away from its grasp!" Emperor Ki was shouting instructions to his men as loudly as he could, but the crashing and splintering of the deck as the boat twisted and rolled in the surf drowned him out. "Aim for the eye! Archers! Aim for the eye!"

One of the archers must have heard his leader's call above the din for a single arrow flew out of the darkness, the sharp tip glinting in the moonlight, and punched hard into the single, staring eye. The kraken reeled back and bellowed with pain. As it thrashed out, its long arms hammered against the side of the boat and sent it into a roll. Skye felt her stomach turn as the floor disappeared beneath her feet and she rolled and eventually dropped against the railings on the far side of the deck. She watched helplessly as Weard fell hard against the mast before spinning and falling into the boiling waves. The towering wall of polished wood that had formerly been the deck of the *Dragonfire* rose up into the sky as the emperor's prize ship continued to capsize. Like an avalanche storming down a mountain, the wall closed in quickly and it was all Skye could do to throw herself from the railings and into the freezing water. She felt the solid wood of the handrail press into her back as the *Dragonfire* crashed into the water and the clanging echo as water filled her ears.

Skye twisted under the water and forced her eyes

open. She could feel the cold salt water stinging and blurring her vision and her lungs burned, desperate for another breath but she was trapped. The *Dragonfire* was sinking quickly, and she was being carried with it.

Above, she could make out the bright white circle of the moon. She desperately clawed out, trying to grab hold of something, anything, to pull herself towards the air. She would sooner fight the kraken than endure another second of this desperate hell. Gradually the bright circle started to fall away. Skye felt herself giving in to the surrounding darkness as the black tunnel stretched away into the distance.

On her finger, the ring started to burn, and she felt the familiar tingle of Akeldama's power coursing through her arms. It was weak, though. There was no strength left for it to use.

I can save you, Skye, but there will be a cost! The voice rang clear in Skye's mind, undisturbed by the fathoms of water above.

I have nothing to give! Skye screamed into the darkness yet her mouth remained shut.

You have everything to give!

What is it? What you want from me? She was desperate. She could see only darkness and feel nothing but the biting cold. The distant thrashing of the kraken had long since disappeared.

You! Give in to the power, Skye! Let me help you and then let me lead you to greatness!

"*Never!*" She screamed louder than ever, and this time she screamed out loud and regretted it instantly as the last bubbles of air in her lungs escaped to be replaced by ice cold water.

Then you will die, you stupid girl!

She felt the ring burn hotter than ever on her finger. Even the ice-cold water did nothing to calm the heat. But she fought back. She wasn't going to die here at the bottom of a watery grave. She felt the power still raging through her aching for an escape. She knew that she would be fighting whatever it was that was talking to her, but she had to fight no matter what. She concentrated and allowed the electricity to flow into her mind. She felt it fizzing behind her eyes, and she felt the familiar buzz warming her from her core. She felt alive again.

She found herself free from the railings and felt herself soaring skywards buoyed on a pillar of bubbles that seemed to rise from the darkness. She felt the cold night air against her skin and gulped down deep breaths as she was ejected from the waves and then the engulfing coldness of the waves once again.

This time she had a chance. She kicked her legs and pushed herself back to the surface and grabbed hold of the first piece of flotsam that she could reach. Gasping for breath and through blurred vision, she was surprised to make out shapes in front of her. A cold hand reached out and grabbed her around the back of her shirt and dragged her onto the raft. Skye rubbed her eyes until she could see once again and was surprised to see Emperor Ki and Roke sat aboard a few pieces of wood strapped together with thick rope.

Skye embraced them both, partly out of affection but mainly for warmth. Then she panicked and started to scour the waves around them.

"Weard?" she asked desperately. Roke shook her head sadly.

"We have not been able to find her, I'm afraid."

Skye screamed into the darkness. Not Weard. She had been her friend despite what had happened in the end. Skye instantly regretted everything that she had said to the healer on the bridge. Of course, she would have forgiven her. What had she been thinking? And now it was too late. Now there would never be chance to say those unsaid things that she wished she had said before.

"Goodbye, my friend," she whispered to the ocean. Sadness washed over her like the tempest that the kraken had so recently wrought. "I forgive you."

History Of The Elves

"Before us lies the valley of Yulrin, once home to the magnificent elven city of Kanthor. It is said to be invisible to all but the most noble of elves, but we must do our best to find it nonetheless." Snudge was stood atop a gently rolling hillside, and Arthur couldn't help but stand in awe at the majesty of the woodland that stretched out below them, dipping gently into the valley of Yulrin before rising sharply in the south.

"What happened to the elves?" Arthur had been wondering about that since he'd heard that they'd left their home. Now that he saw how beautiful it was, he could understand even less why they would leave it.

"They grew tired of the greed and viciousness that surrounded them," Geldrig answered, taking over the story from Snudge. "For a thousand generations, they had watched as the orcs grew stronger and more evil in the Orcwood and yet they did nothing. For age after age, they saw the magic of their world twisted and turned to darkness.

"In our world, much as there is dark and light, there are dark elves and high elves. Dark elves are not named because they embrace the dark forces that the Dark Queen enjoyed, but rather because they choose to live in the shadows of the darkest places. Some even live underground. High elves, the elves that most people know simply as elves, embrace the light and airy woodlands such as this. They couldn't bear to see it shrouded in shadow. They felt it as a physical pain.

"Elves were the first race to harness the magic of Ithilmir. Legend has it, they rose from the ground in the first years following the Before Time, when the scars left by the Spirit Voices were still raw and unhealed. Oh, some say the Shrunken arrived first, but it makes little difference. They were both amongst the first to walk the battered landscape that they found, and certainly, history would be a lot different had those wretched rats never lived. Or maybe it wouldn't be. There will always be evil ready to rise to the top.

"Back then, unfiltered magic leaked into the world in ways we can't even begin to imagine, and the elves of Kanthor were there to capture it and bend it to their will. Though they now have a tendency towards cruelty when angered, an understandable reaction to the great pain they've suffered at the hands of other races, the first elves were pure and noble and vowed to use their new power to drive the world forwards in search of harmony. They saw the damage that the wars between good and evil had caused and knew that, if the world was to avoid a second such age of unrelenting violence and destruction, it would need a shepherd to guide it. They saw themselves as that shepherd."

Arthur looked at the Eden stretched out in front of him and could understand a little of why they had left. Here and there were deep scars in the hillside where nothing grew, a legacy of the damage that magic and power could do. "So what happened?"

"Akeldama. I don't know how much of our history Skye has told you, but the Shrunken were certainly the first creatures to find and use the dark orb known as Akeldama. Its power gave them the chance to grow and spread quickly and with devastating results. The elves were here in Kanthor, on the other side of the world to the Shrunken. Still, they must have sensed that something so evil was growing, but if they did, they did nothing to stop it. Instead, they built themselves a fortress and buried it deep within this valley. You have to understand, Arthur, the elves were naive, and they will be the first to admit that. Had they marched on the Gloom back then and wiped out the Shrunken, who knows how history would have worked out. But they didn't, and the darkness rose and grew until it consumed most of the northern lands."

"What stopped it? Why didn't it consume everything?" Arthur was surprised to hear Brack ask the questions. He'd assumed that this history would be familiar to the goblin. The goblin answered Arthur's confused look with a smile. "I am too young to know everything."

"The elves, in the end. The darkness soon spread far enough to reach the edges of this valley. By then they could no longer bury their heads in the sand. They knew they had to act, and so they marched. There were more than ten-thousand elves that set forth from these woods, but the size of the army that awaited dwarfed them by a factor of ten. The first few battles were bloody and catastrophic, and soon they were forced to retreat back to their stronghold at Kanthor. It was there in their desperation that they made the decision to use their power, to use the magic that they had sworn only to use for the good of their world, to destroy the army that lay before them.

"They set out again, this time with their most powerful mages. Within a generation, they had beaten back the darkness to the edge of the Wandering Place. I suppose had they acted sooner they might have finished their job, but it was around this time that the other dark stain on the world, the Nelapsi, found themselves on the edge of the Gloom. Their leader, Liorath, made his way into Alastor and stole Akeldama, and so began another period of evil. The elves were exhausted and depleted from their years of fighting and they retreated swiftly back to their homeland. The rest is as we told Skye when she first arrived here.

"Since then, the elves have played their part in some small skirmishes outside of their realm, but something about them changed after their long campaign against the Shrunken. They were damaged and distrustful of anything beyond their borders. They found that several of their mages had grown fond of the power they wielded, and they were banished into the darkness. Some of the most powerful sorcerers to mark this land were elves. It wouldn't surprise me if Damphir was part elvish somewhere in his history."

"Is that when they left? When they realised that they couldn't guide the world in the way that they wanted?" Arthur asked with a whisper.

"Not quite. They stayed here, secluded, for a thousand years or so but nobody has seen them in many generations. My guess is that they left across the ocean, looking for something that could never exist. Good and evil cannot live in harmony; there will always be too much friction. The best we can hope for is to quash evil as far as possible and keep it locked away in a box."

"But for now, we must hope that the rumours of their return are true." Snudge had been growing impatient at Geldrig's lengthy history lesson and had finally had enough. "There will be time for more of your tales when all of this is over. Let us head into the woods and see what we can find."

Nobody dared to argue with the goblin leader, and they headed down into the wooded valley. The air quickly turned damp and chilled compared to the airy sunlight they had been enjoying not long before. Arthur found himself pulling his cloak tighter to his shoulders to ward off the cold. They walked for what felt like hours over tangled roots and damp, rotten leaves that seemed to suck at his boots, but Arthur didn't dare to moan. Skye was respected and almost revered by his companions, but he felt distinctly that he would be more disposable if he became a burden. So he pushed on quietly, making sure he never slipped behind or deviated from the path that Snudge was beating in front of them.

The farther forward they pushed, the lower they descended into the valley, and the warmer the air became. The humidity never left them, and soon Arthur found himself enveloped by annoying midges that took every opportunity to bite him. He was somewhat relieved when they emerged from a thicket of trees and stumbled to the edge of a deep ravine.

Arthur stepped forward to see just how deep the crevice was but staggered when the ground shifted uneasily beneath his feet. For a second, he felt his foot float in mid-air before something seemed to rise up to meet it and support him for long enough to gain his balance and fall backwards.

"Careful there," Geldrig said with a laugh. "I shan't be coming down after to you to find the body."

Arthur glowered but broke into a smile when he realised that Geldrig was right. It would be a pointless way to die after coming this far.

The dark abyss in front of them wasn't the main focus of the group. The ravine was easily half a mile wide and formed an empty moat around an island that seemed to float in the middle of the great gap. On top of the platform, a vast walled city rose high and reached for the sunlight high above the surrounding trees. It looked old and worn with some walls barely more than holes held together with ancient stones, but it was easy to see how magnificent it had once been. A dozen turrets rose from the square walls, and a broad, squat keep stood proud on a hill towards the back.

Each tower was punctuated by tens of thin slits, arrow slits to allow their archers to fire out onto anyone foolish enough to attack the fortress. The banner of Kanthor stood fluttering at full mast wherever there was space with a golden fist clenched against an azure blue background. Out of the eastern wall, a waterfall cascaded over the edge and disappeared noisily into the inky blackness below.

True to the beauty of the elves, the walls were covered in thin silver markings that spread out from the heavy wooden gateway and seemed to entangle and ensnare the building like a spider's web. Even after all this time they still shone in the sunlight.

"They are magic." Geldrig seemed to be reading Arthur's thoughts. "They are a spell cast to protect the castle and the town within from any dark magic. Kanthor cannot be breached by magic even after all this time. We must find a way to cross over to the gate."

The fair ones told
Of a city of old
Their magic they save
For only the brave
With closed eyes
Yet darkness to rise
Only then will the fair ones awake

Brack looked uncomfortable as they all turned to look at him as the last notes of his song drifted away over the dark void. "It's an old song I heard many years ago," he muttered, half apologising for his intrusion. "Maybe it has some clue. Their magic is saved for those who are considered brave. Maybe that is how we cross the ravine. Bravery."

"What are you talking about?" Geldrig's voice was filled with scorn as he waved away the goblin's suggestion.

"Maybe he's right," Arthur said, almost to himself. He'd been wondering about something since he'd almost slipped over the edge, and he saw a chance to prove to the others how useful he could be. Without giving himself time to back out, he strode forwards and stepped over the edge of the darkness. For a second, he fell forwards and his stomach lurched but then, like before, something rose up to support his foot. He took a deep breath and turned round to face the others. He was stood a yard out over the darkness, but he wasn't falling. His companions all looked shocked except for Brack who wore a look of smug pride.

"Only the brave, indeed." Snudge gave Arthur a quizzical glance, as though he were a pet who learnt a new trick. "Well done, both of you. We may make a warrior of you yet, Arthur!"

Arthur smiled at the goblin leader and, tentatively at first, they made their way across the ravine.

Draconia

Skye found herself standing knee deep in snow. A snowstorm was adding more depth to the powder and obscured her vision on all sides. Slowly, feeling her way forward with each step, Skye made her way to what turned out to be the edge of a mountaintop. As she stepped down a few feet from the top, the snowstorm stopped and the air cleared. Stretching out a mile or so below her was the endlessly barren Shadowlands. She knew this place well by now. She knew every rock and valley, and yet she had never been here before. She had never been so high above the wasteland.

Skye waited. It was clear to her that she had been brought here for a reason, but the way down the mountain seemed treacherous, and so she sat and watched the horizon. Time was different here. Every second felt thin, as though it had been stretched out over a year. Soon the familiar thick mist started to pour into the valley from behind her shrouding the mountainside like a calm sea. When the valley had filled, the fog started to take the shape of a vast army of goblins. Millions of ghostly grey-green creatures stood to attention and stared intently at Skye.

We are here to fight for you, Skye Thistle! The voices spoke as one, softly enough to be nothing more than a whisper on the breeze, and yet loud enough for Skye to believe that every single goblin had spoken at once. *We are the lost goblins. We have already fought for our causes throughout the ages. We are the ones who paid the price for war. We are the ones who have given all that we can give. But we will give again if that is what you ask of us!*

Know this, Skye Thistle. If you command us to fight, then you will see our ranks swollen tenfold before the war is done. The Shadowlands is the final resting place for those of us who believed in our Elders and who sought peace through war. There are songs sung of us, poems written for us and still we go on living here. It is said that nothing will bring us back! And yet, within you, there is the power to do so. You have felt the power of the stone. You have felt what it can do. It could bring us back, Skye Thistle! We could return for one last glorious battle!

Think of the songs that would be written of the army of the Shadowlands risen once more to quell the evil that has risen!

Do not be afraid to be all that you can, Skye Thistle, but let others fear what you will be to them.

Skye coughed hard and choked up a mouthful of salty water. She opened her eyes and was relieved to see the welcome faces of Roke and Emperor Ki looking down. The loss of Weard struck her hard again, and she felt the warmth of tears on her icy cheeks. She struggled to sit up on the wobbling wooden platform and regretted it instantly. Her back and arms were sore from being thrown around on the *Dragonfire's* deck the night before and her head throbbed from the cold. Luckily the morning air was still, but there was no escaping the icy numbness of the water that surrounded them.

"We have seen several other rafts through the night," Emperor Ki informed her in his usual, light voice. He pointed to the westerly horizon where a jagged coastline was growing slowly closer. "We believe those are the cliffs of Serpent Bay. If we are correct, we should be close enough to swim ashore within a few hours. We will not be far from where we intended to land. That will be an unlikely success given the circumstances."

"What about the other ships? Where were they last night?" Skye asked, finding anything to talk about to distract her from the cold that seemed all-consuming.

"We were at the rear of the fleet as planned in case of attack," the emperor explained. "It appears that when the winds dropped, the others were far enough ahead to lose track of us in the darkness, but we were caught in the drag of the kraken. We were trapped, Skye. The kraken traps its prey by diving very quickly to the bottom of the ocean, drawing down with it all of the water above creating an irresistible current. Even had our oarsmen been rowing last night, we would have been snared.

"We were very lucky to survive. There are not many sailors who can say they have survived an attack by a kraken."

"There are even fewer who can say that they were able to fly through water and air in order to escape a sinking ship." Roke raised her eyebrow as she looked quizzically at Skye.

"The ring tried to bargain with me again. It asked me to surrender myself to its power so that I may be saved."

The two others looked shocked, but she continued quickly. "I refused. I fought back, and it left me to die. I remembered what you said, Roke, about me being in control of it and not the other way around. I managed to control the power before it killed me and instead it carried me to safety.

"I don't like the way that this is going, Roke. I feel like whatever is talking to me is evil and is getting stronger and more insistent. It started as a whisper, but it is getting louder each time."

"Do not fear, little human." The emperor tried to calm Skye down and placed his hand on her wet shoulder. "No seer, druid, shaman or sorcerer has ever had an easy relationship with their power. It is a constant struggle, but it is one that you must continue to fight. Remember, this is no longer about you. This is about the future of our world. It is about you returning home. For now, rest a little if you can. We will wake you when we near our destination."

Skye allowed herself to relax back onto the raft and tried to close her eyes and shut out the pain. No matter how hard she tried, the vision of Weard joining the ghostly ranks of the Shadowlands filled her with a deep hurt. Now more than ever the idea of bringing the army back to fight for her appealed; if only to see Weard once more. She knew that she couldn't allow her personal pain to cloud her judgement though. If what Emperor Ki had said was true and the wizard Damphir had raised an army of the dead, would bringing back even more lost souls be such a wise move?

Skye drifted into a fitful rest, never fully asleep and always listening and waiting. Roke and Emperor Ki continued to talk about what would happen when they arrived, but nothing they muttered could convince Skye that their cause was anything other than hopelessly lost.

Around midday, Skye awoke to the druid gently shaking her shoulders. The raft had come to a halt against a bar of bright sand as white as snow. Emperor Ki was already ashore and scouting the area from the top of a tall dune.

"The tide was with us. We had no need to swim in the end. Thank goodness for small blessings." Roke was smiling, but Skye could see that the druid was in pain. She was bleeding from an open wound above her hip, and her eyes looked sunken and tired.

"Where are we?"

"We think somewhere a little north of Draconia. You can see the northernmost peaks of the Orctooth range in the distance. If so, we should be able to meet up with the other ships before sundown."

It took Emperor Ki over an hour before he finally slid down the side of the dune and reported that they were in fact much closer to the port city of Draconia than they had even dared to hope. He reported seeing the towering masts of at least a thousand ships dotted in and around the harbour. It appeared that most of the rest of the armada had survived the night.

Even though it was only a few short miles to the port, the going was hard. Sand dunes littered the coastline, and Skye's legs moaned with every forced step against the loose sand. Her boots were soon filled and rubbed against the sides of her ankles. Every step forward seemed to be followed by a long slide back, but they somehow managed to conquer each white mountain that rose to meet them. Every now and then something would scuttle or slither away as they approached, but not all were quick enough to escape the blade of Roke. On the top of a particularly high dune, the druid lit a small fire of desiccated scrub and cooked a thick-skinned lizard that she had managed to kill. The meat was tough and bitter, but Skye welcomed the feeling of food in her stomach and felt a little lighter when they pushed on again into the seemingly endless sand.

The sun was setting low behind them when they finally scaled the last peak and slid happily down to the crystal-clear water that marked the top of Serpent Bay. From here to the port, the ground was hard and covered in stinging bushes that ripped at their clothes and scratched their skin, but they barely felt it after the ordeal of the dunes.

Draconia was like all harbours, busy and mixed with the heady smell of fish and salt water. Skye could feel the strong breeze blowing in across the waves rejuvenating her. But something felt wrong, like a discordant note in an aria. Emperor Ki had become increasingly agitated as they'd crossed the scrubland. He constantly looked up to the sky and darted at the quietest of noises. On the dunes, Skye had put it down to being nervous after their attack at sea, but here in the safety of his army, it seemed out of place, as though he were waiting for something to happen. She tried to find a time to mention it to Roke, but they were never left alone.

A trio of heavily armoured soldiers were waiting for them as they approached the harbour itself and embraced Emperor Ki with relief. Each wore a long sword at their waist and carried a tall spear topped with a battle axe; a halberd. Over the armour, they each wore the gold cloaks of the Army of Enlightenment. Skye and Roke received only a nod of greeting from the guards, Skye didn't care. She just wanted to sleep and rest.

The soldiers spoke to their leader in a strange tongue, and even Roke seemed confused. So far, Emperor Ki had spoken only Skye's own language, but now he spoke quickly with an anger and urgency that worried her. Suddenly, the kindly elf that had reassured her back in Dragorith seemed a distant memory.

Emperor Ki turned urgently to the two of them and spoke, once again, in words that they understood. "I apologise for that." Skye noticed him playing with the hem of his robes. Something was wrong. "My guards only speak old Elvish. We have arranged lodgings for the night."

Skye was relieved. The dull greyness of night had started to take a strong hold on the harbour, and she didn't want to be out in the open any longer than necessary. Roke looked equally pleased at the news and even turned and gave Skye a warm smile. It did little to ease her worries.

Emperor Ki continued: "*Dragonfire* is lost to the ocean, and I have taken the ship *Serpensis* as my main vessel. You will sleep in the captain's quarters tonight, Skye. You may have the master bed. May it bring you much rest and comfort."

Skye thanked the emperor and asked where her friend would be sleeping.

"Roke has a room at the Tentacle and Ink, an inn on the other side of Draconia. She will rest well there."

"Nonsense." Emperor Ki flinched at Roke's outburst. "I will stay with Skye. I consider her my responsibility, and I will protect her."

"I must insist—"

"And so must I." The druid made it clear that she wouldn't be moved on her position.

"So be it." Emperor Ki gave a nod.

One of the guards lowered his halberd and led Skye and the druid along the seafront to a huge wooden boat that dwarfed the sunken *Dragonfire*. A thick, wooden snake wrapped itself around the hull from stern to bow where a snarling head reared up into the night sky. Flaming torches had been lit along the ship's deck and hideous shadows danced on the towering sails as the crew finished preparing the boat for a stay in port. Skye had no doubt that any navy foolish enough to come under attack by the *Serpensis* would be frozen with terror when it burst out of the fog. They were led quickly up a wooden plank that bowed and bounced underfoot. Skye saw the deck was lined with enormous war drums painted black with gold edging and skinned with a dark leather. She shuddered as she thought of the ominous sound that they would produce; the rhythmic heartbeat floating across the waves foretelling death to anyone unlucky enough to hear it.

The soldier shouted something undecipherable to the crew, and they all dropped whatever they were doing and scurried from the deck; rats leaving a troubled ship. Once again, Skye felt that something was out of place. So far, Emperor Ki had been nothing but accommodating, but the hairs on the back of her neck stood on end as she stood on the slowly swaying deck. She tried to put it to the back of her mind as she was led to the captain's quarters and left alone with Roke.

Before she could mention her worries to her friend, the druid turned to her and whispered, "I feel it too, Skye. Something isn't right. Don't worry. I will take the first watch. Get some sleep, and I will wake you in a few hours."

Though she felt a little better at Roke's reassuring words, Skye still struggled to fall to sleep. She could hear the gentle rustle of Roke's clothing as she settled into her post outside the door and the creaking of the thick wooden planks that twisted in the gentle waves. The awkward creases and buckles of her clothes and sword belt made it even harder to find a comfortable position, but she knew that she needed to rest quickly in case they needed to flee. She didn't dare relax fully, and she kept her hand on the hilt of Burrower even as she eventually drifted into a weak sleep.

Skye had no idea how long she had been resting before she woke suddenly, going from sleep to alert as quickly as a startled cat. She knew immediately that something was very wrong. Without thinking she rolled on the bed and dropped onto the splintered floor. Overhead, she heard the hiss of metal and the soft thud as a sword cut into the mattress just where her head had so recently lay. She scrambled to her hands and knees and tried her best to crawl along the swaying floor. The wood cut into her knuckles as she gripped Burrower tightly.

There was a sudden creak to her left and threw herself forward. This time she was too slow, and she felt the tip of the sword graze her leg. The cut was shallow, but she felt the sting and warm rush of blood over her ankle. She rolled away from where her attacker stood and felt something against her neck. She reached above her and grabbed the thick curtains that lined the main window. She tugged hard and pulled herself to her feet. The curtain rail gave way in her hands just as a shadow moved out of the corner and lunged.

Skye screamed and threw the curtains over her attacker. She saw him stumble and stagger under the weight and she took the chance to run past him. She headed towards the soft glow of the door; the torches on the deck had burned low during the night and only gave the barest illumination. Skye was through the doorway when her foot struck against something heavy and she fell forwards. She turned mid-fall and landed on her back, her sword ready to block a blow that never came. She looked down and choked. Roke lay across the doorway; her eyes fixed and staring at the stars, her hands gripping the hilt of a dagger that had been thrust into her heart. Her own sword was still in its scabbard.

Skye fought back a sob. She took a second to close her friend's eyes and dragged herself to her feet just as the attacker burst through the door. The curtain still hung from his shoulders like a golden cape in the flickering torchlight.

Seconds passed but no further attack arrived. Skye stood and waited. She could sense more soldiers behind her, taking their time as they boarded the boat. In front of her, the attacker from the room drew closer. She could see his face clearly now. She saw the scars and rotten flesh. The drawn back lips and withered hair. Most of all, she saw the piercing blue dot at the centre of his eye socket. The other was covered with a black strip of cloth. She shivered despite the warm night air. Skye considered herself battle-hardened by now and thought she'd fought the worst that Ithilmir had to offer, but there was something else about the figure stood in front of her. Something that terrified her even more than looking into the Dark Queen's eyes and seeing her mother stare back. She turned and ran in the only direction that she could, towards the edge of the deck. She didn't stop when she reached the wooden gunwale, and for a fleeting moment, she flew.

Icy water seared her limbs and forced the wind from her lungs, but Skye knew that she had to fight her body and swim. She would die in the water before she drowned if she wasn't careful. Taking care to keep hold of Burrower, she kicked off the rest of her thick outer clothes and heavy chain-mail and swam down into the inky blackness. Above her, the low light of the torches outlined the keel of the boat, and she kicked hard towards the stern. She knew there was a small wooden rowing boat strapped to the side in case the ship went down.

A fire was burning in her lungs by the time Skye broke through the waves and managed to grab hold of the ladder that led up to the wooden boat, roughly halfway up the stern of the *Serpensis*. She managed to pull herself clear of the water and stopped to regain her composure. Suddenly, a shadow fell across her, and she looked up into the one blue eye of the dead soldier. In his hands, he held a thick crossbow, pulled tight and loaded. The small metal tip of the arrow filled Skye's world. For a dozen heartbeats, she held on and waited. Then, with a loud slap of leather on wood, the crossbow fired.

Kanthor

The air inside the lost city of Kanthor was still and silent, broken only by the occasional hum of a passing insect, but even they seemed to give the innermost sanctums a wide berth. All around there were signs of ancient life. Broken market trolleys still held ancient and rotten produce or baskets filled with foreign gold coins where the traders would make change. A wooden podium had been set up against one of the city walls, and a set of juggler's sticks lay abandoned on the ground.

"It's almost as though they left in a hurry," Brack whispered to the others. None of them had dared to speak above a whisper since they'd entered the unlocked gates. A sense of foreboding hung over them all like a thick mist.

The gates had led into the outer ring of the city

which was lined with tall, heavily branched trees. Within these branches, the elves had built their ornate houses made entirely of materials harvested from the surrounding woodlands. Thin silver ladders led up into the canopies, and Arthur had made a point of climbing them to see what he could find. Disappointingly, the tree houses had been stripped bare, or else the elves had never bothered with personal possessions. Beyond the wall of trees, the open marketplace dominated most of the space before giving way to the vast stone keep beyond.

Criss-crossing the entire city and encircling the marketplace was a wide canal filled with inky water. Shallow-bottomed boats slowly floated endlessly around the city, reminding Arthur of an abandoned roller-coaster ride. Further on, the canal made its way to the eastern wall where it slipped through a metal grating and continued over the waterfall and into the great abyss beyond. Above the metal grating and powered by the flowing river, a wooden paddle wheel hooked any boats that found their way to the end of the course and lifted them up before dropping them back into the canal on the other side of a low brick wall. A well of water bubbled up from somewhere deep in the ground, and so the canal was continually filled and stocked with moving boats.

Arthur found the whole thing fascinating, but he knew that Skye would have enjoyed the mechanical genius even more. He felt a sharp pang of guilt that he hadn't thought about her since Carak Tak.

"There is nothing for us out here. We should try the keep. At the very least, there may be some food that is still edible." Geldrig urged the group onward across the marketplace. The keep stood no taller than Arthur's house back on Earth, but the walls were thicker than those that surrounded the city. This was a building designed to keep its treasures locked away against all comers.

It took Geldrig over an hour with his sword to hack through the lock that kept the keep's gate shut. Once it shattered onto the cobbles, the gate swung easily open. Darkness enveloped them all as they stepped into air choked with dust. For a while, they groped around blindly before Curglaff found a reed torch that still held enough oil to light. The smell of sulphur momentarily filled the air as he struck a thick match. Arthur had to shield his eyes against the sudden brightness when the torch burst into flames.

The keep was vast, much bigger than they'd imagined from the outside. The reed-strewn floor ran away from them at a steep decline until the ceiling towered far above them. The stone walls were lined with richly coloured tapestries showing first the great battles of the elves but turning darker as they progressed further into the keep. Here they showed a darkness spreading over the world. Strange symbols picked out in gold and silver swirled over unrecognisable monsters standing over the corpses of thousands of fallen elves. In all of them, a crude outline of an eye had been scratched in red ink so as it might watch over the entire scene. Each shadowed monster held a black circle in its outstretched hand.

"They tell the rise of Akeldama, the Shadowed Eye," Snowbroth said. "They saw what was happening, and they wanted nothing to do with it."

Arthur felt sick with fear at the thought of all the death and destruction that had come before and that threatened to come again if they didn't defeat Damphir and destroy Akeldama. He took himself away from the others and explored the rest of the keep or at least those parts that he could see by the flickering torchlight. Stone chests littered the floor, but they had all been ransacked at some point in the past and stood empty but for a few cobwebs. As he walked around, something metal clinked under his feet. He bent down and swept away the dusty reeds. It was a metal ring attached to a wooden trapdoor.

"Over here," Arthur called out to the others as

he pulled on the ring and lifted the door open. A set of stone steps led down into darkness. Without the torch, he had no idea how long the steps went on for but, even as Curglaff lowered the torch into the hole, they still appeared to be endless.

Snudge led the way down slowly. The steps were well worn and uneven and after a few minutes descended in open air. There were no railings or ropes to hold on to on either side, simply an endless drop into nothingness. Without warning, the torch spluttered and went out, and they were plunged into a darkness deeper than Arthur had ever experienced before.

Suddenly, as though a switch had been turned on, gentle spots of light appeared and floated through the darkness, and thin whispers of silver danced and twisted as they descended further and further underground. The light they gave was only weak, but it was enough to outline the steps ahead of them. They pushed on with greater pace, unsure when the guiding lights would disappear and they'd be stranded in the darkness on their precarious perch.

It took a long time to reach the bottom of the stairs. When they did, they found themselves at the entrance to yet another room. This time, the door was unbolted and swung open easily. Beyond it lay a seemingly endless corridor lit only by small candles resting on stone plinths in the middle of the floor. Polished white marble reflected their weak light, but shadows still lurked in every nook and cranny. On each side, the walls were lined with alcoves cut out of the rock, each roughly six feet long and bathed in shadow. Arthur edged closer to the one nearest to him and was horrified to see that each crevice held the body of an elf. Thousands upon thousands of bodies were contained within the walls stretching away almost to infinity and towering high above them.

"It's a mausoleum." Curglaff spoke quietly, but the echoes of his voice carried away on the still air.

"Not quite." Arthur and his friends drew their swords as the strange, high voice drifted out of the shadows. "The elves of Kanthor are not dead. My name is Aefor and I should know, I am one of them. My full name is Aefor the Elderly, Sublime and Venerated, but Aefor will do for now."

As they watched, an elf clad in the azure blue of the Kanthor banner moved into the light. He was old, and it showed in the lines on his face and his grey, thinning hair, but he still looked powerful. He walked with the aid of a black stick carved from the wood of the forest and inlaid with the same silver lines that had embraced the city walls and floated through the darkness not long before.

"Our magic." He spoke as if to answer Arthur's unspoken question. "These silver streams of light show us anything that has been touched by our magic. They aren't strictly necessary, but, if you're going to use magic, why not add beauty to the world at the same time?" He spoke with a light-heartedness that belied their surroundings, and Arthur couldn't help but think that the old elf was almost joking with them. "Our magic is also how you managed to be here."

"The ravine? It wasn't about bravery?" Arthur couldn't help but ask.

"Bravery? No, I don't think so." Aefor chuckled. "It is not brave to step over the edge of an endless canyon. It is simply foolish. No, I have been guarding this vault for many, many years and, I have to say, I was glad to see you arrive. I used what little power I have left to create a bridge for you to pass. You may find that it is no longer there when you leave. Alas, my strength is not what it once was." Again, he smiled and chuckled. Arthur couldn't help but think that he wasn't taking the situation as seriously as he should. "Whilst it is always nice to have company after such a long time, I fear that you are not here with glad tidings and for idle chit-chat."

"Unfortunately, we are not." There was no disguising the irritation in Snudge's voice. He was clearly as annoyed as Arthur at the lack of urgency in the old elf's manner. "There is a darkness rising again in the south. A great war is coming, and we shall need all of the help that we can get. We had heard that the elves of Kanthor were returning, but…" The goblin leader waved his arm to take in the sleeping elves.

"My dear goblin," the elf suddenly took on a more serious tone, "we never left. Why should we leave our home? Instead, we went to sleep until the day arrives when there is no darkness left to fight and we can continue to live our lives in peace."

"Folly!" Geldrig's booming voice seemed to fill the cavern. "There will never be peace, not completely. All we can do is push back against the darkness whenever it comes."

"I wonder what it is about the south." Aefor's musing caught them all off guard. "You say that the darkness is rising in the south? It's always the south. I wonder if it has something to do with the weather. Or perhaps it is something to do with the darkness that fled there so long ago." He spoke almost to himself, and nobody graced him with an answer. "No matter. I have sworn an oath to only wake my people when the darkness has passed."

"There is no time to argue." Snudge was clearly angry, and he made no effort to whisper. Echoes merged into echoes as he shouted. "This war will destroy our world. There will be no chance of peace when this is done, there will be no lightness left, only shadow."

"We fought for many years against the darkness and lost many noble elves. Our time for fighting has gone. Let us sleep our days away. Sometimes the light can only be seen in the darkest of times."

"There is a sorcerer, Damphir. He has raised an army of the dead."

"Damphir?" Suddenly the elf looked worried.

"You know of him?"

"He was foretold. His legend had slipped out of memory long before we went to sleep. He is here?"

"And he has Akeldama."

The old elf sighed and leaned against his stick. "Leave us. I must think on this. If things are as you say, then these are grave times indeed. I shall wake Aymeric, the last King of Kanthor, and I shall seek his advice. You may rest in the keep until I have my answer."

Snudge bowed his thanks and turned and led Arthur and the others back up the towering staircase. Once again, the specks of light and floating magic guided their way and before too long they were back in the dusty keep. They laid out their beds, and Arthur tried his hardest to sleep under his blanket.

Arthur woke suddenly to the sound of rustling reeds next to his head. He reached quickly for Siorraidh, but his hand was gripped tightly by thin, cold fingers. The strength in the arm was surprising, but he soon relaxed when he heard the voice of Aefor whispering. "Don't fear, Arthur. It is only me." Even in the darkness, Arthur could sense the smile on the elf's face. For somebody with such a serious task, he appeared to take nothing too seriously. Arthur felt immediately at ease in his presence.

"Why are you here? Have you woken the king?" Arthur asked as he sat up and rubbed the sleep from his eyes.

"Patience. It is not a quick task to wake somebody up from such a deep sleep. I have read the incantations, mixed the herbs that need to be mixed and read the prayers that need to be said. All in good time. For now, I wish to talk to you a little more of the history of Ithilmir."

Arthur sat up straighter, eager to learn whatever he could. He nodded for the elf to continue. "You know of the Dark Queen Camarina, I assume. The first human to arrive on Ithilmir many years ago?"

"That is what Snudge has told us. My friend Skye, she helped to defeat her not too long ago."

"Correct. And that is as much as Snudge believes to be true. However, he is both right and very, very wrong. Carmine, Queen Camarina's name before she rose to power, was the first human to arrive here from your world and yet, she was not the first human on Ithilmir by a long way."

Arthur was stunned. If what the elf was saying was true, how long had humans been on Ithilmir?

"The race of men continues to live in the furthest reaches of the Frozen Wastelands in the south. It is said to be so cold there that blood freezes as they cut down their enemies. They are cold, hard people, but they are men, true enough. Nobody knows where they came from. They may have arrived as travellers from your world, or they may have risen from the ashes of the Before Time along with the elves and the Shrunken. We are not so different after all, men and elves."

"Are they still there? These other humans?"

"Who knows? There used to be reports of raids into the north for our gold and our cattle, but they haven't been heard of for hundreds of years. They may still be there, trapped in their frozen hell, or they may have moved even further south into the great unknown lands that lay beyond the ice. Or they may have died out and disappeared forever and good riddance to them."

"Why?" Arthur asked.

"The race of men is corrupt and evil, and darkness is in their soul. When the Shrunken found Akeldama, it was bad, terrible in fact, but it was nothing to the devastation that would have been caused had men found it."

"Is that what you meant by the darkness that fled to the south?"

"Correct. When they finally stopped their raids on the north and fled forever to their wastelands, the darkness seemed to leave with them. The Shrunken seemed to lose their strength, and we were able to attack them swiftly and with devastating effect. If the Nelapsi hadn't come along and stolen the orb, we would have defeated darkness for good. Anyway, that is enough talking for tonight. Get to sleep and we shall see what Aymeric has to say in the morning."

Aefor bowed low and made his way back down through the trapdoor. Arthur didn't even attempt to get to sleep. His mind was filled with great armies of men running wild over Ithilmir and destroying everything in their path.

An Attack Of Crows

"It's just a story told to scare young children, that's all. There are no men on Ithilmir, Arthur." Arthur had barely slept all night and told Snudge the story of the men in the south as soon as the goblin leader had woken up. He'd scoffed at the idea and immediately told Arthur to concentrate on the matter at hand.

"But what if it is true? What if there really are more humans here on Ithilmir?"

"What if I told you that dragons and vampires and, for that matter, goblins, lived somewhere on Earth? Would you believe me?"

"No, but—"

"Exactly. It's preposterous. We have far more important things to be dealing with rather than the silly fantasies of the elves. I have half a mind to have a strong word with Aefor. He had no business filling your head with such nonsense."

Arthur was angry. How could Snudge know for sure that there were no men further south? He didn't see the sense in arguing any further. He knew he'd get nowhere, so he simply packed up his bedding and sat sulking under his cloak. For the next few hours, nothing happened and Arthur soon grew bored. He took to wandering the dusty keep looking for anything to keep his mind busy.

Several large braziers had been lit in the middle of the floor and the heat soon became uncomfortable, but they were under strict orders from Snudge not to leave the keep. Even though the magic that allowed them to pass over the abyss had been removed, there was no saying where the eyes of Damphir could see, and Snudge didn't want to risk exposing their mission before they had to.

After many hours had passed and just as Arthur's stomach was starting to protest about the absence of food, the trapdoor slowly opened and the smiling head of Aefor emerged. He made his way out into the keep and lowered the door behind him with his usual slowness, and it was all Arthur could do not to scream out in anger, so desperate was he for any news.

Snudge saved him the job, however, when he said

with undisguised irritation, "Well? What has your king said?"

Aefor smiled and sat down in front of them before he made any effort to speak. "Be calm, my goblin friend. Aymeric has awakened, and we have spoken at length. He has agreed, and I must say it is against my better judgement, that something must be done to defeat the sorcerer Damphir. Throughout the night we have been receiving news from our many eyes in the world, many of whom have been waiting for the waking of the elves much longer than you can imagine. The news that they bring is not good, worse even than you know.

"Damphir possesses Akeldama, this is certain. He has moved into the relics of Horongor, many days' march to the east of us here in Kanthor. Queen Camarina found her way to him not too long ago in her quest to regain Akeldama. He tricked her into agreeing to marry him under the guise of sharing the power of Akeldama. Instead, he killed her and absorbed her power. It is a trick he has used before to great effect. It is part of the reason why he is so strong and has lived for so many years."

"How do you know all of this?" Geldrig asked. Arthur could hear the concern in his voice. Snudge looked dumbstruck but kept quiet.

"He had a slave. A sneaky and untrustworthy hobgoblin calling himself Salismir. It was he who first stole the orb from Queen Camarina in the south. For a while, he was its master, so far as anyone can call themselves a master of such evil. He found his way to Horongor and relative safety, or so he thought. Damphir soon found him and took the stone for his own. There is no doubt that somebody so evil could sense the whereabouts of Akeldama, and no doubt it drew him to it.

"At some point, the wretch creature fled his new master. Our spies picked him up on the outskirts of the Orctooth mountains and he told them all he knew."

"What became of him?" asked Snowbroth. "Somebody marked with the curse of Akeldama could surely not be allowed to live."

"He has no hands and his mind is a shell. Our spies let him loose into the mountains again. He will no doubt die before long. There was no need to hurry his passing." Snowbroth snorted his disdain for their weakness but said nothing. "Aymeric has instructed me to wake the Kanthor from their sleep. This is no small task and will take some time, but you have your army, Snudge. I hope that you realise how lucky you are."

"Thank you. I hope you realise how lucky you are

that we found you before the darkness. History and allegiances aside, we are in a battle for our world, and it will soon be time for every leader to decide how they want to be remembered. Did they help rid the world of this darkness or did they sit idly by and allow the shadows to reign forever. Aymeric will know that he has made the right choice soon enough. The army of darkness must be met before another winter falls. Otherwise, I fear we shall never see another spring."

"I sincerely hope that you are wrong, Snudge, for the sake of us all. However, I fear that you may well be right. For now, I must ask that you show us a little more patience whilst we do what must be done. Aymeric has agreed for me to open the royal chambers in the West Tower, and you may make up your lodgings there until we are ready. Do not worry too much just yet. We have a little time. We will march within a week. Damphir has not left Horongor yet and doesn't appear to be in a rush to do so. Use the little time that we have to rest and prepare yourself."

Aefor guided Arthur and his friends to the wooden door that led out onto the market square. "I will take you to your lodgings, but then I must return to assist Aymeric. It is left to me to do what needs to be done next. The quicker I can cast the magic, the sooner we will be on our way."

The heavy doors swung open without a sound, and Arthur had to shield his eyes from the bright sunlight that streamed in. Once they had all recovered their sight, they stepped out into the market square. Before they even had chance to take in their surroundings, Aefor was screaming at them "Run!" and had started to sprint across the cobbles at a speed that belied his age. As they chased after their guide, Arthur noticed why they were running. A thousand black crows lined every wall, each one as big as an eagle. Thousands of beady shadowed eyes stared down at them from their perches and then they attacked. "They're spies for Damphir. He knows we are here!" Aefor continued to shout as he ran. His long elven legs outpaced even Geldrig. Before long, they had become separated from their guide.

The crows were all in flight, circling the square in ever-tightening circles. The noise was deafening, a thousand calls to attack encouraging each other into a frenzy. Occasionally, one of the birds would break from the pack and swoop down like a bomb towards the group. Some tried to attack with their beaks. Other crows tried to use their razor-sharp talons to take the scalps from their heads, but these were easier to see coming and bat away with their swords.

Arthur screamed as one managed to take a bite out

of his arm before he threw the bird to the ground. Before he could react, Geldrig stamped down hard. "One down, a thousand more to go," the Felmir said with an ironic grunt.

They had stopped running, and Snudge had ordered them into a tight circle with their swords drawn. Aefor was nowhere to be seen. The crows were flying low, swirling in the air and forming a black mist as they almost scraped the ground with their wings. As they got lower, the attacks increased, and Arthur's arms started to tire as he fought back wave after wave of beaks and talons. The air was thick with feathers that choked his lungs and caused his eyes to stream. The pressure was unrelenting. The birds were difficult to kill; Arthur noticed with dismay that even seasoned warriors like Geldrig and Curglaff were lucky if they did anything other than bat the birds away. Every time a bird was killed, it was met with a shout of triumph, but a dozen more soon took its place.

Arthur felt like his arms were filling with lead and his lunges became weaker and lower with each attack. Eventually, he struggled to raise his sword above his neck and, in anger, he threw it to the ground. Without its extra weight, he could swing his arms more freely and waved them around his head as though the crows were simply mosquitoes annoying him on the beach.

Without his sword, though, his arms were vulnerable and he screamed in pain as a talon sliced through his forearm and he felt his blood rush over his hand. He grabbed at it with his other hand and squeezed hard to stem the flow, but that left his face open to his latest attacker. He saw a black blur before he felt the full force of the bird hitting him in the face. He howled as the bird pecked and scratched and felt something sharp cut across his eyelid. He managed to roll over and shake himself to his feet. His attacker was long gone back into the angry swarm, but he suddenly felt weak. His knees buckled under him, and he fell hard to the cobbles. He could feel the cold stones against his cheek and the warmth of his blood flowing from his face.

Then, Arthur saw a thin river of silver flowing between the cobblestones, filling in the cracks and illuminating the marketplace. He blinked in the brightness, but watched as the silver web rose like a fishing net and, within it, he saw the murder of crows trapped and entangled. In such a confined space, they turned on each other in a deafening row. Once the net had captured those that had been too slow or too vicious to flee, it collapsed in on itself with a sound like thunder and the square was plunged into silence.

Nothing remained of the crows except for a few feathers floating on the soft breeze and a few lucky birds that had escaped the net. They fluttered onto the battlements of the tallest towers before calling out a warning and disappearing into the forest.

Gentle hands picked Arthur up and tended and bound his wounds. A patch was tied over his left eye and voices reassured him that wouldn't lose his sight. He struggled to place any of them until he looked up and saw Aefor standing over him with his usual wide smile. He had suffered in the battle as well. His face was crossed with deep cut, and he'd lost a finger, something that he proudly showed off and laughed as Arthur paled at the sight.

"We were very lucky to escape such an attack," Aefor said. His tone didn't match his smile. "Not lucky enough, though. Some of his birds escaped and will tell him of what they saw. He will soon know that the elves are woken and that you are here with us. He must know that war is coming and he will prepare.

"If there was any doubting the strength of his army, we now know that it is not only the dead that Damphir controls. From this point forward, we must assume that he has eyes and ears wherever we go and that any creatures may be turned against us. Your warning has come just in time, Snudge. I must report back to Aymeric and insist that we leave as soon as possible."

True to his word, Aefor showed Arthur and the others to their rooms within the West Tower and immediately left to consult with King Aymeric. Under other circumstances, Arthur would have relished the large, stuffed mattress and comfortable sheets, but now all he could think about was what he had been dragged into that fateful day in Skye's bedroom. When he eventually fell asleep, his dreams were filled with images of Skye being attacked by swarms of birds as she screamed out for him to help her.

Faileas

Skye blinked and braced for the impact of the crossbow bolt, but it never came. She opened her eyes and looked up into the face of her attacker. He was on his knees howling in pain and desperately trying to pull a thick wooden bolt from his shoulder. His own crossbow lay some distance away from him on the deck of the ship, its bolt still securely in place. Seeing Skye, he pushed himself to his feet and ran cursing into the darkness. Just as Skye was thanking her lucky stars and wondering what had happened, a familiar face appeared over the edge of the deck.

"Weard!" Skye cried out loudly, almost letting go of the wooden ladder in her excitement. She quickly climbed the last few rungs of the ladder and grabbed the goblin's outstretched hand to pull herself up onto the deck and embraced her friend. "I'm so sorry for what I said. I didn't mean it. Well, I did, but I'm still sorry. When I couldn't find you, when I thought you were…" She trailed off and caught Weard's eye. "Where have you been? I thought you were dead?"

"At times I wished I was. After the ship was attacked, I ended up in the sea, far adrift from the rest of you. There wasn't much near me, but I managed to grab hold of some flotsam to keep my head above water. It was colder than I've ever felt, but we goblins are a tough bunch and I soldiered through until at last the current washed me ashore somewhere north of Draconia where the mountains cast out into the sea like the open mouth of a dragon.

"The sea took a lot from me. I'm weak, Skye, too weak to join you on the next part of your journey. But it's important you know what happened here. The attack of the kraken was unlucky, but the attack tonight was not a coincidence. The wretch that killed our friend Roke and who so nearly killed you is a servant of the evil sorcerer Damphir."

"Emperor Ki mentioned him when we spoke before," Skye said, suddenly remembering the name.

"Exactly. It could just be coincidence that his minions are here tonight just as you arrive, or it could be something more sinister."

"You don't think that Emperor Ki would betray us,

do you?"

"I don't know. I made no secret of my distrust of the emperor, and I'm still not sure where his loyalties lie. As soon as I have seen you safely away, I will pass on a message to Snudge. He will want to know this latest development. If Damphir has agents this far abroad, then he is much stronger and much more confident than we all feared."

A loud noise erupted behind Weard, and a dozen more soldiers appeared on the deck. Each one was dressed in the same thick black cloak that her attacker had worn, and each one had a face covered in rotten skin that hung from their dead skull. Some were carrying long swords whilst others swung heavy, spiked maces or giant war hammers. Only one had a single, piercing blue eye, and he walked with a stiff gait. Skye was pleased to see the wooden shaft still protruded from his shoulder.

"You must go now before they attack." Weard shimmied down the ladder and cut the ropes that held the small wooden boat in place. It splashed into the surf below but bobbed on the waves waiting for Skye. She gave her friend a quick hug and scrambled down the ladder as quickly as she could before leaping for the boat. She fell short and plunged into the icy blackness. She felt her breath forced from her body and struggled to the surface in time to see Weard stand tall and place her hands together.

As the swarm of undead soldiers descended upon her, Skye smiled as the healer stretched her hands apart and engulfed herself in a pale blue sphere. It was a trick she'd seen her do many times before and allowed her to disappear before appearing somewhere else. Back in the days before the war, Weard had used it mainly as a parlour trick to entertain Skye and the younger goblins, but Skye had secretly wondered whether this was how Weard had managed to visit Earth.

With a crack, the light disappeared along with the goblin.

The small boat rocked precariously when Skye grabbed onto the side, but mercifully it stayed upright whilst she pulled herself into the relative dryness of the hull.

A pair of wooden oars had been wedged under the plank that would serve as her seat and Skye tried desperately to free them with numb fingers. All the while she was expecting to hear the thud of a crossbow releasing a bolt towards her, but it never came.

Suddenly, the oars sprang free, and Skye locked them into the rests and plunged the ends into the water. She had no time to think about a rhythm. She just swung the oars up and down, up and down as fast as she could to try to get away. Looking back towards the deck, the soldiers were pacing back and forth screaming with rage. A single dark shadow stood on the bow of the ship watching her leave. There was a single point of blue in the darkness.

Once she was out of bow range, Skye reached under the seat for the thick woollen blanket that she had seen whilst she freed the oars and wrapped it around her shoulders. Despite the thickness of the wool, she still felt frozen to the bone, and a chill unrelated to the weather washed over her whenever she glanced up at the *Serpensis*.

The boat was stable enough, especially once Skye slowed her rowing down and fell into a relaxed rhythm. She had no idea where she was heading. She knew that there was another town a little further south and along the coast, and so she decided to head that way. If what Weard had said was true, and Emperor Ki had betrayed them to Damphir, then she needed to be as far away as possible as quickly as possible. She also needed to be alone. That way, she hoped, she'd be able to disappear into the crowds more easily.

It took a long while and Skye's arms were sore and leaden, but eventually, she was far enough away from Draconia that the blue eye in the darkness disappeared. Once she felt like she wasn't being watched anymore, she allowed herself to rest back into the curve of the boats hull and close her eyes. She must have fallen asleep because she soon felt the familiar feel of the Shadowlands pulling her closer.

A cloying mist filled the endless plains. Skye made her way down from a rocky precipice and into the white sea below. The mist didn't move when she pushed her way through it. Nothing reacted to her touch. It was a constant reminder that this was all a dream. Skye knew better than to assume that this meant that it was any less real. Normally, spirits would appear and talk to her, and she had grown so accustomed to this happening that it took her a while to realise that something was different this time.

Skye pushed further forwards into the barren landscape, expecting at any point for the mist to form into the souls of dead goblins, but nothing happened. At one point she stumbled on her ankle and her old wound throbbed painfully. There was no sound, even the sound of her feet on the rough grit underfoot seemed to be sucked into nothingness. It struck Skye that it was darker than normal. Even though it was called the Shadowlands, the white mist had always seemed to reflect light into the darkest corners whenever Skye was here. Normally there was never darkness. The landscape was always more grey and white than black. And yet this time, there was undeniable darkness. It wasn't obvious, just shadows underneath the mountains and hidden behind the towering rocks that sprung from the mist like teeth.

The darkness seemed to have a life of its own. Now that Skye knew what was wrong, what she was looking for, she started to pay more attention. Wherever she looked, the shadows seemed to twist and recoil away from her gaze. She could sense the fear in the air. Something was here with her, hidden away but watching and waiting. The back of her neck tingled but each time she spun around she was still alone.

Further into the wasteland, the mist rose higher. Soon it reached Skye's neck, and she stopped, afraid to go any deeper. She closed her eyes, but still she saw out into the endless whiteness.

Then the voice came out of the air. "Welcome, Skye Thistle. I have watched you for a long time, longer even than you have existed. You have been a mark on this world for thousands of years." The voice was strong and powerful and deep, but there was a hint of fear in there as well. Whoever was speaking to her wasn't sure what she might do. She stood very still and fought her body's natural desire to turn around. She knew there would be nothing behind her anyway. The voice sounded as though it had come from far away.

"Who are you?" she asked calmly. She was surprised that her voice didn't break until she realised that she wasn't actually nervous. This was only a dream, after all. And then she remembered how much her ankle had hurt when she'd stumbled. Dreams didn't hurt.

Silence fell again. It felt to Skye like a blanket was resting over the valley deadening any noise. As she stood and watched, the white mist slowly started to swirl and flow in an unfelt wind. It rose higher and surrounded her head and obscured her vision. She held her hands to her face to shield herself though she didn't know why. The mist never touched her.

Here and there, shadows darted through the swirling void, like dark fishes in an ethereal pond. Every now and then they'd merge with other shadows and grow larger. Sometimes they'd take on vague shapes that were both recognisable and yet alien. Skye allowed her hands to drop and she spun on her heels. All around her, shadows were joining and merging and growing until there was only blackness. The mist had disappeared leaving Skye in darkness. She waved her hands in front of her face, but there was nothing but the endless void.

The voice spoke again. "You are strong. I have seen what you have achieved so far. There are many here in the Shadowlands who you put here." In front of Skye, a small army of white, ghostly soldiers floated into view. Each one was barely a foot high. "The Shadowed Eye looks favourably on you as well. You would do great things together. You are powerful even without it, but, together, the world would tremble." Skye noticed the fear voice again. It wasn't obvious. The speaker was hiding it well, but it was there all the same.

"Show me who you are. Or are you too afraid of me?"

A storm rose in the shadow, and it swirled away from Skye before re-forming in front of her. It took the shape of an enormous dragon, a hundred feet high and broad as an elephant. A long tail that was tipped with vicious spikes whipped back and forth in the distance sending rocks through the air whenever it connected. Rows of pale blue and white plates made entirely of ice ran the length of the creature's long, serpentine spine and along its neck as thick as Skye's body before forming a crown on top of its snarling head. Fierce blue eyes burned with cold flames. Everything that wasn't ice was made up of flickering shadows. There were no defined edges to the beast. It flowed as it moved and darkness leaked out of its body.

As Skye watched, the dragon lunged forwards, mouth open and icy teeth bared, and stopped an inch from her face. She could feel the beast's breath against her cheeks. It was freezing cold and painful as it touched her skin. She didn't flinch, though. Whatever this monster was, she knew that it was afraid of her. If she cowered away, it might lose that fear and attack.

"Afraid?" This time the voice was angry, and it echoed through the mountains. There was no mistaking where it came from, either. The head snapped and bit the air. Its thin, snake-like tongue slipped between its teeth and slowly slid across Skye's forehead. It burnt with cold wherever it touched, and she felt her skin blister, but she stood still as the mountains and stared deep into the blue eyes. "I am not afraid of anything, Skye Thistle. Least of all a little girl."

"Then tell me your name."

"I am Faileas. I am the guardian of Mithrostan, the portal to the Shadowlands. Nobody enters without passing through me, and yet here you are, and here you have been, many times without even knowing who I am. Am I to allow this trespassing to continue?"

"I didn't choose to come here. It just happened. I didn't want any of this. I didn't want to kill goblins or anything else, and I didn't want to have whatever power it is that I have. But I'm not afraid of you, either."

"And why is that?" Faileas pulled his head back, and Skye saw him look confused for a moment.

"If you wanted me dead, you'd have killed me before now. You said you've been watching me for a long time. You know where I've been and what I've done and what I'm capable of. I think you need something from me."

Faileas cocked his head and looked curiously down at Skye. "Not need. I don't *need* anything. I *desire*. I have a deal for you, Skye. I want to send you home."

Eragor

It took Aefor and King Aymeric a little less than a week to raise and ready the rest of the elven army, and Arthur had started to move more freely after the attack of the crows. His eye had scabbed and was still bruised, bloodied and bandaged, but he had adapted to fighting with one eye after many hours practising in the market square with Brack and the other goblins. Geldrig and Snudge often sat on the old carts and watched and guffawed whenever Arthur was sent tumbling to the ground by one of the others.

Their laughs spurred him on, and soon he was sending Curglaff and Snowbroth into the dust. He never managed to get the better of Brack, though. The small goblin was too quick and nimble, but Arthur swore he would floor him before the adventure was done.

All the time they fought, they kept one eye fixed on the skies overhead. By the third day, they grew used to the crows visiting them on the battlements, but they still used them for target practise whenever they could. Arthur soon earned a reputation as a top shot with a thrown cobblestone, and he would often run a victory lap around the square whenever he sent one of the birds tumbling with a loud explosion of noise and feathers.

Eventually, as dawn broke on the sixth day, Aefor met with Snudge, and word came out that they were to march for Eragor at noon. The plan was to march hard and reach the old city by nightfall and start to build a base from which to attack Damphir at Horongor. Historically, the Burnt Fort was not built for strength and would be easy to break in a siege; however, with Damphir's powers and his army of the dead, King Aymeric wanted somewhere to retreat to if their siege dragged on for months or they came under attack.

"Remember," Snudge warned Arthur and the others as they readied themselves to leave, "if we can contain Damphir in Horongor, then the dark power of Akeldama is also contained. Right now, he is the biggest threat to our world. In time, even he will grow hungry and be forced to leave his hideout. We can defeat him. But be careful."

They set out for Eragor under a cloudless sky. It wasn't long before Arthur was hot and bothered. The pace was intense, and he struggled to keep up with everyone. More times than he was comfortable with, Geldrig picked him up and planted him firmly on his shoulders with a grumble. As much as he moaned, the Felmir never asked Arthur to walk until Arthur told him that he felt he could keep up for a while.

Food was sometimes passed along the cavalcade, but they never stopped or rested. King Aymeric rode a stunning white stallion at the head of the procession along with his mounted guards, but the rest of the elves were on foot. They never seemed to tire, and Arthur begrudged their apparent endless energy.

Sooner than Arthur hoped, the sun started to set and dusk blanketed the land. As far as he could tell, they were nowhere near Eragor or any other big city, for that matter. They'd been meandering along a winding track between tall grasses getting higher and higher with each step for hours. All Arthur could see in every direction was grass. Even on top of Geldrig's shoulders, the thick, bulbous seed heads obscured his vision.

His world was split into two colours; the greens of the grass and the eye-aching blue of the sky above. At least dusk brought some respite from the heat, but it also brought out the insects. Crickets filled the darkening air with their raucous songs, and midges started to bite any area of exposed skin. It took all of Arthur's courage not to burst into tears and demand they set up camp.

Just as he was about to snap, a call came from the head of the line that they had spotted Eragor. Arthur's spirits lifted instantly. Along with the rest of the soldiers, he sprinted to catch up with King Aymeric to see the magical city for himself. The tall grass ended at the crest of the hill and beyond lay an enormous stone city. Eragor had been built from the local red stone, and it glowed warmly in the growing darkness. It seemed to radiate with a brightness that belied the time of day, as though it had stored up the sunlight and was now releasing it as a beacon of hope for the weary travellers.

Almost as one, each and every elf, Felmir, goblin and human raced out of the grass towards the city. The gates were unlocked, and Geldrig made short work of pushing them open despite the protests of the long-rusted hinges.

They opened onto an octagonal courtyard lined on six sides with two rows of squat red houses. Each row had three dozen such houses, all painted with amazing, abstract artwork. Colourful swirls and lines crisscrossed the red stone forming patterns and ornate designs that added yet more light and energy to the city.

In the middle of the courtyard was an octagonal fountain. The eight short walls contained a crystal clear pool of water, and a jet of water erupted high into the sky before crashing back noisily. On one side of the pool, a stone spout allowed a slow trickle of water to escape into a shallow rill. The rill was only a foot wide and maybe a few inches deep, but it had been coloured black, and the water served as a mirror to reflect back all of the colour and light. As the water flowed from the fountain, it spiralled outwards until it reached the first row of houses where it detoured between the rows and disappeared beyond the thick outer walls of the city.

"It's truly beautiful, isn't it?" Aefor asked Arthur, noticing his look of wonder and wide-open eyes. Arthur simply nodded. "The fountain is fed by a natural spring that erupts deep under the ground, so I'm told. It certainly looks like magic to me. Eragor was originally built by men, before they fled to the south. I know Snudge has told you it is nothing but a fairy tale," he said quickly before Arthur could argue. "Look around you. This is evidence that men were here. They built this. Of course," now the elf had his usual glint in his eye, "when they built it, it was nothing but a dull red city. Practical and strong, but there was no love or magic here. When the elves, my ancestors, moved in, we had a lot of redecorating to do!"

Arthur couldn't help but laugh at the elf's poor joke, but he still wasn't sure whether he believed him about there being an ancient race of men somewhere on Ithilmir. It just didn't seem possible.

"What's through there?" Arthur pointed to another large gate set into the wall on the opposite side of the courtyard. The gated walls were the only ones not lined with houses.

"That leads to High Town. Here, we are in Low Town, where the citizens who worked within the city would live. At its busiest, there could be more than a thousand people living here. Often the houses were filled by two or more families who shared the space as best they could. Sometimes they'd break out and set up camps in the courtyard. Outside these walls is some of the best farmland and richest mines in the north. Every day men and women would head out to sow or plough or whatever it is that people do on farms and every night produce would come back through the gates. It wouldn't stay for long before being sent out to sell to other cities. It was a very rich city, and the elves prospered because of it."

"What happened?" Arthur asked.

"Wherever you have that many people living so close together, disease will always be a risk. Long ago, a plague fell over Eragor. Elves fell ill overnight and were dead by the morning. Their bodies erupted in boils and their skin started to blister. Many said they felt that their blood was boiling in their veins, but most were too ill to talk at all. Within a month the entire city was dead. We cleared out our dead and left the city to the shadows. Nobody dared to live here again."

A shiver ran down Arthur's spine at the thought of all that death in such a beautiful place. "What's in High Town?"

"That's the business end of the city. There's the keep for all of the food and weapons and other things that a thriving city needs to keep safe. There's the Palace of Apostles where our most gifted mages would train and live. Nobody other than the most magical elves ever set foot in the Palace. There is also a town hall and the necropolis for the powerful dead. Perhaps the most important building in High Town is the church."

"I didn't think elves were religious."

"We are not. The church was built before the elves arrived." Aefor looked knowingly at Arthur who stood and looked concerned. "Arthur, it is not my place to make you believe what I tell you. That is for you to decide. All I ask is that you listen to what I say and consider it. Will you do this?"

Arthur nodded. "Can I see High Town?"

"Indeed. I believe that King Aymeric and your friends have already headed that way whilst we've been talking. The king won't want to wait around for long before attacking Damphir. His plan has always been to leave tomorrow at first light. So maybe we should follow our leaders and see what they would have us do tonight? If, on the way, we happen to take a tour of High Town, then so be it."

Arthur laughed again at the elf's sense of humour and followed him through the second set of gates. The church had been built directly inside High Town so that the big stone steps that led to the imposing wooden doors were all that was seen when stepping through the gates. The church was built on a scale to rival any back home on Earth and the tall spires and steeply pitched roof hit Arthur with such a sense of familiarity that he nearly fell to his knees.

Brilliant stained glass windows punched through the side of the dark stone, and a large bell swung gently in the breeze at the top of a thin tower to the rear of the church. There was no mistaking the fact that this church had been built by men. It was too familiar to have been anything else. Arthur was convinced that, no matter how it had happened, and whether or not they still lived, humans had been on Ithilmir for a very long time.

A Blue Eye

Paper erupted from Emperor Ki's desk. The emperor stormed across the austere room in the nondescript inn on the outskirts of Draconia and stood glaring out of the window, daring the world to answer back.

"How dare they attack us aboard my ship?" he screamed at the elf who had brought him his supper. The elf cowered, her golden hair and steel eyes flaring brightly in the darkness of the cabin, but said nothing. "Where is Skye?"

"We don't know. They attacked her as she slept. They killed Roke."

"Who the hell were they? Why are they here?"

At that moment, the door was thrust open with such force that it was torn from its hinges and splinters of wood flew across the room and shattered the window.

Emperor Ki and the servant ducked as quickly as they could, but they were still showered in broken pieces of glass. Sunlight streamed through the gaping doorway and picked out the silhouette of a towering warrior.

"We are the Azrul," the silhouette said. "Our reason for wanting that filthy human is none of your business. I am here for you now."

The elf leapt to her feet and rushed towards the doorway. A single blue eye flickered for a moment, and there was a sound like a wet sack being beaten against a tree trunk as the attacker struck her down. She tumbled across the room and lay still. Her bones were broken beyond repair, and her eyes stared emptily into the distance. Emperor Ki huddled into the corner shaking.

"My master, Damphir, orders you to join him in battle. The girl is dead. There is nothing left for you to fight for. He is not a man to take no for an answer."

Emperor Ki watched as the Azrul soldier moved around the room. He limped slightly, and his sword arm seemed stiff. There was an open wound through his shoulder though there was no blood. The soldier had spilt his blood long ago. He turned his one glowing eye on the emperor.

"What is in it for me?" the emperor asked. "Why should I trust you or your master? I have an army here ready to destroy you yet you dare to enter my room alone?"

The creature shrugged his shoulders. "Why don't you call them?" Before Emperor Ki could answer, the cold dead fingers of his attacker were wrapped around his neck as he was thrust against the wall. A soft breeze blew through the shattered window beside him.

He felt the bones cutting into his skin. A trickle of blood crept towards his collar. He smelled the putrid breath and recoiled at the sight of the hollow eye socket, empty but for the spiralling blue vortex. He struggled to breathe. His lungs burnt as he desperately tried to gulp down some air, but the grip was too tight. His arms and legs fell limp and numb, his body desperately pumping oxygen to his brain. Then freedom as the creature released its grip and turned around. The wall scraped against his back, and he thumped to the floor and greedily gasped and wheezed. Overhead he heard the Azrul warrior chuckling to himself.

"You are weak, emperor. Your army is weak. I could kill you tonight, and nobody would ever dare to question my master or me."

"Why does he want me? If my army is so weak, what use am I?"

"I did not ask. I cannot see a reason to allow a worm like you into our ranks, but my master has his ways, and he is *never* wrong."

"What happened to your shoulder?" Emperor Ki grabbed hold of the window frame and pulled himself to his feet.

The warrior winced at the mention of his wound. "Don't worry yourself with my injuries. It will heal."

The emperor made a mental note. They could be wounded. They may still be as strong as iron, but anything that could be wounded could be weakened. "What will happen if I choose not to bend my knee to Damphir?"

For a while, nothing happened. Emperor Ki watched as the decrepit creature limped over to the window on the other side of the room and swung it open. He whistled into the darkness. The emperor had to strain his ears, but he soon heard a soft, leathery sound of something big beating against the wind, and then it was on top of them and enormous, scaled feet with claws as long as his own arms were crashing through the timber ceiling and splintering the floorboards underfoot. There wasn't enough space in the room for the dragon, and it exploded out into the rest of the inn.

Screams from the ground floor meant at least some were escaping into the darkness but, for Emperor Ki, there was no escape. The dragon turned its head to and fro trying to focus on its tiny prey. The emperor tried to dig his shoulder blades into the wall but felt himself leaning out of the broken window. The air shimmered with the heat of the dragon's breath. Every time it yawned, Emperor Ki winced and waited for death.

The Azrul soldier walked over to the dragon and tenderly stroked its neck. Tiny flames leapt from its nostrils and threatened to burn what was left of the inn to the ground. Then it opened its mouth wide and took a deep breath. Emperor Ki covered his face against the heat and in doing so covered his eyes. He heard a soft hiss and felt his skin burn and blister, but it wasn't the death he had expected. He forced his eyes open and saw the dragon spitting fire towards the Azrul soldier.

When the flames died down, there was nothing left but bone. The curtains crackled and were engulfed in fire and soon the entire room was ablaze. The Azrul emerged from the other side of the yellow and orange wall and stepped up to Emperor Ki. There was no flesh left on his body. It had all been stripped away. The bones that remained were charred and blackened, but he still exuded strength. As if to prove this, he grabbed Emperor Ki by his cloak and lifted him until they were face to face.

"You want to know what will happen if you say

no?" the warrior growled. "There is no alternative." With that, he threw Emperor Ki from the burning building. The walls of the inn spiralled sickeningly as he fell until he landed with a crash in the icy blackness of the dock. The cold water at once soothed his burned flesh and seared his lungs, but he fought his way to the surface and dragged his injured body to the shore. He looked up and watched as the sky burned orange. He knew the path he had to take.

He already felt responsible for Roke's death. If what the soldier had said was true and Skye was also dead, then there seemed to be little hope. He had to lead his army to Crazak D'Ur but not to fight with Damphir, to lead an army against him. Unfortunately, that meant heading through Keredor's Pass, a desolate and unwelcoming place.

The water froze his limbs, but he didn't dare climb back up onto the wharf until he was sure that the Azrul had left. Once he saw the dragon flying off into the night, he scrambled up the stone wall and grabbed the nearest elf that he could. He ordered him to fetch all of the captains and to report to his chambers on board the *Serpensis*. He had to tell them of his new plan.

Caught

Skye swallowed hard and looked up into the shadowed face of Faileas, the large dragon that guarded the Shadowlands. For the first time since he had appeared in front of her, she felt nervous. Going home was everything that she had wanted since Weard had told her that the spyglass had been destroyed. Emperor Ki had mentioned using Akeldama to return home, but the cost had been high.

To embrace the power of something that had caused so much evil would test Skye's strength in ways that she had never been tested before. And what of the men that the emperor had spoken of? He spoke as though their existence would mean that Skye could control the stone. After all, they were the ones who controlled it in the first place. But he'd also said that they had succumbed to its power and been punished for their greed. What if Skye lost control?

Here she was being offered a way home without any of those strings. A free pass back to her life.

"And what is the deal?" she made sure she sounded calmer than she felt. This was no time to show weakness.

"You return home now and never return."

"And Arthur? You will send him home as well?"

Faileas nodded. "He will return with you."

"Why?"

"My reasons are my own."

"What will happen to my friends? They need me to fight alongside them. You said it yourself. With the power of Akeldama, I can destroy the evil that is rising."

"Many of your friends end up here with me. Look at Brabble. It seems that fighting alongside you is not good for their health."

Skye stood and thought. Faileas was right. So far she had achieved nothing, and her friends were still dying. But she knew she still had a purpose on Ithilmir. She needed to do what she had set out to do before she returned home. If that meant risking her soul with Akeldama or risking not being able to return at all, then that would be the price she'd have to pay. To leave now and sacrifice the souls of her friends who had trusted her with their war was a price she wasn't willing to pay.

"No," Skye whispered.

Faileas screamed with rage and lunged forward again. This time he didn't stop, and Skye felt his icy breath engulf her head and his sharp teeth scrape against her skin as his head engulfed hers. Darkness surrounded her, but there was no pain, only cold. Her skin was wet and she shivered to keep warm, but nothing helped. Something splashed against her face, and she jolted upright and out of her dream. Her wooden boat was banging against a pebbled shore, and brisk waves were lapping over the side soaking her blanket.

Skye struggled to come to terms with where she was. She reached for the paddles as the surf picked her boat up and slid it onto the beach. The hull scraped against the pebbles and tipped sideways. She rolled out and pulled herself quickly to her feet. She hastily stowed the oars under the seats, though she didn't expect to need the boat again, and fled into the shadows created by the tall harbour walls that surrounded the beach on three sides. The fourth was protected by the crashing waves of the ocean.

Above, the noises of the town waking up drifted on the sea breeze. Market stalls were being erected in the half-light, and fishermen were trying their hardest to sell their catch by shouting louder than the man next to them. A large painted sign indicated that Skye had landed in Sunport. She'd heard Emperor Ki mention it before they left Dragorith, but he hadn't given much information. Allegedly it was a friendly port for smugglers, but Skye could see no other boats around her.

At the back of the beach, a set of iron steps had been hammered into the thick wooden sleepers that made up the harbour wall and formed a basic ladder to the promenade above. Skye didn't like the idea of climbing into the middle of a bustling market, but she had no other choice. She'd just have to be quick and hope that nobody noticed a small girl running through the streets. She'd pinned the wet blanket from the boat around her neck and tied the top into a simple hood so at least she looked fully cloaked, even if she only had a thin gambeson on underneath.

It didn't take long for Skye to scramble up the iron pegs, and she was soon peeking above the wall. The market stalls surrounded her, but she could see a dark alleyway a few hundred yards to the left if she could make it past the stalls unnoticed. Taking a deep breath, she pushed herself up onto the cobbled street and made a run for it. Her cloak billowed around her and more than once she nearly tripped over the hem. The familiar weight of Burrower banged against her thighs as her legs carried her as fast as they could. She could hear voices around her shouting their surprise, but she ignored them all and focused only on the alleyway.

Skye reached a couple of fruit stalls and turned slightly to squeeze through the gap between them. As she did, she bumped against the wooden frames and sent their wares tumbling the ground. Apples and oranges bounced away across the stones, and she stumbled to a halt to help pick them up. She knelt down and immediately felt the sharp point of a sword in her back.

"What do you think you're doing, you filthy beggar?" Even without looking, Skye recognised the gravelly voice of an orc. "'Appens I've caught myself a little thief!" This was directed at the other traders who had gathered around to see the spectacle.

Skye stood and turned around to look at the orc. He was old and weathered by the sea air, but she could see that he was still strong. His eyes were filled with vicious spite, and she knew she'd get no mercy from him. She tried her best to explain that she had only meant to pass through the stalls, that she hadn't meant to knock over his fruit let along steal any, but he didn't believe a word. A large crowd was gathering around them, and everyone was calling for Skye's blood. For a town allegedly filled with smugglers, they didn't like thieves.

"I'll take her." The voice came from the back of the crowd. A passage was made to allow the speaker through. A small hobgoblin stepped forward and introduced himself to the angry trader. "My name is Miloris."

"I knows who you are," the orc snarled. "I want justice. This little beggar stole half my apples."

"I must wonder where she is keeping them all. No, don't answer that." The crowd laughed at Miloris's joke, but the orc didn't see the funny side.

"She stole from me," he repeated.

"And she must be punished. Let me buy her from you, and I will make sure that she serves her time in the Pit. I think three gold coins should about cover all of the apples that she stole and immediately ate." This got another laugh from the crowd. Skye didn't like the sound of being bought by the hobgoblin, and her hand fell instinctively to Burrower. There were too many people to fight her way out, but, if she could get herself alone with the hobgoblin, she felt confident that she could kill him and escape. For a moment, she was shocked at how easily the thought of killing somebody had come to her.

The orc nodded his agreement and quickly pocketed the gold coins before returning to his stall. Skye watched as he grumbled and picked up what fruit he could find on the ground. Ironically, most of it had been pocketed by the crowd when they'd gathered round to call for the thief's head.

"Come with me, beggar girl, and don't even think about using that sword you'd got hidden away under there." The voice was stronger than Skye had expected from the small creature. She blushed at the thought that he'd spotted her reaching for Burrower. She pulled her hand away but kept it close to her side. She didn't know when she'd get a chance to strike, but she was determined to be ready to take it.

Miloris led Skye away from the marketplace and along the alleyway that she had been heading for in the first place. It weaved its way between two rows of tall, wooden buildings with thick thatched roofs. It was filled with the smell of old fish and damp fabrics, but mainly it was filled with shadows. Sensing her chance, Skye grabbed hold of Burrower and drew it from its scabbard. She spun on her heels and held the blade against the hobgoblin's neck. Or where his neck would have been if he hadn't ducked between her legs as she spun. Skye felt a sharp point in the back of her knee.

"Don't worry." The hobgoblin didn't seem angry, more amused. "If I cut you here, it won't kill you. You'll never walk again, though. And I need you to be able to walk. I'll give you this. You're quick, whoever you are. Let's just put that sword away nicely, and we'll carry on about our business."

Skye slowly sheathed Burrower and turned to face Miloris. He was smiling at her in a funny, lopsided way. She was surprised he was letting her keep her sword, but then she thought that maybe he'd made it clear that she was no more of a threat with it than she was without. She'd been fighting and practising with the goblins for over a year now, on and off, and she thought they were quick on their feet. They were like tortoises compared with Miloris. He'd saw her attack and ducked between her legs before she'd even reached the hilt of Burrower. She'd never get the better of him. For now, he didn't seem to want to hurt her, and so she decided to take her time thinking up her next steps.

For a while, they meandered between the tall buildings. Occasionally they would step out into pools of weak morning light that hurt Skye's eyes, but mostly they walked in shadows. The alleyway snaked upwards towards the top of a heavily populated hill. Every now and then, Skye would get a glimpse between the buildings. She saw row upon row of wooden houses wrapped around a peninsula and blanketing the hillside down to the harbour front. Up ahead, they had been built on any available patch of land all the way to the top of the hill, maybe a thousand yards ahead. Sighing at the distance and noting how steep the hill became, Skye set off again following Miloris at his quick hobgoblin pace.

Morning had fully broken by the time they reached the top. Loud bells started to ring throughout the town below them. At first, Skye thought they might be prayer bells, but then she saw something extraordinary. Swarms of creatures erupted out of the buildings and started to make their way to the crest of the hill. There were goblins, orcs, hobgoblins and many more besides. Sunport was typical of every port town everywhere. Everyone was welcome regardless of the colour of their skin or the shape of their face, so long as they had money or things to sell.

Skye could feel the weight of expectation in the crowd. She had a horrible feeling that they were all heading to the same destination. She didn't like the idea at all.

Battle For The Fort

When he was younger, Arthur had enjoyed playing hide-and-seek with Skye in the woodlands that surrounded their small village. He'd always enjoyed the mixture of the cool, damp air and the hot smell of damp leaves and ferns. Now, it just made him uncomfortable. He was crouched down behind a rotting tree stump and surrounded by tall trees and waist-high bracken, but there was none of the sense of fun that he had enjoyed before. This was mainly due to the heavy chain-mail and sharp sword that he wore as well as the thousand-strong army that he could see just beyond the tree line.

They had marched from Eragor earlier that morning, making sure they left before the sun rose and the crows came out to spy on them. For a while, they'd marched alone, but soon the birds were flying overhead mocking them with their cries. Every now and then a bird would swoop down and try the patience of the elves, but they never attacked with any real aggression.

By midday, they had arrived at the bottom of a gently rolling row of hills. King Aymeric had ordered his troops to stop and rest. Arthur, Geldrig and Aefor had been sent on ahead to see what lay in store for them. Over the top of the hills, they had found a dense but welcoming forest and had slowly made their way between the trees.

Aefor had them stop every few paces to listen for any noise or indication that they weren't alone. They didn't expect to encounter any of Damphir's army, but Aefor had heard rumours of a nest of Shrunken hidden away in this area and they didn't want to fight any more enemies than they had to.

Soon enough, they found themselves blinking in broken sunlight that streamed through the last few trees between them and the open grassland beyond. Aefor had silently called for them to stop and crouch down and had showed them what he had spotted in the distance. Up ahead, a thousand Azrul soldiers were lined up in battle formation. It was formidable.

That had been nearly an hour ago, and Arthur's legs were screaming in pain. He knew he'd either have to sit down or stand up soon, but neither Aefor nor Geldrig had spoken a word since they'd stopped. They'd both kept their gaze fixed on the rows of soldiers lined up maybe a thousand paces beyond the edge of the forest. Arthur gave up and sat down quietly, making sure not to sit too heavily on the dry twigs underneath him. He could make out the wooden walls of the Burnt Fort in the distance through the hazy air. The day was turning out to be very hot.

In front of the walls was a tight ring of soldiers on horseback. From his vantage point, Arthur could see how rotten and decayed they were. Even the horses that the cavalry rode were skeletal and broken down. They didn't look weak, though. Far from it. The horses whinnied and pawed the dirt in anticipation and generals rode back and forth along the lines. Standard bearers bore the simple plain-black flag of Damphir; a black shield on a black background, the true mark of a dark army.

In front of the mounted soldiers were row after row of infantry. Their weapons were rusty and twisted, but Arthur doubted they'd be blunt. They stood perfectly to attention and didn't move a muscle. There was no twitching or stretching of arms and legs that living soldiers so often had to do whilst waiting at attention for such a long time. These soldiers were dead and only under the power of their master. They didn't even have power over their own bodies.

"Do you think there are more on the other side of the fort?" Arthur asked in a whisper that broke the long silence.

"I doubt it. His crows will have told him which direction we were coming from. I think that what we see is most of his army," Aefor whispered back.

Arthur couldn't help but think that maybe it was more what Aefor hoped than what he actually thought. Whatever he was thinking, the elf had clearly seen enough as he rose to his feet and signalled Arthur and Geldrig to follow him back into the forest. He retraced their earlier steps without saying a word and picked up their pace as soon as they left the cover of the trees. They practically sprinted down the hillside to the encampment below. Aefor wasted no time in heading straight for the king's tent. Arthur and Geldrig knew better than to follow him, and so they made their way to one of the cooking fires where they sat down next to Curglaff and Brack and gladly accepted the small portion of boned meat handed to them.

"Crow," Brack said with a gleeful smile.

Arthur paused with the meat halfway to his mouth before his hunger won out, and he wolfed down the tender meat. Overall, it wasn't as bad as he'd expected.

It didn't take long for Aefor to pass on what he'd

seen to King Aymeric, and they were soon back out and mustering the troops. Word came round that they were all to march to the south where they would be able to round the hills and avoid the thick forest which would be impassable to the horses. Once they were to the south of Horongor, they would attack swiftly and try to reach the city before Damphir had time to move his soldiers from the western wall where Arthur and the others had spied them. The king had made it clear that they were to march hard and fast to try to arrive before the crows had chance to forewarn the sorcerer of their plans. Most of the evil spies had flown away when the elves had started hunting them for dinner, but there was no doubt they'd be back before long.

The goblins and Arthur quickly finished the rest of their food whilst a group of elves raced around stamping down all of the cooking fires. Arthur checked his chain mail and loosened Siorraidh in its scabbard and sprinted after his companions. He caught up with them just as they were reading the king's main guard unit, and they fell into a swift march that kept pace with the mounted king.

It took less than an hour for them to round the southernmost point of the tall hills. Soon the entire army were formed into strict regiments and staring out across open grassland towards the main gate into the

Burnt Fort. Aefor had been wrong. The line of Azrul soldiers encircled the fort. What they had spied from the forest had been only a quarter of his entire army. Even as they stood and watched, dark crows circled above Horongor crying out to each other. The soldiers were moving. They were retreating from all other sides of the fort and re-formed into one enormous unit at the southern wall.

"We must attack now!" cried King Aymeric. "Attack before they have chance to regroup!" As he shouted, the king spurred his horse into action, and Arthur was carried forward by the press of elves behind him. There were no tactics, no orderly attack with targeted units. It was chaos, and Arthur had to fight just to stay on his feet. If he fell, he knew he'd be trampled to death by his companions.

And then the crowd thinned out as elves veered off to the left and right to attack the flanks of Damphir's army. Arthur found his feet just as the Azrul fell upon them. They were inhumanly strong and ruthless. Arthur watched as a foot soldier swung his arm into an oncoming elf and sent him tumbling away through the air. The elf didn't get back up.

Instinctively, Arthur ducked as a rusted sickle cut through air where his neck had been seconds before. He turned and swung his sword upwards and felt it cut into the leg of the animated corpse behind him. He looked up and the soldier just smiled and swung his fist. Arthur dodged, but it clipped his shoulder and sent him spinning away. He was sweating heavily and his wounded eye stung, but he had no time to wipe the sweat from his brow as the Azrul soldier rushed him once again. This time he feinted to swipe at the creature's legs before swinging his sword up and cutting through its neck. There was no blood, just the sound of the ancient bones cracking and the thud as the head hit the floor. As he stood and watched for any sign of life, an elf raced past and thrust a burning torch into the midriff of the corpse. A dark yellow flame engulfed the body.

"Just to make sure," the elf said as he raced off towards another body to repeat the macabre act.

Here and there, the elves were making headway. Some of the undead were falling but, overall, the battle was being lost. Dead or dying elves lay everywhere on the battlefield. The skeletal horses were running amok stamping and biting at anything that got in their way. Arthur watched as an elf hacked both arms from an enemy only to succumb to the soldier's teeth and hard skull as it flung itself forward in a rage.

No matter what they tried, the Azrul were too strong and too numerous for their small army. Soon

Arthur heard the heavy sound of King Aymeric's war drums signalling a retreat. They'd arranged to meet back where they'd set up camp if the enemy allowed them to get away unmolested, and so Arthur sprinted for the tree line at the edge of the forest. He dared to turn his head once and was relieved to see that Damphir's army were not pursuing them. They'd simply returned to their ranks surrounding the fort and stood like statues waiting for further orders.

By the time Arthur made it through the forest and back down the hill to their campsite, most of the surviving elves and his friends were already milling about looking lost. Snudge was sat in a corner with Geldrig and Brack looking particularly angry, so Arthur made his way over to his friends and sat down.

"It was a stupid folly to attack with such speed," Snudge was ranting. "We've lost good goblins in a battle that we could never have won."

Arthur turned to look at the others. Brack just looked at the ground, but when Geldrig spoke his voice was broken and sad. "Curglaff and Snowbroth were killed."

"They died defending me." Brack's voice was small and lost. "It's my fault they died. I'd been knocked to the ground and had two of them on top of me, but Curglaff and Snowbroth grabbed them from me and killed them. They didn't have chance to see the others behind them. It all happened too quickly for me to do anything."

"They would do it again in a heartbeat, Brack, and you would do the same for them." Snudge's voice was calmer when he spoke to Brack, but the anger was still there in the background. "The fault for their deaths lies solely with King Aymeric. I urged him to be patient, to wait for Emperor Ki and his army before attacking, but he wouldn't listen. Now we are all the more weakened for it."

"What will we do now?" Arthur asked. "Will we try again tomorrow?"

"Even the king is not that reckless. Once we are sure everyone who is able has returned, we will head back to Eragor and regroup. There, hopefully, he will heed my advice and wait for Emperor Ki to arrive. The Army of Enlightenment is vastly superior to ours in both numbers and readiness. Don't forget, these elves, as brave as they are, were frozen in time not so long ago. They are still weary and weak from their hibernation. The Army of Enlightenment are well trained and ready for battle. Hopefully, we will hear from the emperor before long."

Cockatrice

Skye stood at the top of the hill overlooking Sunport and watched as thousands of its citizens made their way from the town and over the hill and beyond. Loud calling bells echoed from towers dotted around the hillside. She was eager to see whatever it was they had gathered for, and she pushed past Miloris and made her way to the end of the alleyway where it reached the peak of the hill.

On the other side lay a large, shallow crater, perhaps half a mile across and a hundred feet deep. Around the edges, rows of seating had been carved into the rock, and a large wooden shelter had been erected at one end. Even as Skye stood and watched, the seats were being filled with the citizens of Sunport. They were all shouting and cursing and working themselves into a frenzy. Skye realised that she was looking down into a stadium. The flat earth in the middle of the arena was littered with bones and rusting armour. The dirt was stained red with old blood.

"The Pit!" Miloris exclaimed with undisguised pride. "The jewel of Sunport. Gladiators fight to the death for the honour of the queen." As he spoke, the spectators jumped to their feet and the noise increased tenfold. Skye could see a beautiful girl, no older than herself, stood in the sheltered box waving at the crowd. "That is Queen Luaite. She is a Nelapsi and the queen of Sunport. Those who win their fights may ask her forgiveness for their sins, and she may choose to be merciful."

"And if she chooses not to?" Skye didn't like the direction this was heading.

"Then they must fight again, the next day. If they win, they may ask her once more. And so on. Some are condemned to fight day after day until they die, such are their crimes, but others may find Queen Luaite merciful in the extreme."

"This is why you brought me here, isn't it? To fight."

Miloris said nothing but nodded. "You have your trusty sword and you are no slouch. Your crime was not particularly grave, and so I see good things in your future." Again he smiled his awkward smile and took Skye by the hand. He led her swiftly down a set of stone steps at the rear of the crowd and into a small room lined with battered armour. He handed Skye a light shirt of chain mail and a helmet that was more rust than metal. She took both and put them on along with a pair of rough Hessian trousers. They scratched at her legs, but they were better than fighting bare legged. She'd considered fighting her way free again, but there were too many spectators looking for blood. She still had no doubt that Miloris would have the better of her before she even drew Burrower. This time, he might not be so generous.

Through a barred gate at one end of the room, Skye could see the arena. She could hear the roar of the crowd. Down at ground level, the volume seemed to shake the rocks in the walls and rattle the iron in the gate. The smell from the old blood and bodies on the ground outside the gate clung to the back of her throat, and the noise from the flies nearly matched that of the crowd. And then the gate swung open, and she felt a sharp push in the back from Miloris. She stumbled forwards and fell to her knees shielding her eyes from the bright, blinding sun. She heard the metal gate slam shut behind her, and then there was silence. The crowd were waiting. They knew the routine well by now. Even though the small girl in front of them was small and slight, she would fight like a warrior.

They all did when it came to it. None of them wanted to die in the Pit surrounded by crowd baying for their blood. Opposite Skye on the other side of the wide arena, another, much larger gate, swung open.

Skye had no idea what to expect to come out to fight her, maybe a troll or a group of bloodthirsty orcs. The ground shook underfoot, and the crowd erupted into cheers as a jet of fire erupted from the darkness and a tall, scrawny creature burst out into the open space. Even from this distance, Skye felt the warm draft from the flame blow against her face.

The beast walked on two legs and had two enormous clawed wings that it flapped and thrashed as it screamed at Skye across the arena. It looked like an enormous bird covered partly with black feathers and partly with dark red scales. It had a large head with a cruel, hooked beak and beady yellow eyes. When it screamed, a forked tongue lolled from the side of its beak. It was a cockatrice. Skye had read about them when she'd studied Greek mythology. Only the fiercest could breathe fire. Most killed their enemies with a petrifying stare, but she wasn't dead yet. The one thing she remembered most of all was how ridiculous it all sounded. Now that one stood in front of her, she wished she'd paid more attention.

The warm gust of air from the cockatrice's flame

had filled Skye's face with sand, and she blinked away the dust in her eyes and stood up. She didn't draw Burrower. What would be the point? It would be useless, and it would give the audience the spectacle they craved. She knew there was only one way she would survive this, and she didn't like it.

Whispers spread around the crowd when Skye closed her eyes and knelt. She held her arms out to her side and pointed her chin to the sky. She knew this wasn't necessary, but the longer she could keep the crowd guessing what she was doing the more likely it was to work. She twisted her mother's ring on her finger and concentrated. Normally she was angry when she felt the power of Akeldama rising inside her, and now she needed every ounce of willpower to bring it forward when she was filled with fear.

A cold rush of ice filled Skye's veins, and she felt the surge of power inside her. She dared to open her eyes a crack. Not enough to lose concentration, but enough to see where the beast was. It had come closer, nearer to her than the tunnel it had exited. It was approaching cautiously. She figured it wasn't used to seeing its prey act like this. Judging by the scattered bones, running and screaming wouldn't help either.

Up close Skye could see how big it was. It wasn't nearly as big as the dragon Faileas had been, but it was taller than a horse and broad across the chest like a buffalo. It had the same serpentine neck and tail as Faileas, but there was no fire in its eyes. There was plenty in its beak, though, and Skye knew better than to let it get too close.

Out of the corner of her eye, she could see a ring of soldiers forming in front of the front row of the crowd. Each soldier was armed with a long war bow and a heavy shield. They weren't happy about Skye's refusal to run, either. She knew she didn't have long before the spell broke and the crowd erupted in anger. If that happened, everyone would be her enemy.

The flood of ice ran through her body, and Skye felt the power building inside her aching to get out. She was just about to release it in a ball of energy when she had a change of heart. Another thought struck her, and she bit back the power and concentrated even more. Now she felt the ice turn to fire and sear the back of her eyes. She suddenly felt more in control of the magic than she had ever done before. It was hers to do with as she chose. She was no longer controlled by the sliver of Akeldama that she kept in her ring. Now, she controlled it.

She felt part of herself step outside her body like it had done once before in Weard's shack when she'd first arrived on Ithilmir. She looked back and saw herself kneeling in the dust staring into the heavens up above. She had to admit, she was giving the crowd a spectacle, even if it wasn't the one they'd expected.

The cockatrice stopped in its tracks as Skye approached it. The crowd may not have been able to see her spirit, but it clearly could. Without stopping, Skye walked up to it and climbed aboard its back. It offered no resistance to her advance and made no effort to remove her once she was straddling its shoulders. The skin felt warm under her fingers but smooth like a snake. The feathers were coarse and slid over and under each other whenever the creature tensed or moved beneath her. She leaned forward and placed her head against its neck and felt herself melt into it until suddenly she wasn't Skye anymore; she was the animal.

Now she was the inside the monster's head, was the monster, she could see herself kneeling down and felt the boiling tension in her gut as the fire fought to be released. She could sense the anger and frustration that the cockatrice felt at being locked up in a cage and brought out only to fight. Then she felt the cold metal ring around her ankle where it was tethered to the arena. Skye took control and turned around until she could see the long iron chain that led back down into the dark tunnel. She took a deep breath and exhaled. Flames spat from her mouth. She watched as the metal turned first red, then yellow before it snapped under the intense heat.

The audience were scared. She could hear their screams around her as the arena erupted in panic. She had no time for them, though. Her plans lay elsewhere. Even though she was controlling the creature, she could sense its presence in its own head alongside her. She spoke to it without words, simply exchanging thoughts and ideas. She promised it that it would be free if it helped her. She needed one thing from it; one last journey and then it would be free to live wherever it chose. Free from the tyranny of Queen Luaite. She felt the cockatrice's answer and knew that it would keep its promise. As quickly as she had slipped into its mind, her spirit left and raced back to her own body.

Skye opened her eyes and blinked a few times to make sure she was back in control. She hadn't enjoyed being behind the mind of something so powerful, but it had served her purpose for now. She sprang to her feet and drew Burrower as the crowd burst past the guards and stormed into the arena. The guards responded by drawing swords and cutting into anything they could get their hands on. She sprinted across the dusty ground and grabbed hold of the enormous bird's strong leg and scrambled aboard its back. Like before, she straddled its shoulders and gripped onto its feathers.

She pressed her head into its neck and kicked her heels into its side. This time, it knew what to do and the pair of enormous wings erupted from its side with a loud crack. The thick leather clapped against the air and strong muscles rippled under its skin. Skye fought hard to maintain her grip.

The creature pumped its legs and flapped its wings and sprinted towards the royal box. Skye heard bodies crack and scream underfoot, but that was their fault. She had no time to pity them now. Up ahead Queen Luaite was screaming for her guards, and Skye had to duck as arrows whistled past her head. Those that hit the cockatrice simply bounced off into the dirt.

And then they were airborne. It wasn't a clean take-off. It had to claw the air as it rose. Skye laughed when the royal box crumbled underneath its clumsy feet. She saw the queen running away over the crest of the hill and looked back to see most of the crowd fighting amongst themselves. The soldiers had gathered together and were aiming their bows straight for Skye and her mount. The air buzzed as arrows whipped past Skye's head like angry wasps, but at this distance, they didn't pose much threat.

Soon, Skye was shivering and cursing leaving the blanket behind as the air cooled above the clouds. Once she was sure that they were well away from

Sunport, she guided the animal lower until they were skimming the trees. Here the air was warmer, and the cool breeze on her face welcome. She made sure that Burrower was safely back in its scabbard before rearranging herself into a more comfortable position on top of the cockatrice's neck. She knew they had a long journey ahead of them. She was going to raise an army. She was heading for the Shadowlands.

The Army Of Enlightenment

Salismir was hungry. He had been hungry for as long as he could remember. It wasn't just a hunger for food. His soul was hungry for power. Ever since he'd been cast aside by his ungrateful lord, he'd been searching for someone to follow. In the mountains, there were pools of stagnant water and even more stagnant fish, but there was no magic. He felt the scar of Akeldama inside his head like an itch that couldn't be reached. He felt that if he found even the smallest amount of raw magic, he'd be able to control it.

Even better would be to find somebody who could deliver him back to the most coveted prize. He hoped he'd found them. The perfect means to an end. They needed him even though they didn't know it yet. He'd looked on from the darkness as the army entered Keredor's Pass days before and smiled as they immediately got lost.

The tall, dark elves had no idea how to find their way through the treacherous mountains. Salismir had watched eagerly whilst they meandered from one valley to another, from one desolate mountain top to the next. He'd even had his fill of those stragglers that fell behind and were left for dead. He was still hungry. He'd found an old pair of metal gauntlets that he'd strapped to his wrists in place of his hands. He couldn't bend or use the fingers, but they worked well enough to hold things. They'd long rusted into position anyway. He didn't need them to eat the dead elves, he just pounced on them like a wild animal.

He'd bid his time and listened patiently in the shadows for any information he could use. He learnt of their leader's name, of their empire back on their island in the sea, of their reluctant allegiance to the dark sorcerer. His ears had pricked up at the mention of his former master, and he knew then that he had his leverage.

Darkness fell swiftly in the mountains. The elves soon began to set up camp long before the sun fell below the peaks. Salismir used the lengthening shadows to his advantage and moved swiftly amongst the tents and fires. He had a plan, and he couldn't be discovered. He'd seen how hungry- and thirst-crazy the elves had become with nothing but dead birds and stale water to fill their bellies in the mountains, and he knew that they would kill and eat him as soon as they saw him. He'd seen the power of their bows as they'd tried to pluck the carrion birds from the sky with little luck.

At tent after tent, the little hobgoblin pulled a set of small silver bells from his felt-lined pocket and jangled them softly in the still air. He saw the soldiers spin around and grab for their weapons, but he was always long gone before they got to their feet. In the end, the panic spread more quickly than he could keep up with and the first part of his plan was complete. Fear gripped the elves like a vice around the gut, and Salismir started to squeeze that vice shut.

The bells hadn't been the only thing that Salismir employed at each stop. An observer from above would have mapped his progress around the camp as a circle encompassing all of the outer tents. As he scurried from one frightened elf to another, he'd sprinkled a black powder on the ground. He'd first encountered the powder in the forest with the Brotherhood of

Grield. When lit with a wick the powder would ignite rapidly and, if used in enough quantity, explode. Back then they'd used it to blow the wheels from carts or to topple trees for building timber. Now, Salismir intended to make some magic of his own. Hidden away behind a tall rock, the hobgoblin struck a match and pushed it into the powder.

There wasn't enough to explode, but a hot white flame sprung upwards and raced around the ring of powder until the entire campsite was trapped behind a wall of white-hot fury. Within minutes, the elves were all on their feet and screaming into the darkness. Salismir seized his opportunity and scrambled up onto a low-hanging ledge that he'd picked for just this occasion. He knew how sound travelled in the mountains, and he knew that from this ledge his voice would bounce and echo and grow in volume and spirit until it filled the entire valley with his haunting chanting. Only once the elves were rigid with fear and crying for help would he reveal himself and offer them a way out.

Salismir cleared his throat and took a deep breath. He'd chosen a song from his childhood. A song that had been sung around the Eve of the Spirits, the night when his folk celebrated the spirit voices that ruled their world. A song that had filled his young head with a terror that had never left him. He began:

Within the mountains sings a voice
Cast aside by Yllgadow
A voice of spirit magic pure
Wearing a blanket made of shadow
From here within the mountain song
The bells of darkness pierce the night
And fire burns of Faileas
The source of all his might

Yllgadow was the gatekeeper of the spirit voices, the only thing keeping the forces of true evil from returning to the world and destroying everything in their path. Salismir remembered being terrified of the voices in the mountains singing on the wind, cast into darkness by the gatekeeper midst the fires of the soulless guardian of the Shadowlands.

He sang the simple, melodic verse over and over until the echoes merged into one long, continuous noise. Only then did he drop from his perch and slip between the wailing elves and make his way to the largest tent in the centre of the camp. There, he slipped through the canvas flaps and stood face to face with the leader of the elves.

"Emperor Ki." The emperor had watched him

enter but didn't move a muscle when the hobgoblin approached him.

"Who are you and how did you get past my guards?" The emperor gave a scornful look to those he had trusted to protect him and who were only now reacting to the intrusion and scurrying back into the tent. They reached out to grab Salismir, but something of his magic show was still affecting them. They hovered a few feet away and looked to their leader for further instruction.

"My name is Salismir. I am the voice in the night, and I have reduced your army to snivelling beasts with nothing more than trickery."

"Never mind the voice in the night. You are the hobgoblin who stole Akeldama from Queen Camarina. You are famous." For a moment, the emperor looked confused. "But I had heard that you weren't whole anymore, are the rumours false?" With a grim satisfaction, Emperor Ki grabbed one of Salismir's gauntlets and snatched it away, revealing a festering and scabbed stump.

Angry but managing to stay in control, Salismir grabbed back his metal hand and thrust it back into place. "My hands are not important. How I can help you is. You are hopelessly lost, and most of your army is on the verge of death. I have been watching your progress since you entered the pass, and you have so far moved in the same circle several times. You are going nowhere fast, and only I know how to find you food, water and, more importantly, a way through to Crazak D'Ur.

"It is true that I served at the feet of Damphir the Sorcerer for a time, and it is true that I once sought the power of Akeldama. I am humbled now. I know that I can't control it and that it will never be truly mine, but I will not see it be used by that dark magician. I can help you defeat him."

"And how can you do that? How can I trust you? You are twice branded a traitor. My spies tell me you not only betrayed your friend and leader, Jorn, but you killed him and many more of your companions before fleeing into the darkness. Then, even after finding somebody else to put up with your snivelling behaviour, you betrayed him as well, why else would you be here and not with him?"

"You probably can't. But what I tell you is true, nonetheless. I'll wager that Damphir has asked," at this the hobgoblin let out a sarcastic laugh, "or rather ordered, you to join his army. He expects you to ride straight into his arms at Crazak D'Ur and swear your undying allegiance to him. I can help you to avoid this." Salismir looked into the hopeful eyes of the emperor. "Unless you've already decided that this is what you wish to do."

"I would rather die than join forces with him. Speak your mind. I promise to listen whilst it interests me. Beyond that, I make no guarantees."

"First, you must send a message. This is vital."

"A message? To who? And saying what?"

"To your goblin counterpart who even as we argue rides north with the elves of Kanthor."

"King Aymeric? He has returned?" asked Emperor Ki, momentarily stunned.

"You know as well as anyone that elves will never willingly leave their halls. They never left. They simply went…elsewhere for a while. Snudge has awoken them and convinced them to re-join the fight against the darkness."

Salismir explained his idea to the emperor and smiled as his plan was put into motion. The means had begun its inexorable journey to its end. Before he left the elven leader's tent, he had one more point to make.

"If you still don't trust me, Emperor Ki, remember, I could just as easily have killed you tonight or else left your army to tear itself to pieces in terror. My intentions here are simply to help."

A few minutes later, a white dove soared upwards

out of the mountains and disappeared into the west. For the rest of the night, Salismir slept cradled by shadow in the mountains. When dawn broke, the Army of Enlightenment broke down its camp and set out into the mountains. Salismir made sure that they didn't get lost. He was hungry.

All the time, a familiar voice called out.

I am waiting.

March Of The Dead

By the time King Aymeric's army had returned to Eragor, they had lost over a quarter of their numbers. None of the losses were felt as keenly by Arthur as those of his fallen goblin friends. He'd never grown as close to Curglaff and Snowbroth as he had to Brack or Geldrig, but they were still his friends and allies. He knew, if he'd ever needed it, they would've died for him just as they did for Brack.

The mood around the town was solemn, and Arthur rarely left the room that he had been given in the town hall in High Town. Aefor had made sure that they had food brought to them regularly, but mainly he passed the time sparring with Brack and Geldrig. They barely saw Snudge who spent most of his hours in deep discussion with the elven king in the darkest depths of the keep.

At first, he would emerge angry and frustrated, but day by day his mood lifted. Arthur never knew if it was because he knew more of why King Aymeric had led them to their slaughter or if he felt that the king was finally listening to his counsel, but they were glad of his change in mood. With a more positive Snudge to lead them, they felt more hopeful themselves.

One morning the goblin leader sat Arthur down and spoke to him in private. "Damphir isn't the only one with spies in this land. We have been monitoring him since our attack. It would appear that we rattled him, even if we didn't much dent his numbers. He has left Horongor under nightfall and is making his way to the castle at Crazak D'Ur. It is currently under the rule of King Camut Dri, a Felmir and a trusted ally. I doubt Damphir will have too much trouble seizing it. Either Camut Dri will die, or he will succumb to the greatest leveller of all, money.

"I have also received word from Emperor Ki. He doesn't say much but writes that his army left Draconia nearly a fortnight ago. He says that they are currently making slow progress through the Orctooth mountains and should arrive at Crazak D'Ur within the week. King Aymeric has agreed to ride out tomorrow and meet them on Damphir's doorstep. Together we can defeat him. The emperor commands thousands of dark elves, and many are skilled in the ways of magic. There are ways to kill even those that have died once before. Make no mistake, we need their support."

Arthur was confused. "Why are you telling me all of this alone? Surely everyone needs to know?"

"And they shall be told. But I need something different from you. They will fight for me and do their duty, but from you I need information. You are quick and nimble and know how to listen and think. These are valuable skills. We will be riding out at first light tomorrow. I would like you to already be half a day ahead of us.

"You will need to leave as soon as you can and travel lightly and alone. A group, however small, will be easier to see. You can hide in the shadows and avoid the moonlight. You will head towards Crazak D'Ur and see what you make of Damphir's new home. If you can, walk around the outskirts and see if there are any points that may be breached. Are there any weaknesses that he may have missed in his arrogance? If his army is deployed outside the city walls, how many are there and what formation have they taken?

"It is unlikely that his crows will fly this far from their master, so we may have some secrecy in our approach, but make no mistake, he will know of our arrival before we even set eyes on the city walls. We need all the information that we can get."

Arthur nodded and thought better of arguing. Snudge obviously felt he knew what he was doing and Arthur was determined to repay this faith. He kept his light chain mail hauberk over his clothes but removed the heavier over-armour. He made sure that Siorraidh was strapped firmly to his side and walked silently out of his room and out into the shadows. He passed unnoticed through High Town and slipped through a small gate at the back of the necropolis that Aefor had shown him on their brief tour all those days ago.

The shadows were just starting to lengthen as he made his way out into the flat open lands that surrounded Eragor. Snudge had told him to follow the shadows to the east until he found the well-worn Longman Trail that led to the coast. He was to follow the trail until he found the high mountains of the Orctooth range where he was to head due north to Crazak D'Ur. He found the trail easily enough and set off at a steady jog. He knew he would be on the move for the whole night and didn't want to tire too soon, but he also knew that he had to put as much distance as possible between himself and the others.

Night had well and truly fell before Arthur found himself at the foot of the forbidding eminences that were the Orctooth mountains. There was the merest sliver of moonlight in the sky, but it was enough to pick out the towering peaks in front of him. Thankful that he wouldn't have to climb them, Arthur left the trail and set out north.

He hadn't been travelling north for longer than a few hours when he heard a soft rhythmic noise up ahead. It sounded like a heartbeat within the mountains, but as he drew closer, he realised it was the war drums of Damphir's army. Had it not been for the weak moonlight, Arthur would have stumbled right into the rearmost soldiers and given himself up. Luckily he saw them in time and scrambled behind a low run of rocks that seemed to run parallel with their taller brothers in the Orctooth range.

From his vantage point, Arthur could see the Azrul as they approached Crazak D'Ur. He could see the thousands upon thousands of undead marching in eerie time with each other, their footsteps echoing the drums. In the distance, he could just make out a tall man in a dark cape riding at the head of the army. There was something about the way he moved that worried Arthur. He moved too fast and swung left to right too quickly to be on horseback. Then a bright yellow flame erupted from underneath him and crashed into the high stone walls of Crazak D'Ur. Arthur had no doubt who it was and what he was riding.

Damphir beheld the wondrous city of Crazak D'Ur in all its might. He could feel the frozen, dead stares of a thousand Azrul on his back but ahead of him was nothing but potential. Even the wretched and weak Felmir who inhabited it would be useful if they could be persuaded to bend the knee and join him.

King Camut Dri was considered a good man by his people and those who traded with him. Damphir liked good men. They were often weak. Give him a bad man and he could make him into a leader, but a good man had morals. Damphir had always known the limits that morals placed on a soul.

Crazak D'Ur really was a city worth fighting for, he reflected. Protected to the east by the imposing Orctooth mountains, and sheltered to the west by the engulfing shadows of the Orcwood, the only real attack could come from the south. Malagao's Folly, a stone watchtower that stood over three-hundred feet tall, was well placed to the north so that an observant lookout could report any movement there. It was perfect.

Or at least, it was nearly perfect. For now, it was

still in the hands of the Felmir, and Damphir wasn't about to let that stand. His trusted crows had been circling the city for the better part of a week, and he'd spoken at length with them on the journey here. He knew their routines and the layout of the city, even down to the narrow alleyway that led in from the gate and wound around the outer wall before depositing visitors into the open courtyard.

Damphir had smiled when he'd heard about this. It was designed perfectly to stop invaders. Anybody breaking down the imposing front gate would find themselves in a stone corridor just wide enough for a single horse. By the time they'd wound their way into the city, they were in single file and ready to be slaughtered from above. This had kept the Felmir safe for centuries. It was said that the city had never fallen to an invading army.

Tonight, we change that. Akeldama had been a constant companion for Damphir, and he could sense excitement in the stone's voice. He didn't blame it. They were so close.

Underneath Damphir's legs, the dragon buckled and twitched. It wasn't used to standing still. It wanted to be up in the air or scouring the land. Above all, it wanted to be free. Each time that Damphir had to enter the mind of the dragon, it would plead with him to be set free and each time he made a new promise. After this battle or the next, he made a promise that it would be free, and each time he broke it. It didn't matter. Dragons were for taming. Their time as wild beasts had passed.

Do it! The voice of Akeldama was growing impatient. Ever since Damphir had absorbed the power of the queen, he'd felt stronger but somehow more exposed to the power of the stone. He wasn't sure if it was because the queen had been so weak, or because the stone had held such a strong hold over her in the past, but he felt like he had to tread carefully. *You must act quickly. There is danger in the sky.*

Despite himself, Damphir looked up. At first, he saw nothing until suddenly, the stars started to move. They flowed in endless rivers of gold across the black canvas forming into pools before separating and heading off in different directions. Wherever they went, they left soft trails that slowly started to form into a moving image of a girl astride a great beast. She was holding on tight to its back and flying low over a desolate plane.

Damphir watched as the stars continued their dance and re-formed as a towering range of mountains topped by a twisted gateway. He recognised it all too well. He had once made a pilgrimage to the very same place and had been cast away as if he were nothing. He knew too well who the girl was. How had his captain been so careless? She should be dead.

The stars were re-forming again, only this time they showed Damphir, down on his knees and bowing before a mighty queen standing beside a majestic dragon, far bigger than his own. Around its neck was a flaming collar and a chain. The queen had tamed a dragon. Only he could tame dragons. Who was she?

Dumfounded, he watched on, his mind awash with unfamiliar feelings of fear and panic. Wordlessly, the queen clicked her fingers and the collar clicked open and fell to the floor. The kneeling Damphir looked up in time to see the ice-cold flames engulf him.

As quickly as they had formed, the images disappeared and the stars aligned themselves in the sky. Damphir bellowed and lashed with his hands. Next to him, his captain fell to the ground screaming and clutching at his face. His flesh was re-forming on his charred skull. Soon, he looked as he once had when he lived, young and strong with a head full of auburn hair. His one eye still burned with a swirling blue flame. Wordlessly, he looked to his master, unsure what to say.

Damphir stared down at him and spoke with a voice filled with anger and betrayal. "You failed me.

For this, I have punished you. I have given you back the one thing you fear to lose, your mortality." He struck out with his sword and nicked the cheek of the Azrul. The soldier howled at the unfamiliar sensation of pain and grabbed at his bloodied face. "From this point on, you will serve me truly. The only way that you will live forever is to honour me and make up for your failure. Get out of my sight."

Like his dragon, Damphir was restless. The visions had shocked him, but he knew they could just be Akeldama gaining a stronger hold on him. He couldn't afford to think about that now. He could sense the victory waiting for them.

It wasn't just the layout of the city that the crows had delivered. The other news had shocked him. So complacent had the Felmir grown in their protective walls that they didn't post sentries at night. This would be their undoing.

With a roar to the Azrul archers, Damphir kicked his heels into the dragon's side and spurred it into the air. As one, a hundred archers nocked their arrows and drew back silver bowstrings. Before they could fire, Damphir guided the dragon down towards them and gave it another kick. A thunderous jet of white-hot fire erupted from its mouth and engulfed the archers as it passed. In its wake, it left a hundred charred and smouldering soldiers and a hundred flaming arrows. Only now did the archers let loose their quarrels.

Like a rain of fire, the burning shafts flew through the darkness and exploded into a hundred small fires inside the city walls.

That will get their attention, Damphir thought.

Now finish the job, came the hissed reply.

He turned his steed to the sky and roared. The army of the dead returned his cry, and the ground shook underfoot.

Bane Of Grimdir

Inside the city, alarms sounded and half-dressed Felmir appeared along the walls. Each man was armed, but none were awake enough to understand what was happening. Arthur felt sick as he saw the future. They were hopelessly unprepared. They didn't stand a chance.

The tall walls that surrounded the city were bordered by a deep, dry moat designed to keep attackers at bay. The Azrul were no ordinary foe, and the trenches were quickly filled with bodies of the undead who sacrificed themselves without even slowing down and threw themselves into the pit so that the others could reach the base of the wall and start to climb.

Horns grew louder, and Arthur heard the screams and shouts of more activity within the city. They had no choice. The city was ablaze under the thunderous barrage of flaming arrows that continued to light up the night. Through them all flew Damphir and his dragon. He soared in swooping arcs and let loose a torrent of fire with each pass. Felmir fell screaming from the walls and added to the bodies in the moat.

Those that avoided the dragon and the arrows were finally fully dressed and armed. They were too late. The king tried to join the battle but fled as his standard-bearer was cut down with a scream by a bolt through the eye halfway through announcing his arrival. Arthur watched him flee the tower and hoped that he had managed to escape somehow.

The Azrul were merciless. They scrambled over the walls like rats. Arthur shuddered at the screams that pierced the otherwise silent night. The Azrul made no sound as they fought. There were no shouted orders or rallying cries. They simply attacked. If they fell, they knew there were more to take their place and those behind them were ready and waiting to fill the breaches. Arthur reflected that this wasn't often. The Felmir made very little impact on the Azrul numbers.

It was all over within a few minutes. As far as Arthur could tell, the Felmir were wiped out entirely. There had been no talk of surrender; indeed there had been no time for it. Soon tall fires were lit within the walls and the city started to glow. The smell of burning flesh wafted over Arthur and made him sick to his stomach.

By midnight, the ragged standard of Damphir had been raised over each tower, and the Azrul had lined the walls shoulder to shoulder in a formidable demonstration of their numbers. There wasn't an inch of space that wasn't defended by the undead. The only relief came when the dragon took to the skies just before dawn, though Arthur made a note of the fact that it was riderless.

It appeared that the army was staying within the walls for the moment. Snudge had made it clear that a siege of the city was their preferred method of attack if they had the chance. Arthur had commented at the time that any attack on the city seemed doomed, regardless of the method.

The hours after dawn passed quickly and without further incident, although Arthur never grew accustomed to the smell. True to their word, soon after dawn he spotted King Aymeric's standard in the distance and the steel tips of their spears trailing off behind him glinting in the low sunlight, a grim echo of Damphir's flaming arrows.

Arthur knew that he had to get to Snudge as quickly as possible. He scrambled down from the rocks and sprinted towards the army. He arrived panting and out of breath but pushed his way through the outer ranks until he found the king riding alongside the goblin leader who himself was riding uneasily on a horse perched in front of Geldrig.

"The army is in the city, but he has a dragon. Damphir was riding a dragon," Arthur stammered out in one long, jumbled breath.

"Very good, Arthur. You have done well. We will deal with this dragon when we have to. For now, we will hold back and look to make camp. No doubt he will be aware of our arrival, but we came here planning a siege, and a siege we shall attempt." Snudge spoke kindly to Arthur, and even King Aymeric offered his thanks.

Arthur walked alongside his friends until it was decided that they were close enough to set up camp and start the siege on Crazak D'Ur. After they dismounted, their regiments started to break out into small groups and began to erect tents and start fires.

"Arthur, once we have set up camp, we will test Damphir's defences. We won't risk another all-out attack. Instead, we'll send ladders up to the walls and try to scale them. We might catch him unawares. You served us well last night, but I am afraid I need to ask one more favour of you. I need you to carefully make your way over to the walls of the city and see if you can find anywhere that we can easily approach with the ladders. Understand?"

Not wanting to be caught in the open, even with the dragon away from the city, Arthur sprinted the thousand yards to the city walls in the shadow of the Orcwood. After their initial show of strength, most of the Azrul had abandoned their sentry on the city walls, and Arthur estimated there were fewer than a hundred in total stationed around the whole length.

Arthur hoped their attention would be focussed on the army amassing a few hundred yards behind him and he might be able to slip by unnoticed. Here and there, dead Felmir littered the ground where they'd been thrown from the castle by the rampaging Azrul. He had to take care to step around their bodies. Every now and again, he'd scare off a flock of crows that had gathered to feast on the dead. Arthur didn't spend too long looking at them; their wounds were too horrific.

The deep trench that bordered the wall had been emptied of all Azrul; those who had initially sacrificed themselves, had scrambled over the wall once the battle was won. Up close Arthur found it was easily a dozen feet deep and just as wide. The bottom was littered with large stones and Felmir corpses. There was no way a ladder could be balanced for long enough to allow an army to scramble up the walls even without the inevitable attack from above.

There was, however, a small wooden gate hidden in the southern wall at the base of one of the tallest corner towers. It was covered by overgrown bushes, but Arthur managed to push his way through, cursing at the large thorns.

Arthur weighed up his options. He'd been sent to spy a place for an attack, but it was clear, even with his lack of experience, that an attack on the walls was folly. The gate might provide another way in, and he really didn't want to head back to Snudge without an answer.

Surprisingly the gate was unlocked, and Arthur pushed his way into the tower. The gate opened into a dark stairwell littered with old armour and rusted weapons. There were a few quivers of long arrows scattered around the ground, but all of the bows looked weak and unstrung. The stairs were made of wood and some had rotted away long ago.

Each step was a risk and Arthur took his time climbing up into the tower. There were no doorways or exits, just arrow slots cut into the wall at every rotation. From these Arthur could see out into the world below. He felt strangely protected from the violence that he knew would descend on the others, despite being in terrible danger. If he were discovered, the Azrul wouldn't even stop to think before cutting him down.

It was through one of these arrow slots that Arthur saw the shining golden banners of the Army of Enlightenment snaking out of the mountains to the east. His heart leapt when he saw their numbers, and he stood and watched as they formed into well-drilled units that covered the battlefield in a chequerboard of gold and red. He felt buoyed with a strange magic, as though he knew everything would be fine now that Emperor Ki had arrived.

With renewed vigour, Arthur pushed on up the stairs making sure to keep a good hold on the wall whenever the steps felt less than secure. The contrast of the bright sunlight caught him by surprise when he burst through a wooden trapdoor and out onto the top of the tower. Immediately, he raced over to the edge and watched as his friends and King Aymeric organised their meagre troops into formation. The few cavalry that he commanded formed the spearhead of each unit ahead of several rows of infantrymen. Though they were few in number, they were well drilled.

In the east, a loud cheer had gone up as somebody in Emperor Ki's army had given a call to attack, and the hairs on Arthur's neck stood on end as he watched them race towards the city. The closer they got the more the thunderous noise of their stampede made the tower vibrate underfoot.

Then at the last minute, just as they seemed intent on crashing headfirst into the stone walls, they veered to the south and headed in a new direction, this time directly towards King Aymeric and Arthur's friends. Bile rose in his throat as he watched on as they drew closer and closer. It suddenly became clear. The Army of Enlightenment wasn't here to fight against Damphir. They were here to join him.

Arthur's attention was dragged away from the battle about to play out below when he felt the sharp point of a sword dig into the small of his back. Without thinking, he drew his sword and spun on his heels. He'd practised the move a thousand times with Brack and Geldrig and it paid off now. His muscles moved without thinking, and he punched the hilt upwards into the jaw of his attacker. He felt the bone break but knew that wouldn't slow the undead Azrul down.

He remembered how he'd killed the last creature he'd fought and tried to hack at its neck. This one was quicker and ducked away to the left and made to swing its own blade at Arthur's ankles. Arthur jumped, but the swing never came. Instead, the Azrul dropped its shoulder and charged, picking him up and carrying him towards the edge. Arthur felt the wind knocked from his lungs and the sharp scrape of stone against his back.

Time stood still. Arthur could feel himself balanced on the edge of the tower and could see the elves and his friends moving in slow motion far below him. They'd noticed the deviation of Emperor Ki's army and were rushing to their stations to deflect their attack. He tried to cry out, but he had no breath to make a sound.

"What a nice little prize. I'm sure the master will want to speak to you personally." The sickening snarl of the Azrul soldier cut into Arthur's consciousness just as he started to black out. The last thing he saw was a single, piercing blue eye and a heavy fist crashing into his face.

Snudge was starting to worry. Arthur had been gone a long time. It wasn't like him to disappear. Suddenly, he didn't have time to dwell on the missing human. The thundering sound to the east had his full attention.

He looked to his right and saw the Army of Enlightenment bearing down. Next to him, King Aymeric hadn't moved a muscle since they had turned course. Indeed, he almost appeared to be smiling. And then Snudge heard a sound not heard by goblins for centuries. He recognised it in his bones like a memory passed down from his ancestors. There had only ever been one horn that could make a sound like. It echoed through the hills behind them. Snudge turned his horse and pointed into the distance.

In the south, thundering over the same hills that they had passed through only hours before, was a vast army that dwarfed in number even Damphir's mighty horde. "Men have returned!" he cried as loudly as he could, desperate for all around him to hear. "That is the sound of the Bane of Grimdir. The race of men has returned to the north."

Even as he shouted, the others were turning and staring.

Again and again, the deep throb of the Bane of Grimdir rolled across the hills and echoed from the mountains to the city walls filling the world with noise. The elves around Snudge clapped their hands to their ears and many fell to their knees.

In the east, the Army of Enlightenment was unrelenting in its stampede. They were close now, close enough for Snudge to see the steaming breath of their horses and hear the heavy clanking of armour rattling as the infantrymen sprinted. And then they were close enough to hear them scream out a mumbled warning and still King Aymeric's men weren't ordered into formation.

But now suddenly it didn't matter. Somehow Emperor Ki drew his horse to a standstill a dozen yards in front of King Aymeric and his knights followed suit. Snudge wondered how they avoided crashing into the backs of each other and how the infantry wasn't crushed under the feet of the cavalry, but it worked. As quickly as the attack had started, the Army of Enlightenment was stood stationary and in perfect formation in front of King Aymeric.

"I apologise for the scare," Emperor Ki said with a chuckle and looked towards Snudge who was sat shaking in his saddle. "I have sworn allegiance to the sorcerer. Had I made my way towards you in peace or made a camp so close to his enemy, he would have destroyed us both. This way, our ranks are swelled and, with any luck, Damphir will be wondering what has happened. I made sure King Aymeric knew in advance, of course."

King Aymeric glared at his counterpart for a long while before breaking into a grin and thrusting out a hand. "The dove arrived not long ago. You were lucky, my friend. Had it not, then you would not still be sat upon that horse!"

"What about the men in the south?" Snudge asked. He was feeling irritated that he hadn't been included in the king's plans. "What do we do about them?"

King Aymeric looked at Emperor Ki and shrugged. "I think it is finally time that we learn on which side of good and evil men choose to dance."

Mithrostan

In the distance, a row of mountains rose from the grassy plains and towered high above the heavy grey clouds that rolled and boiled with endless storms. Flashes of lightning lit up the dark sky and thunder pierced the air. Skye clung to the back of the cockatrice with renewed energy as the Shadowlands rose in to view. She'd never approached from the outside before. All of her visions started with her already inside the seemingly endless peaks. She hoped that she wouldn't have to venture that far in this time. She wasn't here to see the ghosts of the dead yet.

Her heels dug into the beast's sides and guided it lower and lower until she could reach out and pluck the leaves from the few trees that survived this close to the land of souls. Nothing much lived here. There were no birds in the sky and no animals beneath them. Skye had learned on their long journey just how efficient a hunter the cockatrice was.

Each night when they'd stopped to rest, the bird had flown away into the distance and returned hours later with something for Skye to cook over their fire. Sometimes it was small prey, rabbits and such. But often it would bring back whole deer or even wolves for them to cook on a spit. They always ate well, and Skye knew that she would miss the creature when she set it free.

In her darker moments, she had considered not honouring her part of the deal. She knew how easy it would be to slip back into its mind and have it obey her orders forever with no thoughts of its own. She knew actions like that would only lead to darkness. It was sorely tempting in those moments when she was eating a freshly cooked piece of meat, but when they were free in the air and she saw just how majestic the creature was, all thoughts of slavery slipped from her mind like tissue in the breeze. Instead, she spent the time plotting her next move.

Each day, Skye would go over in her head what she knew so far. She still wasn't sure whether or not Emperor Ki had betrayed her and Snudge and their cause and had turned to join Damphir. The sorcerer had an army of dead elves and was searching tirelessly for Akeldama. He might even possess the orb. She didn't know for sure where the Dark Queen fit into all this, but Skye had no doubt that she would be seeking the orb herself, whether that meant joining forces with Damphir or otherwise. Every day she told the cockatrice these stories to remind herself why she hadn't accepted Faileas's deal and returned home. She needed to know that she was fighting for something worth fighting for; that if she died here, alone and away from her home, it wouldn't be in vain.

They were close to the entrance to the Shadowlands. Skye could see the dark entrance to Mithrostan perched on top of the tallest peak. Tall pillars extended the height of the mountain by hundreds of feet and each one was wrapped with dark chains. A bright yellow hell-mouth entrance glowed between two of the pillars and cast-iron teeth barred entry to any who were foolish enough to venture this far.

Beyond the gate and at the top of a wide staircase that led down into the bowels of the mountain there sat a glorious throne carved from ivory. The back rose a dozen feet into the air and was topped with six curved spikes that bowed down over whoever sat upon it and seemed to enclose them in a porcelain cage. The seat was covered in red satin, and a length of the same fabric flowed onto the stone slabs and out onto the unthinkably long wooden drawbridge that led from the mouth of the gate and across a wide gulf to a ledge on a separate mountain half a mile to the north.

This was the only place to set down. Skye cautiously guided her steed down onto the frozen peak and leapt off its back. She sank to her ankles in snow and gasped. She looked up into the eyes of the cockatrice and nodded her thanks for its service. The creature looked at her for a moment, almost to ask if she were sure she wanted it to leave, before it screamed a goodbye and dropped from the mountain. A second later the loud crack of its wings opening was the only sound in the mountains. Skye watched as it disappeared into the darkness.

The drawbridge was wide enough for two carts to pass each other comfortably and longer than most bridges Skye had ever seen, and yet it didn't rock or creak when she stepped onto it. She heard the wind howling underneath and made the mistake of looking over the edge. She reeled back in shock and had to fall to her knees before she toppled over the edge. She couldn't see anything below her except the sheer sides of the mountains endlessly plummeting away into nothingness. It wasn't just that the ground was so far below, Skye knew that there would be no ground at all in a place like this. If she fell, she would never land.

She would just fall forever into emptiness.

Skye took a deep breath and got back to her feet. She made a point of walking down the centre of the bridge from that point on. She had no intention of falling over the edge. It was a long walk to the entrance to Mithrostan, and she walked every step with her hand on Burrower. She had no idea what might be lurking. Even though the drawbridge looked empty, there were enough shadows and pools of blackness to hide an army of orcs or Nelapsi or other creatures of evil.

Just as Skye stepped from the bridge and onto the hard rock in front of the enormous, pale-white throne, the shadows shifted and merged. Once again, she was stood face to face with Faileas. In life, he was even more impressive than in her visions. He towered above her, and his cold breath stank of death and decay whenever it wafted over her. Flames of ice leapt from his nostrils. Skye stumbled as the dragon's thick tail wrapped around her legs and pushed her forwards.

She was stood directly underneath his head, and she watched as his neck coiled like a snake and his head came down to look her directly in the eyes.

"You are very brave, Skye. There are not many mortals who dare to approach my throne. Tell me why I shouldn't destroy you here on my doorstep." The dragon's voice was soft but filled with menace. Skye felt his tail tighten around her waist.

"I'm here to make a deal." She tried her hardest to keep her voice steady.

"It is too late for a deal. You turned me down."

"That was your deal. This time, I'm here to offer you *my* deal. I don't think you'll get a better offer for a while."

Faileas threw his head back and laughed loudly. "You dare to come here to my realm and offer *me* a deal? You are even braver than the legends tell us. Or simply far more foolish. Tell me of this deal. What is that you are offering me?"

Skye looked up into the dragon's burning eyes and rubbed the sliver of Akeldama that she wore on her finger. "I will let you live." It was a statement, but the dragon rocked back on his tail and laughed even harder this time.

"*You* will let *me* live?" Each time he laughed, flames erupted from his nostrils, but his tail never tightened on Skye. She knew that he could crush her in a heartbeat if he chose to. For now, he was intrigued by her: an insect that had learned how to juggle.

"Like I said, you won't get a better offer." Skye was surprised by how calm she felt. She had thrown herself from the mountain and found that she was floating to the ground. There were still dangers ahead, but she felt that she would get what she wanted. If Faileas had been truly offended, he would have killed her by now.

"And in exchange for letting me, Faileas, the *immortal* Guardian of Mithrostan and the Shadowlands and, not to put too fine a point on it, an enormous dragon made of shadow and ice, live? What do you ask of me for this generous favour?"

"I am here to raise an army. I will lead the forgotten dead into battle once more, and we will be victorious. I will need a steed to ride into battle. A beast that will strike fear into everyone who sees it. The sorcerer Damphir has an army of the dead risen to fight again. I want to meet him with an army who didn't bother to leave the grave, and I want his army to fear me! The only thing the dead will fear is a fate worse than death, a fate of eternal damnation and wondering."

"You want me to bow down and allow you to ride me into battle like a common horse?" Skye felt Faileas's tail tighten further. She was struggling to breathe against his thick scales and powerful muscles. "If it's all the same to you, I'll stay here on my throne, but thank you for the offer. And now, for my counter offer. You will die, Skye Thistle. And in exchange, I will give you…nothing. There is nothing left for you here."

The dragon's tail curled around Skye's chest and

gripped her even more tightly. She started to see stars and gasp for breath. She knew it was time to play her final hand. She hadn't expected him to take her offer, but she needed to act fast before it was too late. This time the overwhelming burning at the back of her eyes came more easily. Far too easily. She felt the power flowing through her body and saw the future scribed on the back of her eyelids.

She saw Faileas bowing to her and taking a knee so that she could climb aboard his back. She saw the army of the dead cowering and burning under his glowing flame and those that ran falling to Burrower. Damphir and the Dark Queen tried to flee, but Faileas caught up with them easily and burned them as they ran.

As she watched, everything around her turned to ash. Snudge fell to the dragon's tail, but Skye knew that this was just and proper. He was weak, and weakness only led to darkness. Her other friends followed, Brack and Geldrig, Curglaff and Snowbroth. All weak and deserving of death. And then there was only one left. Arthur stood before her, clad in shining armour and standing tall and proud with a long sword at his side like the knights he'd read about as a child.

His eyes were brave and strong and pierced Skye like an arrow. But he was human and corruptable, and he would succumb to the darkness if given the chance. Skye knew this like she knew herself. She was the only one who could fight the darkness. The only one who could be trusted to live in this brave new world of lightness. She opened her eyes as the flames engulfed her best friend and shook the memories from her mind.

She could never do those things. She knew it was only the darkness of the ring influencing her mind. Yet, even throughout those horrible sacrifices, she'd enjoyed the ultimate power. She shivered and put it out of her mind. For now, she needed the power of Akeldama. She couldn't afford to let doubt slip into her mind.

Skye closed her eyes again and gasped for another breath. The heat of her magic seemed like it would boil her alive from within, but she felt no real pain, more the thought of pain and what it might be. She felt the ball of rage from inside her belly and took a deep breath. She was in control again. For a moment, she'd allowed the stone to gain control of her, but it was back where it belonged.

She opened her eyes and looked up into the inferno that burned in Faileas's sockets. This close they looked like a galaxy of fire and smoke swirling in infinity. In their reflection, Skye saw herself. Her eyes were sunken and drowned in pools of dark shadow, but her pupils burnt with their own green flames. On her forehead, she saw the rough outline of an eye growing on her skin like a scar. Where it cracked and opened, flames tried to force their way out. The Shadowed Eye had her in its grasp.

It took every last ounce of breath, but Skye screamed with rage. She'd fought so hard to overcome the darkness that she couldn't let it take her for one of its own. With her bellow, the power poured out of her fingers and surrounded the dragon. She saw the scales of ice melt in the heat and the shadow twist and contort as the energy ripped through him. And then he re-formed just as before, only now he wore a collar made of fire. It encircled his shadowy neck and moved and grew as he rolled on the ground and clawed at it with his talons. His tail uncurled and dropped Skye over the edge of the cliff.

The clouds in the sky spun as Skye fell into the darkness, and her stomach churned. Something thick and rough brushed against her hand, and she snatched out. She grabbed hold of a branch and her arms screamed in protest. She could sense the emptiness below her willing her to let go and fall into its waiting mouth. She knew there was only way to know whether her plan had worked. If it hadn't, she was as good as dead anyway. She closed her eyes and let go. She felt the world spin, but she held her breath and waited. Far above her, a loud clap of thunder broke the silent night sky.

Just as Skye started to worry that she'd made a terrible mistake, she heard the comforting sound of leather wings beating through the air, and she smiled as she landed with a heavy thud on the back of Faileas. Even though he was made of shadow and ice, he was solid enough to ride and her landing knocked the wind from her lungs, but she had her answer.

She opened her eyes. Below her, shadows distorted her view into nothingness. The collar of fire burned brightly around his neck. She pulled on the collar and guided her dragon back up towards the throne. As he flew, Faileas looked back and spoke. Skye noticed that his eyes burned just as brightly as ever but now they burned green. He was hers to control.

"You have your deal. You will have your army and your steed. You will rule Ithilmir, Skye Thistle, from the Ivory Throne of Mithrostan."

If you haven't read the first installment in the Shadowland Chronicles, The Spyglass and the Cherry Tree, now is a great time to grab a copy and get caught up.

Available from all good bookstores.

Acknowledgments

There are always many people to thank in the production of any book and this one is no different. I want to say a huge thank you to my family for supporting me with this endeavour. To my dad who continues to read everything I put in front of him and for offering advice and guidance. To my mum who never fails to believe in everything I put my mind to. Thank you both.

Pam, with her unlimited patience and unending quest to find the hidden gems in my writing (often deeply hidden), has my endless gratitude.

Even after passing through Pam's desk, there are sometimes little tweaks and errors that creep in. Without the dedication and eye for detail of Lily, my amazing proof-reader, many of these would still grace these pages. She deserves a massive thank you for giving up her lunchtimes and barely putting the book down for several days. Thank you Lily!

Alex, your artwork rocks and makes these books scream out to be read, thank you!

Finally, as always, I owe a debt of gratitude to my wonderful wife, Toni. Her support and encouragement when things get tough are the only reason that any of this ever gets finished. You continue to inspire me and I am forever grateful for everything you do.

About the author

Matt Beighton is a full-time writer, born somewhere in the midlands in England during the heady days of the 1980s. He is happily married with two young daughters who keep him very busy and suffer through the endless early drafts of his stories.

Matt's books have been read around the world and awarded the LoveReading4Kids "Indie Books We Love" and Readers' Favorite 5 Star Awards.

Having spent many years as a primary-school teacher, Matt Beighton knows how to bring stories to life. He regularly visits schools and runs creative workshops that ignite a passion for words.

If you have enjoyed reading this book, please leave a review online. Your words really do keep authors going!

To find out more or to join the mailing list, visit
www.mattbeighton.co.uk

www.ingramcontent.com/pod-product-compliance
Lightning Source LLC
Chambersburg PA
CBHW060943190726
48286CB00005B/1401